Pinned

Pinned

ALFRED C. MARTINO

HARCOURT, INC.

Orlando   Austin   New York

San Diego   Toronto   London

www.HarcourtBooks.com

Library of Congress Cataloging-in-Publication Data
Martino, Alfred C.
Pinned/by Alfred C. Martino.
p. cm.
Summary: Dealing with family problems, girls, and their own competitive
natures, high school seniors Ivan Korske and Bobby Zane face each other
in the final match of the New Jersey State Wrestling Championship.
[1. Wrestling—Fiction. 2. Family problems—Fiction. 3. Friendship—Fiction.
4. Competition (Psychology)—Fiction. 5. New Jersey—Fiction.] I. Title.
PZ7.M3674Pi 2005
[Fic]—dc22 2004014444
ISBN 0-15-205355-7

Text set in Janson
Designed by Cathy Riggs

First edition
A C E G H F D B

Printed in the United States of America

*For every young wrestler with the guts
to step out on a mat and compete*

Acknowledgments

I have had much good fortune and been touched by many wonderful people in my forty years.

I am humbled by the gift of wonderful parents who adopted me as an infant, and who, two years later, graced our family with my adopted little sister. My mother and father instilled in us the idea that we were "chosen," and I have held this belief, not as a sense of entitlement, but with humility and pride. I thank my parents, especially my mother, for a remarkably happy youth and for providing me with the confidence to move forward through the rest of my life regardless of what difficulties I might face.

There are many others who have had an important influence on me, including (but certainly not limited to) my grandparents, my Aunt Mary, my aunts, uncles, and cousins, Elizabeth (a best friend for as long as I can remember), Alisa (the best business partner anyone would want), Cheryl (who believed in me at times when I didn't believe in myself), and my friends from Short Hills whose families, wives, and children are a source of love and support.

I thank my three high school coaches—Mr. Sachsel, Mr. McSorley, and Mr. Miron—each of whom inspired me to embrace the sport of wrestling, and who taught me that sportsmanship was always more important than wins or losses.

I am also grateful to my California writing group— Alexes, Janet, Mary Lou, and Cathi—all fabulous writers themselves, who helped refine and improve *Pinned*. And to author Natalie Goldberg—though we've never met, it was through your books that I came to understand why writing would always be a part of my life.

And, finally, a huge thanks to Karen Grove and Susan Schulman. Without the expertise of both, *Pinned* would have never made it to print. For making this dream (and it is a *really* big dream) a reality, I am forever indebted.

ALFRED C. MARTINO
AUGUST 2004

Pinned

1

Wind rapped against the bedroom window. Ivan Korske stared beyond his reflection, into the shadowy woods that surrounded the family's farmhouse. November, and its chilly prelude to winter, had long arrived. Ivan stretched a thermal shirt over his back, then pulled long johns up his thighs. A plastic rubber-suit top that crinkled when he slipped it over his head came next. Sweatpants and a sweatshirt followed.

Downstairs, a grandfather clock chimed eleven. Ivan vaguely noticed, grabbing a pair of weathered running shoes on the floor of his closet. While most Lennings High School seniors spent Sunday night on the phone, piecing together memories of the weekend's parties, Ivan prepared for his evening run.

Every night, regardless of how tired or hungry he was, Ivan ran. When his running shoes were soaked from rain, he ran. When his fingers were numb from the cold, he ran. The night his mother died last April, he ran.

The final judgment of his high school wrestling career hinged on whether he stood victorious in Jadwin Gymnasium, site of the New Jersey State Championships, the second Saturday of March. Each run, Ivan was certain, brought him that much closer to the dream of being a state champ and a chance to get away—far away—from Lennings.

Anything less would be failure.

Ivan sat at the end of his bed in the sparsely furnished room, dog tired from an afternoon of splitting logs behind the shed out back. There was a dresser and bookshelf, a wooden chair to his left, and the red and white of a small Polish flag coloring one of four otherwise bare walls. Ivan leaned over to tie the laces of his running shoes, then looked up at the photograph of his mother as a teenager in the old country—a sturdy young woman with soft, rounded cheeks and bright hazel eyes. Ivan was proud to have the same. The silver frame glinted from his meticulous care, even under the dim light of the bedroom lamp.

Ivan imagined his mother sitting beside him, as she often had the last months she was alive. "Too many chores for you," she would say. "Your father forgets you are only seventeen. I will speak with him. I know you have other interests . . ." She would smile and give a knowing nod toward the house across the street. "Even besides this wrestling sport."

Alone, in the chill of his bedroom, Ivan closed his eyes. He could hear her words, soothing and familiar, and see her face, robust and healthy, as they once were. He remained that way for some time.

"Ivan." His father's voice bellowed from the first floor. "Are you running now?"

Ivan held back the sadness and hardened his face with unflinching resolve, the same glare he gave opponents before a match. "I'm going."

"Now?"

"Yeah, Papa, now."

He grabbed his jacket from the chair, walked out of the bedroom and down the stairs, its floorboards creaking and the radiator clanking from the rush of hot water through the metal piping. The scent of chimney embers lingered. At the bottom of the staircase, Ivan zipped his jacket and stepped out the front door.

It was a clear night. A crescent moon hung just above the tree line. Ivan looked across the street at the Petersons' house. In a second-floor corner window, he saw Shelley's silhouette, head propped on an elbow, at her desk. Finishing her homework, he knew. Ivan breathed in deeply. Cold wind pressed against his body and slipped beneath his clothing. He felt alive, intensely aware of every inch of his skin, nostrils, and the full expansion of his lungs.

This is gonna be a good run.

With a shiver, Ivan started down Farmingdale Road. His running shoes bounced off the pavement edged by fields of withered grass, beyond which miles of woodlands passed in darkness. Ivan traveled back in time, as he did during every evening run.

. . . Lennings' first freshman varsity starter—108-pound weight class. Going against the captain from Westfield—fourth in the state the year before. Everyone talking about me. Lots of

articles. Always spelling my name wrong . . . Scared to death in the locker room before the match . . .

Forgetting what to do for the fifty-four seconds it took the guy to toss me all over the mat. Struggling to get off my back, while he squeezed the half. So tight my lungs couldn't expand. Can't breathe! Can't breathe! Panic scrambling my head until, finally, giving in. Letting my shoulder blades touch the mat. The referee calling the pin, ending the nightmare . . .

I gave up . . .

Quit . . .

Never again . . .

To Ivan's right, Sycamore Creek snaked its way through the woods before emptying into a pond, a stone's throw wide, where he and the Scott brothers, Josh and Timmy, played ice hockey as kids. Six years ago, the township's new irrigation system began siphoning off water for a nearby corn farm, leaving the pond a bed of damp silt. Not that it mattered to Ivan. Shortly after, the Scotts moved away. He never heard from them again. No letters or postcards, no phone calls. They were just gone. To somewhere in Minnesota was all he knew.

A car came up behind him—illuminating the road ahead, stretching his shadow—then passed by, leaving the crimson of its taillights and the hum of its engine fading into the night.

And his wrestling memories, still raw years later, continued.

. . . first sophomore region champ at Lennings. Dreams of going farther. Riding a nine-match winning streak—all by

pins . . . Quarterfinals of the states—122 pounds. W
by some guy from Newton. Hit a switch, and hit it ha
the guy steps across and catches me. On my back. Fighting to
get out. Then finally do. I score a reversal, later a takedown,
but nothing else.

Time runs out. The humiliation of getting beat 11–4.
Walking off the mat, the crowd staring at me like I'm some
loser. No escape. Freezing-cold nights running. Drilling moves
for hours and hours and hours. Thousands of push-ups. Thou-
sands of sit-ups.

But I lost . . .

Losing tastes like crap . . .

Passing Wellington Farms, Ivan counted 564 steps
along the length of the wooden fence. The night before
it had been 573. He had logged so many miles on this
road, he could run, eyes closed, and avoid all the potholes
and broken pavement. Sweat coated his body, while heat
trapped within the layers of his clothing insulated him
from the cold. Ahead, a row of street lamps shone on
Main Street.

The center of town was desolate. Ivan passed Mr.
Johnston's Florist Shop, a fixture in town for decades;
Burley's Automotive; and the Starlite Deli. In the deli's
front window a poster read: IVAN—BRING HOME THE
STATE CHAMPIONSHIP! A little farther, Ivan passed
Hometown Hardware, then, at the corner, a neon sign
blinked above Evergreen Tavern. The gravel parking lot
was nearly full. Drinking away the last hours before another dreary week of life began, Ivan figured. He crossed

the intersection, and soon, the center of Lennings was behind him. All Ivan could hear was the beat of his running shoes on the pavement and his steady, comfortable breathing.

. . . junior year, undefeated after twenty-four matches— fifteen by pins. Named one of the top 129-pounders by the Star-Ledger *. . . Gonna be Lennings' first state champ. Everyone says so.*

Too many newspaper articles. Too many interviews. Too many people wanting me. Too many distractions. Semifinals of the states, against last year's champ, from Highland Regional. So damn close . . .

Got caught in the first period, but came back in the third. Time running out. Needing a two-point reversal. Sat out, then hit the switch. Leaning back hard against the guy. He's gonna collapse. Ten seconds left . . . nine . . .

Eight . . .

Seven . . .

Six . . .

Five . . .

Four— The buzzer goes off as the guy collapses.

No, there's three seconds left! How'd the buzzer go off too soon? They said the timekeeper made a mistake. That's it. End of discussion.

The timekeeper screwed up.

Lost in the state semifinals.

Lost 8–7.

Miles later, Ivan turned off Vernon Avenue and started up the hill past the Wallens' house. His thighs stiffened, then burned, but he kept pumping. His heart hammered his rib cage. Ivan kept pushing, pushing beyond the pain, beyond any normal threshold, until he was overcome with numbness, still moving, still breathing furiously, but no longer feeling the impact of his feet against the road.

Finally, the hill crested and Ivan was back home. Chilled air rushed in and out of his lungs while baking heat in his body dizzied his thoughts. Ivan staggered a few yards, then stopped at the stone wall that surrounded his house, and bent over. A swell of nausea rose from his gut. His diaphragm jerked tight, and he vomited.

Good run. Damn good run.

A wisp of steam rose from the liquid. Ivan moved farther along the wall, then down the driveway. He glanced back at Shelley's window—a light was still on—then braced again. His stomach jerked a second time. He wiped vomit from his nose, spit the rest from his mouth, and continued around the house.

The back door slapped against its wooden frame. Ivan's father stood in the kitchen with a *Daily Record* in his hand. He was old, silver-haired long ago, but still a bull of a man. Ivan stepped inside, sat on the floor, and began untying his running shoes. His father unfolded the newspaper, nodded, and tapped a page. "Did you see today's paper? There is an article about you." He set his glasses and began reading, "'The township of Lennings—'"

"Papa, not now."

"You will listen," his father said. He again looked down at the newspaper. "'The township of Lennings is nearly invisible on a map of western New Jersey. Hidden on the southern shore of Round Valley Reservoir, fifteen miles from the Pennsylvania border, it is a world away from the bright lights of Philadelphia and New York City. A blue-collar community with small-town ideals, Lennings is again buzzing with excitement for one of its own, Ivan Korske, the odds-on favorite to win the 135-pound state title.'" Then his father said, with a firm nod, "Very nice."

Ivan said nothing. He pulled off his running shoes, tossing them to the corner, then stripped to his underwear. His sleeved shirt and long johns fell to the floor with a wet slap. Sweat glistened on his skin.

"It says teams start practice tomorrow," his father said. "But not Lennings?"

"Remember the *tradition*?"

His father did not.

"That stupid-ass tradition," Ivan muttered, "where we start practicing a few days after everyone else—as a handicap to our opponents." He rolled his eyes. "Someone forgot to remind us we've had four straight losing seasons."

His father sat down heavy in the chair, as if he, too, was very tired. "Are you ready?"

"Ready?" Ivan said, annoyed. "Yeah, I'll be fine."

"Good," his father said, "very good." He then went on. "The coach from Bloomsburg telephoned earlier."

Ivan looked up for a moment, then away.

"He wished you good luck for the season," his father said. "He would like us to drive out for a visit. We will take a campus tour. Before Christmas, perhaps. I think this would be a very good university for you."

A drop of sweat gathered at the end of Ivan's nose, quivered, then dropped to the kitchen floor. "I'm gonna shower," he said, bending down to gather the wet clothing into his arms. Without another word, he slipped into the dark of the dining room and climbed the stairs to his bedroom.

2

His heart pounding, Bobby Zane stood. The thirty-second rest between round-robin shots was hardly enough time to sit down and get up again, let alone catch his breath. But Bobby understood no amount of weight lifting or miles of running would have prepared him enough for the first practice of the season. He slipped the plastic headgear over his head, shifting the halo and earpieces into place, then snapped the chin strap secure. Sweat ran down his cheeks. A drenched long-sleeved shirt clung to his body like a second skin.

"Time!" Coach Dean Messina's voice boomed from the front of the Millburn High practice room. "Look up front!"

Bobby and his teammates turned toward their coach, the most celebrated wrestler in school history, a two-time New Jersey state champion whose wrestling legend crossed county lines as far north as Sussex and as far south as Cape May.

"You guys are *not* executing on your feet," Coach Messina said. He cleared space on the mat. "There are four parts to a single-leg. Stance. Setup. Drop step. Finish."

Coach Messina recoiled in a powerful stance, then lunged forward with his left leg, down to his left knee for a split second, sweeping his right leg under his body and forward along the mat. In an instant, he was back on his feet with the lower leg of an imaginary opponent secure, in a perfect position to finish off the two-point take-down. "Any questions?"

There were none. Or perhaps, Bobby thought, no one dared ask.

"Another set of round-robins, new partners," Coach Messina said. "Seventy-five percent for right now. I want you guys working technique. Perfect technique, understand?"

Wrestlers crisscrossed the mat, motioning for part-ners. Bobby pointed to Kenny Jones, a returning starter at 135 pounds, whose blond hair and freckled skin seemed better suited to a beach than to a wrestling room. But Kenny was a talented wrestler, who rarely put him-self in vulnerable positions on the mat. More than any-one else on the team, he pushed Bobby hard during practice. Bobby liked that.

"You and me," Bobby said.

Kenny nodded.

Bobby then gestured to Anthony Molinaro, hunched over at the side of the mat. "You, me, and Kenny. I'm A."

"B," said Kenny.

Anthony nodded, wearily. "Guess I'm C."

"A and B, on your feet!" Coach Messina barked. "Everybody else off the mat."

Bobby faced Kenny and shook his hand—a ritual indicating each was ready—then crouched in his stance. Kenny did the same. At the whistle, Bobby shuffled laterally, head up, elbows in tight, hands out in front. An opening for the takedown was a sliver wide, but that was all he needed. He attacked, drop-stepping across the mat, his hands clasping behind Kenny's right knee and pulling it tight to his chest. Before Kenny could react, Bobby stepped up.

"Run the pike," Anthony said.

But for Bobby, finishing off a single-leg takedown was as automatic as breathing. He dropped his head from Kenny's chest to Kenny's thigh and stepped back with his left leg, pulling his teammate to the mat and covering on top.

Kenny slapped the mat.

Bobby offered a hand, but Kenny pushed at it, stood up, and turned away for a moment, straightening his headgear and tugging at a knee pad. When Kenny turned back, Bobby extended his hand again. "Ya cool?"

Kenny shook it. "Yeah, sure."

Immediately, Kenny shot a single deep, catching Bobby flat-footed. But Bobby recovered with a heavy sprawl, leaning every bit of his weight on his teammate, driving Kenny's head to the mat and spinning hard. Kenny hung on until the whistle sounded. The two wrestlers slumped against each other.

"Didn't know we were goin' all-out, state finals, hundred-and-twenty percent," Anthony said, putting on his headgear.

"Me . . . neither . . . ," Kenny said, between breaths.

Bobby said nothing. He wanted to stay out on the mat for every shot. *No pain, no gain.* Still, he was feeling the pain, the exhaustion that sucked every bit of strength out of him until even lifting himself up off the mat was a struggle.

"B and C, on your feet," Coach Messina said.

While Kenny and Anthony squared off for the next thirty-second shot, Bobby sat against the wall, gazing beyond the condensation on the windows, catching the last moments of fading daylight. He ignored the brutal heat that rose off his back and the choking humidity that thickened the air.

Things—bad things, sad things—filled his head, and in a weaker moment, he might have let them bother him. But this was his senior year, and nothing was going to distract him during wrestling practice, nothing was going to derail his season.

He stared around the room, feeling little pity for the new wrestlers as they stumbled their way through drills, complaining too much, talking too often, naive to the grueling months that lay ahead. *No need to straighten their asses now,* he thought. In another week or two—if they hadn't already quit—they'd be as dead serious as the veteran wrestlers who would fill Millburn's varsity lineup.

Conference champs again, the Millburn *Item* had predicted. Essex County champs, too, Bobby was sure.

Still, that wouldn't be good enough, he had decided. An entire wall of Millburn's gymnasium was dedicated to the wrestling program, honoring the school's finest teams, with their captains' names stenciled in fiery-red letters: Dean Messina, Bob Nuechterlein, Bill Miron, Buzz Wagenseller, John Serruto, Mark Serruto, Mike Kauffman, Paul Finn. They were names that drew wide eyes and reverent words from the Millburn wrestlers who followed.

That's what Bobby wanted. He wanted his name to stand as prominently as these others, so that in five or ten years, some Millburn wrestler might look up at the wall and say, "Bobby Zane, yeah, I heard about him. One of the best captains the school's ever had."

The thirty-second shot ended. Bobby's heart was still racing, sweat still flowing. He stood and took in a deep breath, waiting for Kenny and Anthony to separate, so he could step in.

The round-robins continued past five o'clock. Bobby's lungs ached; his muscles quivered. Coach Messina had drawn a threshold of exhaustion for each wrestler to cross; Bobby knew he was approaching his own. He saw his teammates looking forlornly at the clock, and even caught himself glancing over once. Then, annoyed, he thought, *Keep pushing . . .*

"Come on, Millburn!" Coach Messina's voice rocked the room.

The wrestling stopped.

"You're tired, I know. You're sucking wind, I know."
Coach Messina walked among the wrestlers. "Fear is
creeping in. Fear of trying new moves when you're tired.
Fear of taking chances. Fear of pushing yourself to that
very edge. Some of you feel like puking, I'll bet. Arms
are dead, legs wobbly, lungs burning. What're you going
to do when you start cutting weight? When you haven't
had anything to eat in days? When you need to drop that
last half pound and still practice hard? How're you going
to stop that fear?

"I see you looking at the clock. Wondering if practice
is ever going to end. Push yourselves! Leave everything
on the mat! Break that fear today, so we won't have to
worry about it tomorrow. Or next week. Or the rest of
the season!"

Coach Messina circled the room. "This is Millburn
wrestling, don't forget that. Since 1965, there hasn't
been a more respected program in all of New Jersey.
Only a few—the chosen—ever get the privilege of wearing a Millburn varsity singlet." He let that idea sink in.
"*Each* of you has a chance to be part of that elite group."

These were the words Bobby waited to hear each season. Ever since he was third-string on the Millburn
Midget team nine years earlier, he had dreamed of a spot
on the varsity team. In that time, wrestling had slowly
but unquestioningly become a part of him. He had, at
first, tasted it. Then chewed and swallowed it. Until it
was inside him and a *part* of him. To the point where he
never questioned tearing his body down practice after

practice, or dehydrating himself so he had too little saliva to wet his mouth, or losing so much weight his rib cage cut sharp ridges across his torso.

It was what a wrestler did.

After a final stare, Coach Messina said, "Grab a partner for double-legs."

Bobby and Kenny paired off again, alternating takedowns. Afterward, fifteen minutes of stairwell sprints, then push-ups, sit-ups, and leg lifts, until—finally— three hours after practice had started, Coach Messina put down his whistle. "Everybody up front."

Bobby sat with his teammates in a semicircle in front of their coach. He had physically given everything. Salty sweat touched the corner of his mouth; some blood, as well. His lips curled into a faint grin. He had stomped all over that threshold.

"Sit up, or sit on your knees," Coach Messina said. "Never crawl, never lie down. Never show you're tired. Not in this room."

He pointed to a stack of papers by the door. "Schedules. Grab one before you leave. It's pretty simple. A match against Morris Catholic in mid-December, the Hunterdon Central tournament during Christmas break, then matches every Wednesday and Saturday until the district tournament. That's it—that's the season. Of course, there is a notable stop along the way." Coach Messina gestured to Bobby. "February tenth."

Bobby nodded. "Rampart High."

"They're back on the schedule," Coach Messina said. "They'll probably be undefeated."

"So will we," Bobby said.

Then Coach Messina, an intense man, turned more severe. "During the regular season, we compete as a team. But starting with the districts, you wrestle for your own glory." His voice was unyielding. "Each one of you should be thinking about being a state champ. It's not beyond anyone's ability. It takes a season of absolute dedication. But it starts with a dream. If you can't *dream* of being a state champ, you won't *be* a state champ."

He held his stare. The room remained pin-drop silent.

"Jumping jacks, then roll up the mats." Coach Messina gave Bobby and Kenny a quick nod. "Captains up front."

Bobby and Kenny faced the other wrestlers. On Bobby's command, the team shouted the count. "One! Two! Three! . . ." At fifty, he and his teammates collected their clothing, knee pads, headgear, and schedules, and dragged themselves down the hall, past the empty classrooms and administrative offices, to the locker room near the gymnasium.

No one spoke.

The season had begun.

3

Black ASICS wrestling shoes dangled over Ivan's shoulders, bouncing against his chest as he walked down the school hallway. "Mr. Korske," he heard from behind him.

Ivan recognized the voice; how could he not? Garrison Holt, who wore the title of new school principal as arrogantly as he wore his pin-striped suits. Yet, despite the fancy clothes, mirrored shoes, and air of pomposity, something was always a little askew. Some days, it was his breath. Other days, a slight body odor.

"I'd like to speak with you," Holt said.

Ivan continued down the hallway. "Gotta get to practice."

"Mr. Korske," Holt said. "I understand it's almost three o'clock, but you can—and will—spare a minute of your time. We both know very well, practice won't start without *you*."

Ivan stopped.

Holt put a hand on Ivan's shoulder and turned him, semi-politely and abruptly. Then he stood, fists at his waist, with the lapels of his suit jacket flared out, material bunched at his elbows—the superhero pose students at school mocked in private.

"We're expecting big things this season," Holt said. "The school, the town—everyone's looking forward to victory after victory. I think there'll be plenty of articles written about you this season. Newspaper reporters, cable TV people, college scouts all visiting Lennings High." Holt grinned. "So," he said, "are you ready?"

Of course I'm friggin' ready, Ivan felt like saying. But he didn't bother opening his mouth. Instead he pretended to be distracted by someone down the hall.

Holt furrowed his brow, annoyed, expecting Ivan to answer. Neither said anything. Students, leaving for the day, walked around them.

"Well, you let me know if you need anything," Holt said, finally. "Anything at all. When this is said and done, I want to be able to say we've crowned our first wrestling state champion. That's very, very important. Understand?"

"I gotta get to practice now," Ivan answered.

Ivan descended the auxiliary stairs to the school basement, turned the corner, and continued through a musty corridor. At the end of a second hallway, past a storage closet, he entered the practice room.

The ceiling was low. A maroon mat covered the floor from brick wall to brick wall. There were no chairs. No benches. No windows. Inside the door hung a board with the twelve wrestling weight classes stenciled at the top— 101, 108, 115, 122, 129, 135, 141, 148, 158, 170, 188, and heavyweight—and below each were two hooks for the names of the Lennings starters and second-stringers.

In an adjacent room, a boiler began to groan and thump in a powerful rhythm, growing in intensity. . . .

Getting louder . . .

When it seemed the machinery might break through the brick wall, the boiler suddenly fell silent. Momentarily. And the cycle began again.

Ivan, wearing his customary black shorts, no socks, and white T-shirt, breathed in the familiar odor of stale sweat. He tossed his wrestling shoes to the side and began stretching. Other wrestlers filed into the room and spread out on the mats. Only one wrestler sat next to Ivan.

"Missed you this weekend," said Ellison Ward, combing his fingers through his spiked reddish hair. "I got wasted. Figured it'd be the last time until March. Ended up at the old graveyard, tossin' beer bottles." He half laughed, then looked at Ivan and nodded dismissively toward a group of wrestlers at a corner of the room. "Freshmen."

Ivan stretched both legs out and reached for the soles of his feet. "They'll be gone by January."

"Think so?"

"We start droppin' matches, they sure as hell will quit." He stared at one in particular, a midsized wrestler with thin arms and a slight gut, his face blotched with acne. "What's your name, freshman?"

Ivan's voice brought an immediate silence to the room. The wrestler looked up from the corner of the room but did not answer, as if he were taking a few moments to pray that Ivan Korske was, in fact, *not* addressing him.

"You," Ivan snapped.

"H-hannen," the wrestler said.

"H-h-hannen?"

Then in a clearer voice, "Phillip Han—"

"Kid, I don't need your life story," Ivan interrupted. "You're not gonna be here long enough for it to matter." He glanced at the clock, then barked. "Tell your girl-friends they better be warmed up. We're startin' practice at three sharp!"

The freshmen wrestlers watched Ivan in awe, while the others looked at him with contempt. Ivan was famil-iar with both looks. Three years ago, early in his fresh-man season, Ivan beat—dismantled, really—Johan Mills, a senior captain and the most popular athlete at Lennings, in a challenge match for the starting spot. While Ivan's name would remain on the top hook at 108 pounds for the rest of the season, his outcast status at Lennings was cemented that afternoon.

Ivan was ignored at practice, before matches, even away from the wrestling room. Out of spite and jealousy, he was sure. The team's coach, Lewis McClellan, saw it and said nothing—something Ivan would never forget. It was only when Ivan won that the team acknowledged him—and then it was only halfheartedly and begrudgingly. He learned the importance of winning for himself, and did so often, setting school records for victories and pins by a freshman. Then as a sophomore. And as a junior. He had learned his four-year quest for a state title would be a solitary one.

Lying on his back, Ellison bridged up on the crown of his head. He rolled forward and backward, then side to side. "Got a letter from the coach at Montclair State," he said. "Gonna visit the campus Thanksgiving weekend. My pop wants me staying close. Coaches must be calling you all the time."

Ivan put on his wrestling shoes. "Too many, too often."

Ellison walked his feet closer to his head, his back arched severely, bluish veins rising from his freckled skin. "Where ya looking?"

"Nowhere around here."

Ivan stood up and began bouncing on the balls of his feet. Immediately, the other wrestlers followed his lead. He saw the hope in their eyes, the hope that this would be the year Lennings surprised teams in Hunterdon County and won a handful of dual meets. He shook his head. They were fooled by the optimism of a new season, when a glimmer of promise still existed.

Don't fool yourselves, he thought. *Nothing's different from last year. Or the year before. Or the year before that.*

Ellison turned to his stomach and began doing push-ups. "How's your weight?"

"A little under 143."

"What weight ya going?"

Ivan shrugged. "One-thirty-five for Hillsborough and the Hunterdon Central tournament. Maybe cut to twenty-nine after. I'll see." He offered a hand to Ellison and pulled him to his feet. "Takedowns."

Ellison nodded, and the two wrestlers faced each other. Behind Ivan, the boiler chugged to life again. His legs sizzled along the mat and his arms knifed into position as he finished off a double-leg takedown, lifting Ellison high off his feet and down to the mat. Ellison did the same. Back and forth they continued.

The practice room door shut.

Ivan turned. The sight of Lewis McClellan knotted his stomach. Another season of him staring, watching every move he made. On and off the mats. In the locker room, in the hallways. It didn't matter, McClellan was always there. The intrusive eyes, the paunch of neglect, the undeserved authority of a mediocre wrestler fifteen years past his time.

McClellan moved to the center of the room. "Okay, Lennings, let's start the season." The wrestlers spread out slowly. "I know those of you returning to the team are all too familiar with the lack of success we've had."

As if on cue, the boiler kicked into high gear, sending a thumping through the room so strong Ivan could feel the vibrations through his wrestling shoes. McClellan raised his voice.

"But there's no reason why we shouldn't be able to change what's happened to this program over the past few years. This season, we're not going to fall into the trap of expecting to lose. We *are* going to be better." He pumped his fist. "Of course, I want each of you to understand there's more to being a Lennings wrestler than simply winning or losing."

The incessant pounding grew even louder. McClellan's voice kept up, until he was shouting. "Each of you will learn teamwork, respect for your teammates, referees, opponents, and—"

There was silence.

McClellan's voice quieted. "And coach. I won't ask for everything, but I will ask for this."

4

Outside the gymnasium, cars of waiting parents lined the school driveway. Bobby climbed into the back of a black Lexus, offering a tired hello to Kenny's mother. The smell of new leather and perfume filled his head as he set down his backpack and slumped against the seat. Kenny pulled the passenger door shut.

"Your coach kept you boys late," Mrs. Jones said, her voice tinged with impatience.

"It's like this every season, Ma," Kenny said.

Mrs. Jones pulled the Lexus to the end of the school driveway, glanced one way, then the other. "Seems later this season." The Lexus darted into the traffic on Millburn Avenue. "Your coach needs to understand there's homework that needs to be done."

"I think he understands," Kenny said.

"No, I don't think so."

"Yeah, yeah . . . ," Kenny said.

"College applications to fill out," Mrs. Jones said. In

the rearview mirror, she caught Bobby's eye. "How'd you do on the SATs?"

"Okay."

"Where're you applying?"

"Not sure," Bobby said. "Dad has that covered."

He was much too tired to get into a conversation about his future when his future didn't seem any further away than tomorrow's practice. He figured Mrs. Jones knew he wasn't going to offer much more. The car was quiet, and as they passed under the stone trestle of the Short Hills train station, up Highland Avenue, then eventually onto Lake Road, Bobby stared out the side window, fighting off the typical early-season exhaustion that left him light-headed after each practice.

Mrs. Jones turned to Kenny. "Are you hungry?"

"I'm always hungry."

"Are you going to eat?"

Kenny shrugged.

"All this starving can't be good," Mrs. Jones said. "I don't know how you boys can concentrate on . . ."

Bobby stopped listening. Any other time, he would have hung onto every word from Mrs. Jones' mouth, following the movement of her red-lipsticked lips as they pursed with each syllable. He would have noticed streetlights glancing off her blond hair and been disappointed that the rest of her was hidden underneath a fur coat. But not tonight. Not fifteen minutes removed from another brutal practice. It was almost Thanksgiving. The first match of the regular season was a few weeks away, the Hunterdon Central tournament not long after that.

". . . you certainly can't take good notes during class," Mrs. Jones said, shaking her head. "I'll say it again if I haven't said it a hundred times before, this wrestling is ridiculous."

The Lexus came to a stop along a corner property where Lake Road angled into Joanna Way. Bobby grabbed his backpack, buttoned his varsity jacket, and stepped out. He thanked Mrs. Jones for the ride.

"Haven't spoken to your mother in a while," she said.

Bobby smiled, faintly. "She's been working hard. There's a house in the Deerfield area she's trying to sell." That was a good lie.

"It's a busy time for all of us," Mrs. Jones said. Almost sadly, Bobby thought. "Have her call me . . . okay?"

"I will."

The Lexus sped away. Bobby swung his backpack to his shoulder and looked across the street at the Short Hills Club, where he could see four men playing paddle tennis. Bobby found the powerful lights above the courts comforting. During the late fall and winter, the lights shone through the barren trees and illuminated his bedroom as he lay in bed waiting for sleep. When he woke up in the dark morning and returned home at night, the lights were a kind of surrogate sun.

Bobby jogged up the brick path around the house. Before reaching the driveway, he heard voices. He stopped in the shadows, peering through the side window into the garage.

The ceiling lightbulb, yellow and dim, cast odd shadows on his father—a "fine attorney," as family friends often called him. His charcoal-gray suit hung limply off his shoulders, his tie undone. His eyes looked dark and tired. And Bobby watched Christopher, his mussed brown hair sprouting from under a crooked New York Yankees baseball cap, swing a lunch box back and forth.

Bobby thought about waiting until his father and brother went inside the house. They wouldn't know he was home. He could be alone, at least for a few minutes. Then join them later. Maybe even after dinner.

But Bobby was cold. And bruised. And tired. And even a little sad. Standing in the darkness wouldn't help that, so he stepped out under the garage lights. "Hey, Dad, didn't think you'd be home this early."

His father unlatched the trunk of the Jaguar and pulled out a briefcase. "Your mother's working late." The trunk slammed shut. "We have to cook for ourselves."

"That means pizza, right?" Christopher said.

"No, not tonight," his father said.

"But I want pizza really bad."

"There are leftovers."

"Stevie's family *always* has pizza for—"

"Enough," his father snapped, "enough . . . We'll eat what we have." He walked out of the garage. "Christopher, help your big brother bring in the garbage pails, then wash up. I have a phone call to make."

Bobby watched his father disappear around the corner of the house to the back door, then he put a hand on Christopher's shoulder.

"You okay?"

Christopher nodded.

"Don't worry about it," Bobby said. "We'll have pizza some other time."

Together they walked to the end of the driveway and carried the empty garbage cans into the garage, setting them along the wall.

As Bobby opened the back door to the kitchen, a car rushed down Lake Road. He looked in its direction, hoping the car would turn onto Joanna Way and up their driveway. But it continued on. He stood at the door for some time, listening for the engine of another.

5

Plastic food containers sat on the dining-room table. Bobby spooned sliced potatoes onto a plate, then jabbed a piece of veal with his fork. Beside him, Christopher ate quietly, while at the other end of the table, his father poured a glass of wine, saying nothing. Bobby glanced at his mother's empty chair. The dining room felt empty, he thought. The damn house felt empty. Ignore it. Throw down some food, go upstairs, get to bed. Period.

Bobby huddled over the dish. It was his only food all day. One forkful after another, he shoveled the food into his mouth. Chew, swallow, take a breath. Chew, swallow, take a breath.

At any other time of the year, his father would not have ignored such table manners. But the calendar had passed into wrestling season. Bobby wouldn't have to sit with the family at dinner. His growing moodiness from cutting weight would be forgiven. And as the season wore on, when he became entirely self-centered, that, too, would be tolerated. All in the name of wrestling.

"Your face is raw," his father said.

Bobby reached up and with his fingers touched an area below his temple where the skin was tacky. "Mat burn."

"Did you return the favor?"

"Of course," Bobby said.

His father nodded, pleased. "This is going to be a special season."

"We'll be good," Bobby said. "Six returning starters. Some of the young guys'll step up, too."

"No," his father said. "This is going to be a special season for *you*."

Bobby shrugged. "Whatever."

"No, not whatever."

"Dad—"

"What about the states? What about *winning* the states?"

Bobby put down his fork. "Do we have to get into this now?"

It was a grueling road to the states, he knew. In late February, thirty-two district tournaments across New Jersey advanced the winners and runners-up in each weight class to the eight region tournaments held the following weekend. The same was true from the regions to the states, a week later, when the top sixteen wrestlers at each weight competed for the title of state champ.

His father shook his head. "That's not the kind of attitude I expect from you."

"Sorry," Bobby said, smartly.

"I'll assume it's because you're tired."

"Yeah, yeah, I'm tired."

And still hungry. And, yes, he had thought about being a state champ. What wrestler in New Jersey hadn't dreamed of standing atop the winner's podium at Princeton University's hallowed Jadwin Gym to have the championship medal placed around his neck? Any wrestler worth a damn dreamed it a thousand times. But Bobby didn't feel that way right then. Not hungry and dehydrated and wondering how many more nights his mother's chair would be empty.

His father's voice was uncompromising. "You weren't 18–5 last year on a fluke, Bobby."

"I know."

"You won the districts and placed fourth in the regions."

"I know, I know. I was there."

"Relax, young man," his father said sharply. "You can be much better this year. Everyone believes it. Now *you* have to."

"I have other things to think about."

"Like what?"

"I don't know, like . . ."

"Girls," Christopher said. He pursed his lips. "Kiss, kiss, kiss. He does that on the phone *all* night."

It wasn't exactly the truth. There was only one girl—

Carmelina Veloso. Bobby had met her at the Livingston Mall the month before, while she worked the perfume counter at Macy's. She was brash but soft, and she seemed to dance without moving. She had a killer smile, semi-dark skin, and eyes that reached out and held his gaze, so that even if he wanted to look somewhere else, he couldn't possibly. Bobby kept a photo of Carmelina in his shirt pocket. During class, he would look at it and wonder what she was doing at that moment in her school. Late at night, they would talk on the phone about nothing in particular, but everything, it seemed, that mattered.

"You shouldn't be up that late," his father said to Christopher, then he turned back to Bobby. "You get one shot at your senior year. One shot, that's it."

"I know."

"You've got to be more selfish. Understand? You want the team to do well—fine—but think about yourself first. The state tournament has to be your primary focus. And enough with the phone."

"Yes," Bobby said. "Focus."

But Bobby knew he had said it halfheartedly, and when his father shook his head, Bobby felt he had to say more. "Dad, it's not like I'm saying I can't do it. But if the team is ranked high in the state, and I win the districts and regions, wouldn't that be great?"

His father stood up, carrying dishes to the sink. "But would it be enough?"

Bobby didn't answer.

"Well, would it?" his father said. "You should certainly win the regions. And the states? Who knows what'll happen once you're at Jadwin."

Bobby still didn't say anything.

"Did you see the Yale application?" his father said. "I put it on the staircase."

"I saw it."

"Don't settle, Bobby. Do you understand me? Don't settle. If you want to be a state champion, then make it your goal and accept nothing less."

The thought of that made Bobby's stomach tighten. His final season of high school wrestling had always been off in the distance. Now it was here. No days to count, no waiting for summer to turn to fall, and fall to turn to winter. It was time to deliver. And now his father was talking about him being a state champ.

6

"D amn, Papa," Ivan muttered, his voice hoarse.

He sat up in bed, awoken by the sound of a grinding ignition as his father tried to start the Chevy Nova. Sunlight fought through the ice-frosted bedroom window, and Ivan could tell it wasn't any later than seven o'clock.

Ivan climbed out of bed, draping a wool blanket over his shoulders, and shuffled across the floor to the window. With his fingernail, he scraped away a patch of ice on the inside of the glass so he could see the front yard and the pile of logs his father had begun moving the day before.

Frost dusted the evergreens along the driveway and made the Nova appear even older than its hundred-and-sixty-thousand miles. His father tried the ignition a half-dozen more times, until the engine finally turned over in a grating screech. Plumes of exhaust chugged from the tailpipe, drifting upward.

His father stepped out of the Nova, wearing overalls, a plaid flannel shirt, and work boots. He *had* to be cold, Ivan thought. Across the road, Mr. Peterson tugged at the leash of his golden retriever, Modine. The two men waved, then continued about their business. Ivan's father walked to the front of the house. A moment later, the door opened.

"We will leave in five minutes."

Go without me! Ivan wanted to say. *I'd rather go by myself.* He sat down hard on the chair, looking around the bedroom as if somewhere behind his closet door or underneath his bed, there might be an escape. The sun slid behind clouds, casting the room in shadow.

Finally, he said, "I'll be down."

Ivan threw off the blanket, opened his closet, and reached along the inside wall, pushing aside a few pairs of jeans, four shirts, and a couple of hooded sweatshirts. He wished he had nicer clothes.

At the back of the closet, Ivan found a hanger with a pressed pair of navy-blue corduroy pants, a neatly tailored white shirt, and a burgundy tie. On the closet floor, he kicked away some rumpled clothing, uncovering a shoe box. He opened the top and pulled out black loafers.

Ivan reached his arms into the shirt, the starched material feeling cold against his skin. He stepped into the pants, pulled on a pair of argyle socks, then wedged his feet into the stiff loafers. His feet felt caged and pinched along the instep, reminding him how much he preferred the nylon and thin rubber soles of his wrestling shoes. Ivan carefully knotted his tie, smoothed it flat, then inspected himself, making sure every stitch of clothing was in order.

When he was young, his mother would tease him about that. She would kneel in front of him, straighten his tie, and give him a kiss on the cheek. "You look like a very serious young man." Years later, he would take great pride when the *Lennings Chronicle* described him as a "very serious" freshman wrestler.

"You have much work to do later," his father called up from the bottom of the stairs. "We will go now."

The front door closed.

A smell of roses filled the Nova. His father handed him a bouquet of long stems wrapped in a cone of green tissue paper.

"These are nice," Ivan said. "Mr. Johnston made them up?"

His father nodded. "Special for us."

The Nova rumbled down Farmingdale Road toward the center of Lennings. At the Starlite Deli, a few townspeople were picking up the morning paper, and the Sunoco station was open for business. Otherwise, theirs was the only car on the road.

His father looked at him. "You are dressed nice this morning. I should have dressed up, too."

Ivan held the bouquet of flowers. He stared out the passenger window. "I don't think Mama will care," he said, quietly. "We're going to see her; that's all that matters."

A half hour later, they had passed through Stanton Station to the outskirts of Quakertown, where a wrought-iron gate marked the entrance to the cemetery. His father turned in and continued up the gently curving roadway. On the sloping hills, rows upon rows of head-stones formed an endless pattern.

Across the way, a young woman, her head hung low, stood motionless. The hem of her dress flapped in the wind as she held the hand of a neatly dressed boy stand-ing obediently still. A headstone overwhelmed his small frame, outlining his brown pants and matching coat.

Ivan's father parked the Nova under a barren maple tree. Ivan stepped out. Wind pressed against him, so he flexed his muscles for warmth and wrapped his wool coat tighter. The grass was firm under his shoes as he walked toward his mother's grave, his father a step behind. Ivan gazed at the woman and young boy—they still hadn't moved. *Who'd they lose?* he thought. *What was* their *pain like?*

Out of the corner of his eye, Ivan watched his father. This wasn't the same man from a year earlier. That man had withered away. Someone had taken his place, some-one bitter and distant.

Passing the graves, Ivan was careful not to read any of the headstones. It was a superstition he had learned years ago when he and the Scotts played capture the flag in the graveyard down past Wellington Farms. "Never look at the names," Timmy Scott had said in a hushed voice, "or you'll be haunted by the dead person for thirteen years."

But eventually Ivan came upon his mother's headstone, where he *had* to look. His father stepped forward and went down awkwardly to one knee.

Ivan held him. "Papa?"

White mist rose from his father's mouth as he whispered something Ivan couldn't hear. A twig lay against the headstone, and a few leaves huddled beside the stone base. His father brushed them away.

Ivan glanced at the etched lettering. ANNA KORSKE, LOVING WIFE AND MOTHER. That was all that remained, her name in stone, her body buried below. And memories.

His father looked back over his shoulder. "This is a nice spot for her."

Ivan handed him the flowers. "Here, Papa." His father laid the roses at the base of the headstone and placed a fist-sized rock on the stems to keep the flowers from blowing away.

Ivan stepped back. His eyes began to well, but he fought back the tears. Two hundred and twenty-six days of unyielding loneliness, of missing his mother so much his temples throbbed, of wishing that somehow it had been a big joke and that one day he'd walk through the back door after practice and she'd be standing there in the kitchen.

"Ivan, did you wrestle good today?" she'd ask.

"Yes, Mama," he'd say. "Let me show ya what I did to

one guy." And he would show her a hip throw, lifting her high off her feet.

And she would laugh, "Ivan, put your mother down; I am too old for this craziness."

April third. A Saturday. Ivan didn't remember whether it had been sunny, rainy, cold, or whatever. It seemed like yesterday, and five years ago, all at once.

April third. That's when her body gave in to the disease. He didn't know its despicable name. Something unpronounceable, something the doctors couldn't explain to him in any understandable way. They stood in their pristine white coats saying things that changed nothing. In the end, they could only delay her death, not stop it. Ivan watched as his mother, over a few months, became weak and brittle, until finally the disease took her away. And through it all, he could do nothing to stop it. Nothing.

Sunlight broke through a seam in the clouds. Ivan welcomed the faint warmth, tilting his head back to let the sun shine on his face. He squinted, searching for the woman and young boy. They were gone. On another knoll, an elderly man took their place. Then, just as quickly, the sun disappeared.

"We should go, Papa."

His father opened his eyes, dazed. "What?"

"We should go. It's cold out . . . for you."

His father nodded and, with Ivan's help, stood up. "Take some time for yourself," he said, starting back to the Nova.

Ivan stood a few feet from the headstone, too tired for more tears, too drained to know what to think. His fingers outlined the engraved letters. She was in his heart. Now and always. But she wasn't here, in the flesh, when he needed her most. *Why her? Why my mama?* But there was no reasonable explanation. Nothing that made sense. And so he cursed God and any belief in Him.

Ivan stepped back and, without another look at the grave, stalked away. When he and his father returned home, he found the only comfort he could, running the roads of Lennings. The same streets, the same routine. Over and over.

Ivan toiled through the afternoon, continuing the work his father had started earlier, carrying logs from a pile behind the shed to the edge of the driveway. Eventually dusk fell, making way for another cold night.

Ivan wedged the logs into a neat stack. His palms were nicked with splinters and rubbed raw, his right thumb smeared with blood. He stopped for some time, wiping the sweat from his forehead.

"What's up, Champ?" Ivan heard from the end of the driveway. He turned.

Shelley's blond hair fell out from under a beret, spilling over a cherry sweater and white turtleneck. Her smile was the finishing touch of a perfect picture on an otherwise colorless day.

"Happy turkey day," she said.

"You, too."

Modine bounded toward Ivan, stopped at his feet, and spun around in a circle, tail whipping back and forth. Ivan knelt down and patted his side. "You just love the cold, don't-cha boy?" He looked up at Shelley. "How's your day been?"

"Holidays at my house are like a day out at the asylum, I swear to God. I barricaded myself in my room to finish up this A.P. English paper, but then I saw you out here. Can't stay long, though." She gave him a curious look. "Why in the world are you working today? Or should I even ask?"

"Papa thinks we're in for a bad winter."

"So . . . ?"

"He wants it done."

"Today?"

"Today."

"Well, okay," Shelley said.

Ivan appreciated that she didn't push it further.

Shelley followed him as he grabbed more logs. "You know," she said, with a whimsical grin, "even when you're doing something else, something totally different, you still look like a wrestler."

Ivan stopped. "And what kinda look is that?"

"Well, first of all, that spiked haircut makes you kind of mean-looking."

"Mean?"

"Very."

"What else?"

"You walk like a wrestler. Shoulders flexed, hands out to the side. It's like you're always ready to grab someone and take them down really hard." She mimicked the walk, shifting her shoulders back and forth, adding a frown. "And, of course, you always look tired, thin, and a bit sickly pale."

"Thanks."

"That's the life you chose, I guess." She picked at a piece of bark and playfully tossed it at him. "So is there any guy out there who actually thinks he's gonna keep you from winning the states?"

Ivan had little desire to talk about wrestling. Wrestling was all around him, day and night, without a break, without an escape. He stood up straight, easing the ache in his back. The pile was much larger than he had figured. He leaned against it for a moment. Shelley stood close. He could smell her perfume.

Ivan nodded toward her house. "So it's crazy over there?"

Shelley rolled her eyes. "My grandparents are here, and my cousin Jean from Philly with her three kids, brats that they are. Later, big—and I mean, big—Aunt Lucy is coming with her fourth husband, George."

"Fourth?"

Shelley smirked. "Yeah, that's what the family thinks. We're used to it now, I guess." She bent down to fish a twig out of Modine's mouth, but he squirmed from her arms and circled the woodpile. "This dog's crazy, too," she said. "I guess he kind of fits in. Anyway, you can take your chances and come over later if you want. I promise I won't make you eat anything."

"Thanks," Ivan said, picking at a splinter.

She reached for his hand, her fingers touching his chafed skin. "Why aren't you wearing gloves?"

Ivan shrugged.

"You should be."

"A little late now," he said.

Shelley held his hand a while longer. They talked about bits and pieces of nothing really, then Shelley got a solemn look on her face. She was quiet, as if waiting for the right moment, then, finally finding it, she said, "How was your visit?"

No one else would have had the nerve to ask Ivan. And if someone else had, he wouldn't have answered. But this was Shelley, the girl who finger-painted with him in nursery school, who was there freshman year when no one else was, who cried when he lost in the state semi-finals last March and, weeks later, when his mother died. She was his closest friend for God knows how long. If anyone was allowed to breach the wall he put up, she was.

"Okay, I guess," Ivan said.

"Tell me about it."

"Yeah?"

"Please."

Ivan drew in a deep breath . . . and exhaled. "It was cold . . . very cold . . . sad. Thought there'd be more people since it's a holiday. I guess they were smarter than us. Staying outta the cold, I mean."

"And your papa?"

"Who knows?"

At least his father wasn't drowning his sorrows in

bourbon, Ivan thought. Like other men in town did. Still, his father was drowning, just drowning in a different way. Most nights he'd come home late from work. They'd exchange a few words, then disappear—Ivan into the basement to practice moves, his father into the television room. For hours on end.

"He's sad," Shelley said.

"I guess."

"Do you talk to him?"

"I ask him what's the matter," Ivan said, "but he just shakes his head."

"He's got so much to think about," Shelley said. "This house, your season. And he's probably sad about you leaving for college. You told him, right?"

"No."

"Why not?"

"I'm not ready."

"Ivan, you gotta tell him."

"Yeah, I know," Ivan said. "The coach called the other day when Papa wasn't around. They don't make a decision for a while, but he pretty much promised me a scholarship."

"Do you have to go so far away?"

"Every night, I dream I'm there," Ivan said. "Warm, sunny, not cold and gray like Lennings." He motioned. "Look at this place." He stepped to the pile of logs.

"It's not so bad," Shelley said.

"School ends, I'm outta here. That week, maybe the week after."

Shelley touched his arm. "Why are you in such a rush to leave? Look how excited the town, the school—everyone—is for this season. You're gonna be the best in New Jersey."

Winning the state championship. Ivan had thought about it every waking moment since a victory in last year's state semifinals had been stolen from him. Yet, he felt chained to it all—the practice room, McClellan, Lennings, the expectations. He breathed in and looked up the road. "The Wallens must be making a fire."

"Smells good," Shelley said. "See, if you go out West you'll miss all that. No crisp, clean air. No beautiful fall afternoons. You can't get *that* in Arizona."

Ivan didn't say anything.

"It'll be hard for us to stay close, you know."

"Nah."

"Yes," Shelley said. "You'll be busy, and I'll be busy wherever I go. And I know how much you hate to write letters . . . But if I did write you, you think you'd write back?"

"I'm not leaving yet."

"But would you? Even when you're absolutely exhausted from wrestling practice and you don't have an ounce of energy to pick up a pen?"

"Yeah, sure."

Shelley touched her finger to his jacket. "Cross your heart?"

He nodded.

"I don't believe you," she said, with a crooked smile. "And I can't believe you wanna go out West. Don't. Stay here. I'll help you with your applications, I promise I will—"

"Shelley!" Mrs. Peterson called out from their front door. "I need your help." She waved. "Happy Thanksgiving, Ivan."

Ivan waved back.

Shelley sighed. "Well, I gotta go. Turkey probably needs more basting." She started down the driveway, with Modine following behind. "Have a nice one with your papa. And forget this Arizona thing. Go somewhere near Philly so we can visit each other."

Against the front porch lights of the Peterson house, Ivan watched Modine scamper inside. Shelley turned. "Gonna come over later?"

Ivan shook his head. "I can't."

"I understand," Shelley said. "Anyway, see you tomorrow, Champ."

Ivan continued his drive toward the bottom of the pile, lifting the logs and stacking, lifting and stacking. . . .

It was late. The pile was finished. Ivan faced his house. Though his father was somewhere inside, the house reeked of emptiness. He would've enjoyed dinner with Shelley and her family. He'd even put up with Cousin Jean's bratty kids and big Lucy. The food would be wonderful—even if he didn't have any—and the banter around the dinner table would be dizzying, and funny, and everyone would be so alive.

Shelley could complain all she wanted, he thought.

But her house lived and breathed. "Come stay in this place," he whispered.

Ivan opened the front door and, for a moment, was surprised, even slightly confused. On the dining-room table, two places were set meticulously with the family's finest china, silverware, and cloth napkins—things he hadn't seen since his mother passed away. He turned the light dimmer on bright.

"The table looks good," he called out.

"The turkey will be ready soon," his father said, walking in from the kitchen. "You should take a shower now." He placed the dish of baked yams and a bowl of pierogies on the table.

"All the wood's in a pile," Ivan said.

"Good."

Ivan started toward the stairs.

"Wait," his father said. "Your hands. What is the matter with your hands?"

"Nothing."

"Let me see."

Ivan stopped, turned his palms up. They were red and swollen.

"You did not wear gloves?"

"Couldn't find any."

"Gloves are in the shed. Do you have a brain in your head?" his father said, poking his temple with his finger. "You could have hurt your hands so they are no good for wrestling. Then what would we do?"

Ivan turned. His father might have said something else, but Ivan closed his ears and mind and continued away.

In the upstairs bathroom, he hunched over the porcelain sink, easing his lower back. Warm water poured over the cuts and scrapes on his stiff hands. He knew Thanksgiving night was not the best time to tell his father he was going to Western Arizona University for college. Then again, he thought, when would be?

Ivan showered and put on a sweatshirt and jeans, using the few minutes that passed to strengthen his resolve. Until it was simply *time*. He marched down the stairs, through the dining room, into the kitchen.

"Papa, I need to talk to you." Without waiting for a response, Ivan continued. "I wanna go away to college. Not Jersey or Pennsylvania."

His thoughts had never been so clear, nor had his own words brought such relief. There was conviction in his voice. Satisfaction filled him. If his father was ever going to accept him as a man, Ivan knew he had to explain himself, then hold firm to what he *had* to do.

His father continued spooning cranberries into a glass bowl, not looking up, and for a time Ivan wondered if he had heard him. He placed the bowl aside, laid the spoon in the sink, then ran the faucet. His father walked over. Standing face-to-face with his father was the only time Ivan ever felt fear. He did now. Finally, his father spoke. "No." The brevity of his response was startling.

"But if I get a scholarsh—," Ivan started.

"You want to be away from here?" his father snapped. "From your home?"

Ivan didn't answer.

"You have pushed my patience."

"This is what I want."

"That's enough," his father said.

"Papa," Ivan said, "it's been eight months. Mama's gone. We need to move on. When are you gonna let me live my—"

The back of his father's hand, in a crisp, sudden arc, sent Ivan sprawling into a chair. In an instant, Ivan bounced back up to his feet like he had done a thousand times on the mat. His reaction seemed to surprise his father, if only for a moment. Ivan didn't touch his cheek or acknowledge the gash on the inside of his lip. He simply smiled, a livid smile.

Every bit of him wanted to raise his fists to return the favor. He was old enough, certainly strong enough, and now pissed off enough to take his father. But he didn't. Instead, he turned, looking over his shoulder, the whole time still smirking, and left the kitchen.

Ivan stared out his bedroom window at the Petersons' house. It seemed every light in every room was on. He imagined Shelley and her family having a wonderful time.

"Happy friggin' Thanksgiving," he whispered.

From the living room downstairs, late-night television programs droned on. Ivan knew his father was sitting in his chair, motionless, not smiling, or laughing, or crying, but staring blankly, a vacant look of loss that worried Ivan with its relentlessness.

And the television screen raining its pity.

7

The house was dark, empty and silent, and unexpectedly peaceful.

Bobby lay in bed, drifting out of a shallow nap, his body exhausted, his head filled with thoughts of Carmelina. . . .

On Sunday morning, Bobby borrowed his father's car, promising that he was going to the library to work on his college essays. Instead, he drove down to Newark to see Carmelina. It was his first time at her house.

At the front door of a brown row house, Bobby pressed the doorbell. He stepped back from under a rusted awning and looked across the street at Branch Brook Park. An elderly woman pushed a stroller along the buckled sidewalk, while trash swirled in the wind, ducking in and out of the passing cars. Police sirens sounded in the distance.

Bobby's stomach cramped, a reminder that he hadn't eaten anything all day and wouldn't until dinner. He checked the house number again, then rang the bell a second time.

There were footsteps and the front door opened. "*Oi*, Bobby," Carmelina said.

Bobby moved toward the door, but Carmelina waved a finger. "No boys allowed in the house. Mama's rules." She put her hand on his chest. "I'll get my coat. You wait here."

Bobby stepped a foot inside. The living room was dark. Still, he could see the sofa cover torn and pock-marked from cigarette burns, and the carpet worn to its padding. Paintings of Jesus and crucifixes hung on the walls. Carmelina went into a nearby bedroom, where Bobby could see a pink vanity cluttered with bottles of hair spray and makeup, and fashion magazines scattered about the floor. She returned quickly.

"I just got back from Mass. Mama's still there," she said, nudging him out. "Nothing to see in here, *meu amor*."

Carmelina closed the door and took a few moments to smooth her turtleneck and skirt, and straighten her wool coat. She started down the front steps, looking over her shoulder. "You came a long way to see me, Bobby."

Bobby followed her. "It's not that far."

"And you keep calling."

"You call me, too."

"So tell me, then," Carmelina said, "why'd ya come down to lovely Newark?"

Bobby shrugged. "Didn't have much to do today," he said with feigned nonchalance. "Thought I'd come see you."

"You mean *stare* at me? Like ya do waiting for me at work. Pretending you're shopping. You don't fool me."

"Well, I guess I won't come and visit anymore," Bobby said.

"It's all right, I'm used to it," Carmelina said. "Just like that first time you stared at me at the mall. You and your little gang of white boys walked by." She smiled. "I knew you'd come back."

"Really?" Bobby said. "I only came back because I needed a birthday present for my mom."

"Oh, Bobby, you're so silly," Carmelina said, shaking her head. "You woulda come back. Maybe later that day, maybe the next Saturday, maybe the Saturday after that. But you woulda come back. I could see it in your eyes. You were looking at this gorgeous, dark girl—like nothin' in *your* school—and couldn't think of anything else."

Carmelina reached her hand out to hold his. Bobby didn't say anything; he knew she was right. She *had* him. Whether it was her auburn curls rolling over her shoulders when she moved, or the way her lips came alive when she spoke, or that everything about her was soft and inviting—she had him.

They walked down the sidewalk. At the corner, Carmelina smirked. "Let's have some fun."

When the DON'T WALK signal turned red, Carmelina bolted across the street. Bobby's throat squeezed. *Oh, no*— Cars in both directions bucked forward then screeched, their bumpers reaching out to within a loose thread of Carmelina's skirt. Horns blared, but she continued on, laughing.

Bobby waited for the light to change, then crossed. "You're crazy!"

"Scared ya, didn't I?" Carmelina spun around, holding her skirt from raising too high. "Come on, this is my only Sunday off this month. I wanna make the most of it."

She grabbed his hand and they ran across an open field in Branch Brook Park. As they reached the swing set, Carmelina turned sharply, and Bobby's arms naturally wrapped around her. Carmelina looked at him. Her fingers touched his cheek.

"Your face," she said. "It's red."

"I got cross-faced in practice yesterday."

"What's that?"

Bobby placed the bony part of his wrist against the bridge of Carmelina's nose. "Like this," he said. "Then jam it hard."

"To hurt you?"

"To make it uncomfortable."

"Doesn't sound like fun," Carmelina said.

"It is, I guess."

"So you like touchin' other boys?"

"No," Bobby said.

"But you *do* touch them? My friend Maria went to a wrestling thing once. She said it looked like two boys doin' it to each other."

"No way! I'm trying to beat the guy's ass, and he's trying to beat my ass. I don't think about anything when I'm wrestling. It's just instinct, pure instinct. You'll see when you come to my matches."

"No, no," Carmelina said. "I'm not goin' to any wrestling matches, or whatever ya call them."

"Yes, you will."

"I won't."

"Yes."

"No."

"Why not?"

"I can't," Carmelina said. "I just can't."

"Can't?"

"Look, Bobby, I work Wednesday nights and every Saturday. *Every* Saturday. I told you that. The other days, I gotta do homework and help my mother. You see where I live. My family is not rich like yours. We don't have a fancy car like yours. I gotta work. I gotta get the grades."

"So no matches at all?" Bobby said.

Carmelina paused. "Probably not."

"Well, I'll work on changing that."

Carmelina shook her head. "Let's just have fun now."

She grabbed Bobby by the front pockets of his jeans and pulled him close. Her eyes started at his forehead, moving to his nose and chin, then downward. She unbuttoned his jacket, lifted the bottom of his sweatshirt, and touched his stomach. She tugged at his jeans again, until her breasts pressed firmly against his chest.

"I do like you, Bobby."

"Yeah?"

Her head tilted slightly and she looked into his eyes. Bobby let Carmelina take things wherever she wanted. He gave up control and didn't care. Her lips floated toward him. He closed his eyes. Wet and warm, she kissed his left cheek, dragged her tongue down to the curve of his jaw, then whispered something in Portuguese.

"You're different than I thought you'd be," Bobby said.

"What'd ya think . . . ," she said, kissing his neck, "I'd be like?"

"Serious . . ."

"I am at the store," Carmelina said. "That's what the rich white ladies want. Just 'cause I live here don't mean I can't act like them. I can when I wanna." Then she softened. "Besides . . . that's work."

"And now?"

"This is play," she said. "*Beije-me.*"

She pressed her mouth against his, and they kissed. And held hands. And hugged. And found a secluded spot behind the swing set, where their hands wandered. There, against her feigned objections, Bobby unbuttoned Carmelina's blouse and lifted the bottom of her skirt. . . .

Bobby opened his eyes. He heard his mother's Mercedes pull up the driveway. He tossed the comforter off, sat up, and scooted to the window.

He watched his mother step from the car, a mink coat draped over her shoulders, a Louis Vuitton valise tucked under an arm. She was an elegant woman, Bobby thought. An elegant woman who wore elegant clothes, drove an elegant car, and lived in an elegant house. She spent her days as one of the most successful real estate agents in town and attended all of the most important charity events in the area. Bobby admired his mother, her drive for success. Someday, he wanted to be as well-known in Short Hills as she was.

But she was changing. It had started at the end of the summer, perhaps earlier, though Bobby wasn't sure. Despite the familiar clothes, her hairstyle, the way she presented herself, she no longer moved around the house as if its queen. Instead she seemed indifferent, as if an occasional visitor.

She walked up the cobblestone pathway to the back door, glancing up at the house. Bobby leaned back from the window, then bolted from the bedroom, skipped down the stairs, and hit the foyer floor with a thud. When he reached the kitchen, he heard his mother fumbling for her keys. He opened the door.

"Oh, you scared me." She put her hand to her chest. "I didn't see any lights on."

"Sorry," Bobby said, giving her room to brush past him. She shrugged the mink coat off her shoulders and handed it to him, then unwrapped a silk scarf from around her neck.

"Did you put your workout clothes in the washer?"

"Not yet."

His mother was not happy. She looked at her watch.

"I don't have much time. I assume you're hungry. I'll put some food together." She opened the refrigerator.

"That's okay," Bobby said softly, walking into the foyer. He was hungry—starving, really—but it wasn't particularly bothering him.

"Christopher should be dropped off by the Browns' in a little while. Make sure he gets to bed early. I have an appointment at the Paper Mill. For a benefit in January. Your father will be home later," his mother said, then added, "He's at the tennis club, I think."

Inside the foyer closet, Bobby switched on a light and grabbed a hanger. Peering between the hinges of the open door into the kitchen, he said, "How come you don't?"

"Don't what?"

"Play tennis anymore," he said, "with Dad?"

His mother stopped for a moment, as if to consider his question.

But Bobby wasn't sure he wanted to hear the answer. He hung the fur beside the other coats, turned off the light, and closed the closet door. He walked into the kitchen. "Got an A-minus on a calc test today."

"That's nice," his mother said. She spooned leftover broccoli and a chicken leg onto a plate.

"Wrestling's going well."

His mother gave him a cursory smile.

And then it seemed they didn't have anything else to say to each other. Bobby leaned on the countertop, hoping his mother would say something more. Anything.

But she didn't. So he fingered, idly, the china figurines lining the kitchen windowsill.

"Be careful with those," she said.

Bobby pulled his hand away. "Mrs. Jones asked after you again."

His mother smiled. "I haven't spoken to Charlotte in such a long time."

"She said that."

"We were supposed to have lunch a few weeks ago. Right around Thanksgiving. I guess I got busy, then she got busy . . ." She slid the plate into the microwave oven and pressed the settings. A soft whirring sound followed.

From the cupboard, Bobby pulled out a pewter baby cup engraved with his initials. It held four ounces, ideal to keep from drinking too much. He filled it with seltzer. The first cup went down quickly. So did the second. His limit.

His mother chopped celery and carrots on a wooden cutting board, then broke up a head of lettuce and tossed it all in a bowl. After a minute, the microwave bell sounded. She pulled out the dish. "Set a place at the table."

"That's okay," Bobby said. "I don't want anything."

"Did you eat already?"

"No."

His mother set the plate down hard on the countertop. "This is starting too soon," she said, her lips tight. "Every year you start earlier and earlier."

"What?"

"Your dieting."

Bobby rolled his eyes. "Wrestlers don't diet, Ma. They cut weight. We all do it. It's simple. Practice. Run after practice. Don't eat. Run. Practice some more. We do it and do it, again and again."

"Don't be a wiseass, Bobby."

"I'm not."

"You can't just starve yourself."

"I've been doing this a long time."

"And didn't you get sick twice last year doing the same idiotic thing?"

"No."

"Oh, you didn't?"

"No," said Bobby. "It was something else."

"Something else," his mother said. She laughed dismissively and shook her head. "I rush home. Rush to put food on the table. All I ever do is rush."

"I didn't ask you to do anything."

"Oh, that's right, I forgot, you can handle everything."

"I can," Bobby said. "And I *do*."

"Don't raise your voice to me," his mother said.

"I'm not raising my voice."

His mother's eyes narrowed. "Shut your mouth. Shut your goddamn mouth right now."

"I'm—"

A wooden spoon slammed against the countertop. "If I tell you to shut your mouth, young man, you'll goddamn do it." She waved the spoon wildly in the air. "You better start showing some respect. I'm not your little Puerto Rican—"

"Portuguese," Bobby snapped. "Carmelina's Portuguese."

His mother pointed the spoon. "I don't give a damn what she is," she said. "You watch yourself with her. And understand this, young man. I'm not a slave here. I work all day and have to come home to this house and make food for you and your brother and your father. And you can't even do a simple thing like put clothes in the washing machine and turn it on. I can't do everything in this house, do you understand that?"

"You're hardly ever here," Bobby said.

"Excuse me?"

His anger flared. "Why aren't you—" But he held back.

"What?" his mother said.

And his anger flared more. "Why aren't you around more like—"

"Like what?" she baited him.

Then his anger exploded. "Like a mother's supposed to be."

In the moment between when the last word left his lips and when his mother wilted, Bobby's throat squeezed and he was suddenly dizzy. A wound was torn open.

His mother sighed. Deeply. Suddenly she looked exhausted. But not from working too many hours or sleeping too few; from something else. Bobby had seen it before, in the eyes of opponents who knew, even before they stepped out on the mat, that they had lost. The look of resignation.

"Ma . . ."

She raised a hand. "I need to go in my bedroom for a while," she said, rubbing her eyes. "It's been a long . . ." She didn't finish. Instead, she put down the spoon and walked past him, out of the kitchen, into the foyer, and silently toward her bedroom door.

"Ma, can we talk?"

"There's no reason to say any more," she said. "Is there, Bobby?"

He watched his mother walk into her bedroom and close the door. She didn't slam it, just a simple quiet click of the lock. Bobby stood alone in the kitchen. A swirl of steam rose from the chicken and broccoli, then dissipated. He listened. The house was empty and silent. And lonely.

8

It was well past ten o'clock. Textbooks, spiral notebooks, and pencils covered the bedspread. Propped up on an elbow, Ivan looked on absently as Shelley explained an algebra equation. "Understand?" she said, tapping the page with her finger.

"Yeah, sure," Ivan said.

"You're not into this."

"I am."

Shelley smiled. "No, you're not. Try to listen for a few minutes," she gently pleaded. "I can't help you otherwise."

Her hand brushed his. She sometimes did that. She'd touch his arm, or hand, or shoulder. Sometimes she'd hug him. Maybe it meant something; maybe it didn't. Ivan wasn't sure. But he always wanted that hug to last for hours, not moments, the way her smile stayed in his mind long after she went home.

"I *know* you understand this," she said.

"I'm trying . . ."

Ivan thought he could finish the problem, probably even get it right. Why, though? Little math was needed on a wrestling mat. Takedowns and reversals were two points; escapes, one; back points, two or three. Short of a pin, the wrestler with the most points won. Pretty simple. More importantly, if Shelley thought he didn't need the help, she might not stay as long. He was *not* going to take that chance.

"I'm just a little tired," he said.

"Me, too."

Shelley turned to her side and reached her arms above her head, which pulled the bottom of her shirt from the waist of her jeans. Ivan couldn't help but stare at her slender stomach. It had been a wonderful two hours laying beside Shelley, following the curves of her ears, the slope of her neck, breathing in her perfumed scent whenever she'd sweep her hair off the pages or turn quickly to say something.

"You're lucky," she said. "My parents watch over me all the time. Every project, every paper. Have to do my homework perfectly, have to get the perfect grades. You'd think they'd trust me." She looked at him. "Let's take a break."

She closed the textbooks and notebooks, pushed them into a pile, then jumped to her feet. "Your papa won't be home for a while, right?"

"Yeah."

"Working?"

"Yeah."

"Your papa's a nice man," Shelley said. "My dad says that about him all the time . . ."

Ivan sat up. "And?"

"Nothing."

"Tell me."

"I don't know. It's just that I worry about him," Shelley said. "And I worry about you."

"Worry?" Ivan said. "Don't worry about me."

"But I do."

"Don't," he said, irritated for reasons he didn't quite understand. He suddenly felt like lifting weights, or running, or beating the hell out of some guy on a mat.

"I just want everything in the world to work out for you, Ivan," Shelley said. "Always have. Ever since we were kids. Even more since your mother . . ."

"Died," Ivan finished.

"Yes," Shelley said. "There's nothing wrong with that, is there?"

Ivan said nothing.

Shelley turned and walked over to the dresser, flipping through a stack of unopened envelopes from college athletic departments. She held one up. "They spelled your name wrong. You'd think they'd get *that* right."

Ivan moved beside her.

"Have you started any essays?" she asked.

He shook his head.

Shelley picked up a quarter-sized bronze medal discarded in the corner of his bookshelf, turned it over, and read the etching on the back. "Bloomfield Summer

Wrestling Tournament, fourth place." She handed him the medal.

Ivan rolled it in his fingers. "My first tournament. They took the four littlest kids and threw us together. Got my ass kicked." He flipped the medal on the shelf, where it skittered under dog-eared copies of *Amateur Wrestling News* and *W.I.N.* Magazine. "I keep it out as a reminder."

"Of what?"

"Getting my ass kicked."

Shelley looked around the room. "Where are the rest?"

Ivan tapped a bottom drawer with his foot. Then another drawer.

Shelley knelt down and pulled one of the handles. Gold trophies lay stacked, one on top of the other, with dozens of medals littering the bottom like coins in a treasure chest. She picked up a fistful of medals. "AAU freestyle qualifier, first place. District seventeen championships, first place. Most valuable wrestler, Old Bridge Wrestling Festival." She looked at Ivan. "Do you remember winning these?"

"A few," Ivan said.

With a sigh, she pushed the drawer closed. "You're so hard to understand."

"Hard to understand?" Ivan said.

"You're better at wrestling than I am at *anything*."

Ivan shook his head. "Doubt it." He didn't want to hear this. It didn't matter what Shelley or his father or the newspapers *said* about how good he might be. There were only results. He had only placed third in the state last year. Not first. Not state champ. There was no consolation prize for *almost* winning. There was only winning. Or losing.

"You're good at the piano," Ivan said.

"Yeah, sure," Shelley said, rolling her eyes. "I'm okay, one of a zillion people who are okay at the piano. I can play at the holidays for my aunts and uncles; I can play at school sometimes." She held her fist to her chest. "It's just not *in* me. Not *in* me like wrestling is *in* you. What you have is special. Can't you find *any* satisfaction in that?"

He didn't answer.

Shelley stood. She leaned her shoulder against his. "It's late," she whispered.

She seemed tired—tired of doing her homework, tired of prodding him to do his. Ivan wanted to kiss her and have his body naked next to hers. He wanted to make love to Shelley, though he didn't know what making love felt like. And, it seemed, she might want that, too.

Then Ivan simply erased those thoughts. There wasn't time to be boyfriend and girlfriend. That complicated life and would certainly steal his focus from wrestling. He wouldn't allow that. They would always be friends—best friends—but wrestling had to come first.

Always.

9

Sun streamed through the kitchen windows, bathing the room in a warm morning haze. Bobby walked in from the foyer, anxious and quiet. At one end of the breakfast table, his father sipped coffee as he thumbed through a stack of legal briefs, jotting notes and separating the papers into piles. At the other end, Christopher shoveled cereal into his mouth, humming along with a Saturday morning cartoon on the television. His mother, dressed for an afternoon open house, stood at the counter, spooning bran and fruit chunks into a blender.

Bobby waited for one of them to notice him and acknowledge that this wasn't a typical morning—that he was just a few hours from the first dual meet of the season. But no one said anything to him, or to each other. They were like total strangers, he thought.

"It's hot in here," he said. He put down his gym bag, walked to the counter, and kissed his mother's cheek.

"I made some ham sandwiches," she said. "They're in the fridge." She returned to preparing her breakfast.

His father, looking over his glasses, asked, "How's your weight?"

"Close."

"A problem?"

"No."

Hunger did claw at his stomach, and his lips and tongue were dry, but Bobby would not put an ounce of food or a drop of liquid in his body until after weigh-ins.

His father tapped the top edge of a handful of pages, making them flush. He secured the pages with a paper clip, then set them in his briefcase. "I have a few more things to look at here. I'll drive you to the school in a—" He stopped and stared down the table. "Christopher, turn the television down."

"But—"

"Turn it down!"

Bobby turned. The kitchen was silent. His mother stiffened as she glared toward the table. Christopher reached out to lower the volume.

"Bobby," his father said, "have you heard of—"

The blender churned, cutting off his words. From the corner of his eye, Bobby saw a hint of a smirk on his mother's lips. She and his father exchanged seething looks.

His father raised his voice above the noise. "Ever hear of Ivan Korske?"

The blender stopped.

"Korske?" Bobby said. "From Lennings. Took a third at 129 last year. Lost a close one in the semifinals. Everyone was talking about it. They said he got ripped."

His father pointed toward a *Star-Ledger* on the counter. "There's a write-up on him."

Bobby opened to the newspaper's sports section and the headline: KORSKE SEEKS ELUSIVE STATE TITLE. Bobby scanned the article, catching parts of Korske's modest background, the death of his mother, and the prediction that no one would score a takedown on him all season. Bobby looked for just one thing and nodded when he found it.

"He's going 135 this year. Can't say I'm disappointed."

"You can beat him," his father said.

"Yeah, well, I'll just worry about today's match."

"You can beat anyone. You just don't believe it yet."

Give it a rest, Dad. How about worrying about our family? Bobby snatched his gym bag and threw on his varsity jacket. "I'll be in the car."

His father pulled the Jaguar onto Joanna Way and rounded the end of their property, then rushed down Lake Road. Bobby stared out the frost-coated side window, clutching his gym bag. This was not how he wanted to start the morning. Part of him wanted to yell *something* at his father, but he couldn't come up with anything meaningful. And when he did, he thought better of it.

"When's your match start?" his father asked.

"JVs go at ten," Bobby said. "We'll start around eleven."

"After I drop you off, I'm going home to finish some work. I'll drive out to Morris Catholic with Christopher," his father said. "How are college applications coming?"

"Fine."

"The one from Cornell?"

"It'll get done."

"When?"

"Soon."

"How about today?"

"Today?"

"Work on it after the match."

His father was serious, oddly serious. Bobby didn't understand why. The applications would get done, there wasn't any urgency. The deadlines weren't until February and March. His father knew that.

"I'm going to the mall later," Bobby said. "Me and some of the guys . . ."

"'Some of the guys,'" his father repeated. His forehead knotted, and when he continued, his tone was firm. "These applications have to get finished, Bobby. I don't want another weekend to slip by. Christmas is a week and a half away."

Bobby didn't look over. "They'll get done."

"You and I both know you won't have much energy to write all the essays once the regular season gets going."

Bobby sighed. "I'll start them tomorrow. No practice, no match. I won't have anything else to think about," he said. "I just can't today."

"You're going to see that girl," his father said.

"No."

"Yes, you are."

"No, I'm going with the guys," Bobby said as convincingly as he could.

"Don't bullshit me, Bobby!"

Bobby felt the heat rise up his sweatshirt. This was serious. He didn't often hear his father swear. "Come on, Dad, I've got a match today," he said. "The applications'll get done. I promise."

"You're damn right they will."

Neither said a word. Soon, his father pulled the car down the Millburn High driveway, coming to a stop in front of the gym. He stared ahead. A distant look, Bobby noticed. Bobby waited for his father to say something, and when he didn't, he opened the door and reached a foot to the curb. Then he felt his father's hand on his arm.

"Hold on, Bobby. Listen to me a moment. This is going to be a difficult winter. Very difficult. There's a lot going on. Now would be a good time to"—he paused, as if searching for the right words—"to prepare for anything that might happen." He seemed to force a smile.

Bobby knew his father was talking about something very different from a tough winter of wrestling. A helpless feeling overcame him, one that had been building for months. Something very wrong had seeped into his family, something destructive and elusive, a kind of disease. He couldn't stop it or slow it down. These were heady thoughts, something Bobby hoped he'd never have to consider. His mind scrambled for answers, not knowing the most important questions.

But Bobby realized that wasn't the truth. He knew the questions. They were crystal clear. He knew the answers. They were just as obvious. Most of all, he knew what was happening to his family.

Bobby didn't want to hear another word from his father; he just wanted to get the hell out of the car. "Gotta go, Dad. See you later?"

"I'll be there," his father answered.

Bobby closed the car door. He watched the Jaguar curl around the school driveway, turn right, then disappear down Millburn Avenue. He might have stood there in the cold for a long while if Anthony hadn't walked up.

"Hey, Bobby," Anthony said. "We gotta get going."

The words nearly slipped by his ears. "Uh, yeah, I'm ready."

Anthony grabbed the sleeve of his varsity jacket. "You're dazed, man. Remember, we got a match today."

10

Bobby raised his eyes. Coach Messina stood before the varsity team in the cramped, musty visitor's locker room of Morris Catholic High School.

"It begins today," Coach Messina said, arms folded across his chest. "Your seasons. Our team's season." He held up the lineups. "On paper, Morris Catholic isn't very strong. We should beat them by a wide margin.

"But we don't wrestle on paper," Coach Messina continued, dropping the lineups to the floor. "Last year's records mean nothing. Reputations mean nothing. What matters is how well you wrestle on the mat today."

Coach Messina took his time, gesturing deliberately, locking eyes with each of the twelve Millburn wrestlers.

"Don't let up at all, not at any moment this season. From the first practice, to today's match, to the state tournament, each of you goes all out. You'll have the spring and summer to relax."

———

Coach Messina was pleased, Bobby could tell. He didn't smile or stand up or say anything, but instead sat back in the folding chair on the Millburn side of the mat and watched.

Damien Eriksen, Morris Catholic's 129-pounder was a tough wrestler—district champ last year, with a third-place finish in the regions. "Don't give him the opportunity to believe he belongs on the same mat as you," Coach Messina had said before the match. "Leave no doubts."

And so, Bobby was doing just that.

The referee motioned. "Millburn's choice for the second period. Top, bottom, or neutral?"

"Neutral," Bobby said. In the first two minutes he had scored a takedown, let his opponent escape, then taken him down a second time for a 4–1 lead. He expected to do it again.

The referee stood at the center circle, motioning for both wrestlers. Bobby stood ready in his stance; Eriksen did as well. Off the whistle, Bobby moved forward to tie up with Eriksen. He dug his toes into the mat and drove his legs, then eased up, allowing his opponent to push back.

Fifteen seconds passed . . .

Then a half minute . . .

And the game of cat and mouse continued.

At the edge of the circle, Eriksen crossed his feet, putting himself momentarily off balance. Bobby reacted instantly, dropping down to his right knee, his right shoulder and arm deep between his opponent's legs, then pivoting sharply to capture a leg. He swept Eriksen down to the mat to finish off the hi-crotch takedown.

But a 6–1 lead wasn't enough. Bobby continued his attack, jamming his hand under Eriksen's right arm and onto his head for the half nelson, then driving forward and cranking in the head. The Morris Catholic wrestler offered little resistance, and for a moment, Bobby was mildly surprised to be so thoroughly dominating an opponent Coach Messina considered to be tough.

Bobby turned Eriksen to his back, scoring two back points. Then held him for a referee's count of five to get the additional point.

"Near fall, Millburn," the referee shouted. "Three points."

Eriksen was ready to be taken; Bobby knew it. He went for the pin, tightening his grip, pressing his opponent's shoulder blades to the mat until both touched and the referee slapped the mat.

11

TEAM SCORE: HOME: 0 VISITORS: 22

Ivan lowered his eyes from the scoreboard. *Another damn season of embarrassments. First match—getting our heads handed to us.* He stood behind the Lennings bench, waiting for time to run out in the third period of the 129-pound match—the match before his. Another Lennings wrestler was being tossed around the mat as if he had no business being in the same gym as his Hillsborough opponent.

... ten ... nine ... eight ...

"At least it's not another pin," Ellison said from behind Ivan. He rolled his neck and stretched his arms.

"Does it matter?" Ivan said.

Out of the corner of his eye, Ivan saw Shelley, sitting halfway up the stands with some friends, wave. Ivan nodded, then fixed his stare across the mat. His opponent was kneeling down behind the team, eyes closed. After a moment, he genuflected hastily and stood up.

You're gonna need that prayer, Ivan thought, waiting to see if his opponent dared stare back. He didn't. That annoyed Ivan. *Don't be a candy-ass. Make this a match.*

. . . five . . . four . . . three . . .

Hillsborough fans began to clap. Ivan unbuttoned his warm-up jacket and pulled off his warm-up pants. He took a couple of deep, relaxed breaths. His vision narrowed. Cropped from the sides. Until the gym's vast space had disappeared. No stands, no spectators. Nothing else; no one else. Just him and his opponent. Bitter anger inside Ivan began to froth and spill over. It was all part of the ritual, and he embraced it. The muscles in his arms, shoulders, and back, his thighs and calves, were warm and loose. Ivan hissed curses under his breath.

The buzzer sounded.

The referee separated the 129-pound wrestlers and raised the arm of the winner. He then motioned to the scorer's table. The individual match score was reset to zero as the scoreboard above changed to HOME: 0; VISITORS: 27.

On the opposite side of the mat, Ivan's Hillsborough opponent adjusted the chin strap of his headgear and brushed aside hair from his eyes. His teammates and coaches surrounded him, patting him on the shoulder and back, offering words of encouragement and strategy.

The PA system announced, "Now wrestling at one hundred and thirty-five pounds, from Hillsborough . . ."

The Hillsborough wrestler bolted from his teammates, sprinting to the center circle. His eyes were wide, his movements herky-jerky. He put a foot on the circle.

". . . and from Lennings, Ivan Korske."

The Lennings crowd roared. Ivan dropped his warm-up jacket off his shoulders. He set his headgear and walked to the center of the mat. At the referee's command, Ivan and his opponent shook hands. Ivan saw the fear in the Hillsborough wrestler's eyes. His opponent knew he was going to get pinned. It was just a matter of how quickly.

"Wrestle!" the referee commanded.

Ivan's drop step was blistering. Before the Hillsborough wrestler could react, Ivan was in on the single-leg, arms around his opponent's knee. Tight. He stepped up, ready to run the pike and finish off the takedown. *Too damn easy.* And it was. Devastatingly so. *Fight me . . . Fight me!* But his opponent's breathing was already strained.

So Ivan loosened his grip. Slightly. Just enough to allow his opponent to wedge an arm underneath Ivan's armpit as a wizzer. *Think ya got somethin'?* Ivan thought, and he nearly smirked, sensing a sudden but shallow confidence in his opponent's movements. The Hillsborough wrestler, balancing on one leg, attempted to hip into Ivan, hoping to knock them both out of bounds so the referee would start them in the center circle again. His attempt was futile. *Weak . . . Very weak . . . You gotta have more than that.*

Ivan allowed the charade to go on for a half minute, then he lost his patience and exploded. Letting go of the leg and stepping into his opponent, with a fury. Wrapping both arms around his chest. Lifting. Kicking out his legs. Crashing him to the mat. Hearing him groan in pain.

"Takedown, Lennings!" the referee called out. "Two points!"

Ivan deftly switched to a headlock, leaning all his weight on his opponent, inching his shoulders toward the mat. *Come on, fight it . . .* But the Hillsborough wrestler couldn't. He had nothing left.

The referee blew the whistle, signaling the pin. The Lennings fans stomped the floorboards of the stands and yelled their appreciation. Ivan stood up, had his arm raised, then walked past McClellan, past his teammates, nodding to Ellison, who waited for his 142-pound match to be announced.

"Another victim," Ellison said.

"First of many," Ivan answered.

12

The evergreen nearly touched the ceiling—white lights and silver tinsel spiraling down from the top, ornaments hanging from its branches—filling the room with a sweet holiday scent. A week ago, Ivan had noticed the tree not far from the old pond. It stood out from the others with a kind of nobility that Ivan thought belonged in his house. Now adorned for Christmas, it was a special tree indeed.

Ivan had always loved Christmas, allowing himself, even during the crucial first month-and-a-half of wrestling season, the pleasure of wishing December away until, on the twenty-fifth, he would wake up and rush downstairs to the living room to eagerly wait for his parents to join him in opening presents.

This Christmas, however, would be the first without his mother.

People hid from their feelings, Ivan thought. He wouldn't allow that. He had learned to face the pain of losing his mother. In his own way. Even knowing she was long gone, he wasn't afraid to feel her presence, her touching his shoulder, kissing his forehead. Later in the day, he would visit her in person.

Ivan unzipped his jacket and pulled off the layers of clothing underneath. Every run had a purpose—to cut weight, to build endurance, to work on explosiveness—but this morning he had given himself a kind of gift, just an easy jog through the snow, enjoying the soft crunch under his sneakers, the powdery wake behind him.

Ivan toweled off, then put on dry thermal bottoms and sat in front of the tree, arranging the presents. There were four: two from his father, one wrapped in shimmering red paper and the other in green; a large flat box from Shelley, which he hoped was a Flyers jersey; and the last, his gift to his father.

Ivan touched a red and green miniature sleigh that hung from the tree. A branch higher, nearly hidden behind tinsel, hung a cardboard sock, tattered along the edges and creased across the middle. Wads of cotton were coming unglued along the top. Ivan turned it over, recognizing the awkward scribble of his childhood, "Love You Mama and Papa, Merrie Chrisstmas—Ivan." Ivan thought he had made it in kindergarten, though all he could really remember were snippets of so many fading holiday images.

He lay back on the wood floor, listening to the house clank and pipes hiss and the wind whistle down the chimney flue. Ivan sat up, pinching the film of skin over his abs. Still more to lose. He lay back down and sat up again.

He did another sit-up, then another, his upper body reflecting in the bulbous silver ornaments. Now faster. Twisting his torso right, touching his left elbow to his right knee, then the opposite. Harder and harder, he jacked his body upright, all the while thinking about the Hunterdon Central tournament and crushing whichever opponent stood before him. When he reached fifty, he did another fifty.

Ivan then turned to his stomach, setting his hands on the floor, shoulder-width apart, and pushed up. Then again. And again. His forearms were engorged with blood, and a network of veins ran elbow to wrist as he pumped out the reps. At fifty, he sat through and did another set of sit-ups. After that, he did push-ups again.

A half hour had passed when Ivan heard his father's footsteps down the stairs to the living room. Ivan turned around, wiping a touch of sweat from his forehead, breathing hard.

"Merry Christmas, Papa."

13

The clock clicked to 12:43 A.M. Bobby was still a long way from sleep. He held his stomach muscles tight, fighting back quivers of nausea, but he couldn't stop the pangs of hunger that wrenched his gut.

Another wave of nausea hit. Bobby sat up and held the edge of the bed. He wanted to yell, but that would have taken too much energy. Heat radiated from his body, but there was nothing left to sweat. He rolled his tongue around to keep his mouth as moist as he could. He ached for water—not much, just a cupful—but his weight was too close to take a chance. Nothing went in unless something came out first.

Bobby stood up, walked across the dark bedroom to the closet, and turned on the light.

He stood naked, his skin puckering into goose bumps from the chilly floor. He set the counterbalance at 129¾ pounds, then stepped gingerly onto the scale platform. The scale arm fell.

He tapped the counterbalance to 129½. The scale arm didn't move from the bottom.

At 129 even, the scale arm floated. And Bobby figured he could probably piss another quarter pound. He'd be able to drink something—not much—but at least something.

In the bathroom, Bobby squinted under the bright ceiling light. From the medicine cabinet, he pushed aside bottles of laxatives and diuretics and pulled out an old glass baby bottle, into which he peed. Urine careened off the inside, filling the bottom. He relaxed, hoping every bit would drain from his body. The yellow liquid moved higher and higher until finally the stream sputtered to a few squirts. Then just a drop or two.

It measured four and a half ounces. Short of what Bobby had hoped, but enough to allow him to keep his mouth wet for a while. He poured the urine out, washed the glass bottle, and set it back in the medicine cabinet. Then he turned on the cold water faucet and filled his pewter baby cup to the top. Four ounces, no more. His thirst was impossibly strong, his hand unsteady. The cup tilted against his chapped lips and the cool water washed over his tongue. He savored every drop.

After a final check on Christopher, curled up restlessly under rumpled blankets, Bobby returned to his bedroom and slid under the covers.

A sprained ankle had kept him out of last year's Hunterdon Central tournament. This year, the 129-pound weight class was his for the taking. With Korske going 135, Bobby was certain no one could keep him from the title. People would take notice. That made him nervous as hell.

He stared at the ceiling. Slight imperfections in the paint began to fade in and out. He felt his chest rise and fall with each breath, and he followed the rush of each pulse down his shoulders, arms, wrists, and fingertips; and his torso, legs, feet, and toes. Then he ran through the catalog of moves in his head.

Again and again.

Eventually, yawns came more often and sleep quieted his tired mind.

14

Sweat beaded on Ivan's skin. He climbed the stairs to his bedroom. The midnight run had been a good one, one that would put his weight at 130 pounds. By morning, he'd be closer to 129¼. By weigh-ins he'd be right on weight.

He'd stay at 129 pounds for the rest of the season. He hadn't told McClellan or his father, and wouldn't until morning, relishing the idea that the 135-pounders at the tournament would be thanking God when they found out, while the 129-pounders would be scared as hell.

Switching on the bedroom light, Ivan listened for his father downstairs, then closed his door. He walked to his bed and reached under the mattress. In his hand, he held the application for Western Arizona University.

Attached was a note from Coach Riker, wishing him good luck for the season. Ivan fixed on the signature, George Riker. The "Gainesville Grappler," a nickname he earned as the winningest high school coach in the state of Florida.

But it was at Western Arizona where Riker had secured his legend. It was Riker who turned the university's nearly defunct wrestling program into an NCAA contender, who guided three wrestlers to national titles, who made the upper echelon of collegiate programs— the Iowas, Nebraskas, and Oklahoma States of the world— sit up and take notice. In a fitting tribute, *Wrestling USA* called Riker "the Dan Gable of the West." Ivan received recruiting letters from dozens of college coaches across the country. None was as important as this one.

A drop of sweat fell on the envelope, smudging Ivan's name. Then another.

This is gonna get me out of Lennings. That's what it's gonna do. Get me away from McClellan, from Holt, from all this crap.

He reached inside the application's envelope and pulled out the essay sheets and personal-information request form.

But a familiar fear stopped him. *I can't do it*, he thought. *Maybe*, he worried, *I'll never be able to do it.* Without another thought, Ivan slid the pages back into the envelope and the envelope, once again, under the mattress.

15

By nine o'clock, weigh-ins had ended, and a buzz of anticipation filled the Hunterdon Central gymnasium. Sitting high in the stands with his teammates, Bobby looked down on the gym floor, where two mats lay side by side, each with a scorer's table and chairs at opposite corners for coaches. Wrestlers from the eight competing schools had begun warming up—stretching out and drilling moves. At a far entrance, a team in maroon warm-ups walked in.

Kenny tapped Bobby on the shoulder. "Lennings."

Bobby sat up. He was curious to see Ivan Korske up close. He watched each wrestler, but none had what the newspapers described as "the musculature of a thoroughbred, the cold stare of a caged panther."

"I'm ready for Korske," Kenny said.

Bobby glanced over his shoulder. "Yeah?"

Kenny nodded. "I don't give a rat's ass if he took a third in the states. Other guys worry about that; not me."

Finally, the last of the Lennings wrestlers walked through.

"Well, that's a disappointment," Kenny said. "Big, bad Korske's a no-show."

It was wishful thinking, Bobby knew. Korske would be there. He'd show up in a big way.

Moments later, a lone wrestler entered through a second door. It seemed the gymnasium hesitated.

"Spoke too soon," Bobby said.

Korske's walk, his gestures, growled, "You know who I am; don't mess with me." Other wrestlers stopped and stared. Korske nodded to a few people, shook hands with the Hunterdon Central coach, then sat down on the bottom bleacher, away from his team.

Kenny leaned forward. "Look at him. Tryin' to be a tough guy. I'm gonna kick his ass from here to Millburn."

"Hope you do," Bobby said.

"Oh, I will."

And so, Bobby had seen Korske and was duly impressed. Perhaps Korkse had glimpsed him and was impressed, as well. Bobby hoped so, but doubted it. He closed his eyes; facing Ivan Korske—or a wrestler of his stature—would come at another time. And when it did, he knew he'd have to be perfectly prepared. But for now he'd worry about his weight class, his opponents. The murmur of background conversations softened as he ran through dozens of scenarios for the opening whistle of his first-round match. He visualized the mechanics for a single, double, and hi-crotch—his body hitting each perfectly, taking his opponent down to the mat. Then duck unders, leg sweeps, hip throws . . .

Soon, he nodded off.

"Bobby!"

Someone was nudging his shoulder. Bobby opened his eyes, blinked, and focused.

"Bobby, wake up," Anthony said.

"Huh . . . ?"

"Did ya hear me?"

Bobby sat up. "What?"

"Korske's in your weight class."

"He's going 129?"

"Must've cut down," Anthony said. "The brackets are up on the wall. He's seeded first; you're second."

Bobby breathed in—his heartbeat had kicked into high gear—and forced air out his nose. *Lousy way to wake up from a nap.* The cobwebs cleared.

Kenny rose to his feet. "Come on, let's look at the brackets."

Bobby didn't move. His body stiffened instinctively, and he stared as defiantly as he could muster at that moment. He would concede nothing, certainly nothing in front of his teammates. *Don't show fear,* he thought. *You're a Millburn captain.*

He saw his teammates hesitate, as if waiting for his response. As abruptly as he awakened, his body was on alert, his mind clear.

"You can; I don't need to," he said. "I'll see Korske in the finals. I'm ready. I've been ready for him."

Beneath the bleachers, hidden among the steel supports, Bobby bounced on his toes, then stretched his arms and shoulders. What looked like a crumpled algebra quiz lay at his feet next to an empty Coke can, pencils, and chewed pen caps.

His first-round match ended in a second-period pin, setting up a semifinal match against Jordan Seitzer from Manalapan, tough on his feet and Region VI champ the previous season.

Sweat coated Bobby's skin. One more win and he would get a showdown with Korske. He unzipped his navy blue nylon warm-up suit. A pungent smell rose from his armpits.

"On deck, mat number one," the PA system boomed. "One-hundred-and-twenty-nine-pound semifinal. Zane, Millburn; and Seitzer, Manalapan." And a moment later, "On deck, mat number two. One-hundred-and-twenty-nine-pound semifinal . . . Korske, Lennings; and Milner, Essex Catholic . . ."

Bobby genuflected. In a quieter moment, he could have finished reciting the Our Father and the first part of the Hail Mary—which was all he knew—but his thoughts were blurred . . . *and forgive us our trespasses, as we forgive those who—* Twice he lost his place, then gave up on the rest when the crowd let out a sudden roar. He stepped out from under the bleachers. Time was winding down in the third period of the 122-pound semifinal match.

Bobby watched Korske standing by mat number two. Korske didn't bounce on his toes, didn't stretch his legs or arms, or practice any moves. He didn't talk to teammates, or his coach, and only acknowledged briefly a girl with blond hair standing behind him. Arms folded, headgear tethered to the drawstring of his warm-ups, he seemed as calm as if he were lying on the sofa at home.

At the buzzer, Bobby stripped off his lucky Yankees T-shirt and put on his headgear. He got a pat on the back from his father and a "Go, Bobby!" from Christopher as he marched his way to the corner of the mat. There, he and Coach Messina shook hands.

"This guy's good," Coach Messina said. "But this is *your* season. Six minutes of hard wrestling. The finals are waiting for you."

Bobby and his Manalapan opponent met at the middle of the mat, each placing a foot inside the center circle. They shook hands. "Keep wrestling until I stop you," the referee instructed, then blew the whistle.

Bobby immediately tied up with Seitzer. For much of the period, he pushed forward and eased up, letting Seitzer push back, gauging his strength. Sensing an opening, Bobby dropped down for a hi-crotch, pivoting to capture a leg. But Seitzer sprawled hard, and neither gained an advantage.

Bobby pressed the attack, shooting a double-leg, settling in deep. Seitzer wedged his arm underneath Bobby's armpit for the wizzer and, with a powerful shift of his hips, forced Bobby's grip to weaken. Bobby tried to repenetrate, but as he did, the buzzer sounded, ending the period scoreless.

"Your choice, Millburn," the referee said.

"Bottom," Bobby answered, adjusting his headgear. He noticed Seitzer hunched over, tugging at the bottom of his singlet, his chest heaving fiercely.

Bobby dropped to his hands and knees. A moment later, Seitzer settled into the top position. Off the whistle, Bobby stood hard, thrusting his hips out, trying to break the hold around his waist. Seitzer tripped him down to the mat. Bobby tried a second time. Then a third time. On the fourth, he was able to get to his feet, cut his arm underneath, and square off.

"Escape," the referee said. "One point, Millburn."

It had taken a monumental effort, but Bobby pressed for the takedown. With time running down, he tugged on Seitzer's head, then drop-stepped into his gut. It was as beautiful a single-leg as he had done all year, and for a moment, he pictured the scoreboard flashing 3–0.

But that was premature. Again, Seitzer threw in a powerful wizzer, driving Bobby outside the wrestling circle as the second period ended.

Bobby walked back to the center, mad at himself for losing the takedown. Now he would be in the top position, needing to ride Seitzer for the final two minutes to protect the 1–0 score.

At the referee's whistle, Seitzer did a roll that Bobby

countered, then sat out and turned hard, which Bobby followed smoothly. Seitzer sat out again, but Bobby kept a tight waist. The two wrestlers battled from the same position, Bobby looking to maintain control, Seitzer fighting for the escape.

Time was ticking away—a match with Korske was waiting. Bobby felt Seitzer weaken, so he drove his opponent's head toward his knees, setting up the snap-back. It was waiting for him. Right there. He could rip Seitzer to his back, score near-fall points, and ice the match.

But unexpectedly, inexplicably, an errant thought—perhaps about Korske, or maybe his parents—cracked Bobby's focus, and he hesitated a moment too long.

Seitzer ducked his shoulder, hips whipping over his head. Bobby recovered momentarily, stepping over the roll, but as he did, Seitzer locked his wrist and hooked his leg. A Granby roll. A move so graceful that, even as it happened, Bobby managed a hint of admiration. Then he braced.

"Hold on, Bobby!" Coach Messina yelled.

Bobby felt Seitzer lean back hard. Bobby scooted his hips toward the outside circle, trying to get out of bounds before the referee made the call. He inched closer. One leg out. He needed to get a shoulder over the line. So close, Bobby knew, but impossibly far.

"Reversal," the referee shouted an instant before the buzzer sounded. "Two points, Manalapan."

Bobby collapsed.

A wave of disappointment crushed him. They were

staring, he was sure. Every person in the gymnasium was staring, mocking his loss. Bobby struggled to his feet but did not raise his head. The referee lifted Seitzer's arm in victory, drawing cheers from the Manalapan fans gathered at one corner of the gymnasium.

Bobby walked off the mat, passing his teammates, Christopher, and his father, who offered a quiet, "You'll get him next time." Bobby gathered his warm-ups and looked over at mat number 2.

Holding an eleven-point lead, Korske was looking for a pin. With his Essex Catholic opponent flat on his stomach, Korske reached around and under the wrestler's waist, trapping his left arm and tightening. *A gut wrench*, Bobby thought. Korske went up on his toes and drove toward his opponent's left shoulder, then rolled and arched, twisting his opponent to his back. The execution was stunning. A sophisticated move against a good wrestler, and yet Korske made it look as easy as drilling. *Incredible . . .* , Bobby thought. As he turned away, he heard the referee slap the mat, signaling the pin.

Coach Messina pointed. "In the locker room."

Bobby shuffled toward the door marked VISITORS. *Here it comes. What's Coach gonna tell me? That I had the match and pissed it away? Damn it, I know that.*

Inside, Bobby threw down his headgear and straddled a locker room bench. He covered his head with his hands, feeling the throb of frustration along his temples. He heard breathing and noticed Coach Messina standing beside him.

"Six minutes of hard wrestling, not five minutes and fifty seconds," Coach Messina said. He slapped a locker with his hand. "You dominated that match, but you let up for one moment, and look what happened. Bobby, you're good enough to beat any one of these top guys. But you can't have a bad match, or a bad period, or a bad ten seconds. Not at this level."

"I wanted a chance at Korske," Bobby said.

"I know you did."

Bobby looked up. "Think I could beat him?"

"Not the way you just wrestled," Coach Messina said. "You have to become mentally tougher. Can't have a lapse in concentration. Not against Korske."

"This was my chance."

"You'll get another."

"Not this tournament."

"No, not this tournament," Coach Messina said. "Beating Korske today wouldn't make your season, anyway. There's a long way to go. But from this point on, promise yourself, no letting up against anybody. Not for a moment. Imagine every opponent is Korske. Every match. Then, down the line, at Jadwin, you *will* get your chance. And you *will* beat him."

It was then, in the dim locker room, his coach looming above him, that Bobby quickly pushed aside self-pity. Coach Messina was coldly honest; Bobby knew he had to be that way with himself. And so, he considered why he had just lost, opening himself up for the truth.

Did I run enough? Bobby knew there were nights

when he could've stretched a three-mile run into a four-mile run.

Did I work hard enough in practice? He remembered drills when he could've pushed himself harder.

If I'd known from day one that Korske was going 129, would I have worked on perfecting my switch? My sit out? My single-leg? Of course.

Finally, Bobby asked himself: *Was I as prepared as I should've been?*

The answer to this was a very obvious no.

Focus, preparation, execution—that's what had to separate him from his opponents. And now Bobby understood, with a feeling that he would not reveal to the others, who looked to him as their captain, there was *always* more he could have done.

Coach Messina put a firm hand on Bobby's shoulders. "We don't have a single wrestler moving on to the finals yet. That's unacceptable. I want you out there preparing the others. Get these guys ready to wrestle. And we need you to win the consolations for third place."

Bobby nodded. "Be there in a minute, Coach."

"No, you're a captain. You get out there now."

Coach Messina was so damn exact. Input information in one end, output some neatly thought-out answer on the other end. No waste of emotion. No extraneous words. Discriminate.

Bobby stood up. He closed his eyes and breathed in deeply. He had to face his teammates, his father and

Christopher, the Millburn fans, the other spectators. He had to face the defeat, then put it behind him. Later, he would watch Korske in the finals. He would get a chance at him, down the road.

Down the road, at Jadwin.

Coach Messina had told him so.

16

The dining-room light flickered. Ivan leaned over the oak table, careful not to disturb the arrangement of silverware and glasses. The bulb buzzed, then blinked off. Ivan tapped it once, then another time, until, after one last annoyed rap, the light stayed on. He shook his head. *Another thing that needs to be fixed.*

He felt neither hungry nor very much like sitting down at the table. Winning the Hunterdon Central tournament so handily—three pins in three matches—left him restless, his body needing to move around, his thoughts wanting space.

He heard the oven door shut. His father walked in, holding a silver platter with two thick pieces of sizzling meat, charred along the edges. "Dinner fit for a champion," he said. He placed two plates on the table, stepped back, giving the room a thoughtful look, then nodded, pleased.

After a long day at the farm, his father had worked hard to prepare the dinner. Though his father would never say it, Ivan was certain it was his way of apologizing for missing the first two matches. Not that it mattered, Ivan thought. Both matches hadn't made it into the second period, anyway. The attention made Ivan uneasy. It was just another Saturday night, just another tournament victory. It was *not* the state championship.

He sat down, unfolded a cloth napkin, and spread it over his lap, as his mother had taught him. He ate quickly, craving the steak and potatoes. After a few bites, his stomach, shrunken after six weeks of cutting weight, felt as if it would burst.

"That boy from Manalapan was strong," his father said.

Ivan shrugged.

"I remember when wrestling was not so easy for you," his father continued. "You were young and it was many years ago, but you should not forget. Tell me about your first matches."

"Not much to say."

"Where were the boys from?"

"Didn't notice."

"Their names?"

"Don't know."

Ivan reached into his pocket, pulled out a medal, and handed it across the table.

His father held it up to the light. "I must build a wood cabinet for all your medals and trophies." He spread his hands wide. "Large glass doors. And one spot in front for the state championship medal. That would be nice."

"Sounds like a lotta work."

"A lot of work?"

"Too much work."

"No," his father said.

"Papa, you come home tired every night. Now you work Saturdays. You're gonna wear out."

His father brushed aside his concern.

"I heard stories, Papa. People are getting laid off; is that true?"

His father hunched forward, spearing the meat with his knife, then cutting a piece and putting it into his mouth, cutting another piece and shoving it into his mouth.

"Saying nothing tells me enough, Papa." Ivan looked down. "Are you gonna lose your job?" he said quietly, almost hoping his father didn't hear him.

"That is not for you to think about."

"How can't I?"

"You must worry about wrestling only," his father said. Then added, "And a good university. That is important, also."

Ivan put down his knife and fork. "Coaches call every day. They send me hundreds of letters. Beg me to take their scholarships. Paying for college won't be your problem."

There was hurt in his father's expression. "You are not a problem to me." His father waved his finger. "No matter what, I will always worry about you. When you are fifty years old, I will worry about you. Understand?"

For a time the dining room was quiet. Ivan watched his father eat heartily, while he picked at the few small pieces of meat he could still force into his stomach.

"You received a telephone call earlier. This Coach Riker," his father said, "do you know where he is from?"

Ivan lowered his eyes.

"The University of Western Arizona," his father said. "I have not heard of this university. He wanted to know if you won today. He asked if you received the application. Do you want to know what I told him? I told this Coach Riker he should not call us."

Ivan sat back hard. "What?"

"Yes, I told him you will attend Bloomsburg University next fall."

"That's wrong, Papa."

"You are not going far away. It is final. We discussed this."

Ivan half laughed. "We didn't discuss a damn thing. You yelled and hit me. That's no discussion."

His father's hands knotted into fists, raised up, then crashed down on the table. Ivan didn't blink. "You will not answer back anymore," his father said through gritted teeth. "Do you understand?"

Ivan stood up, flexed his arms and chest, and leaned over the table. "Papa, you're not gonna hit me again." His eyes never left his father, whose stare—Ivan was surprised—had momentarily weakened. Ivan took pleasure in that. With one hand he swept up the medal and stuffed it into his pocket. "I'm going out," he said, then he turned and left.

Under the porch light of her house, Shelley wrapped a red scarf around her neck, buttoned her coat, then pulled mittens from the coat's hip pockets. She met Ivan in the street and gave him a hug.

"God, I'm glad you knocked," she said.

Ivan gestured to Shelley, and together they started down Farmingdale Road. "Let's walk."

"Know that physics paper I wrote last week?" Shelley said.

"Yeah."

"Got a B-plus on it. Well, my dad freaked. You'd think I'd screwed up any chance of getting into UPenn. Maybe *I* should be the one to go far away to college."

"My idea first," Ivan said.

Shelley held the sleeve of his jacket as they turned off onto a dirt path that quickly disappeared into the woods, curved left, then dipped down a small hill. The scent of pine hung in the cold damp air.

"You know, for someone who wants out of Lennings, you sure know your way around," Shelley said. "Doesn't surprise me, though. Told me once you'd never leave Lennings. 'In a million years' were your exact words."

"Things change."

"I watch you from my window when you go out to run and when you come back," Shelley said. "I see you in school. Down the hall. When you're sitting in class. I haven't missed one of your matches in two years." She tugged his sleeve. "Hey . . ."

Ivan stopped.

"For all I see you and know you, I wanna know even more," she said. "I wanna know everything. It sounds silly, I guess . . ."

Her hair fluttered in a gust of wind; she brushed the strands off her cheeks. Clouds parted, shooting shafts of moonlight through the tree branches to the ground below. Ivan could see the glint in her eyes, the part of her lips.

"Let's keep going, okay?" he said.

"Where?"

"You trust me?"

"Of course."

Shelley followed Ivan through a thicket of birch trees, then another, then stepped over and around the fallen branches along Sycamore Creek. They walked the shoreline of the pond, then turned off, where the path narrowed even more.

"A little farther," Ivan said.

"Until what?"

Ivan didn't answer. Words would be unnecessary, he knew. Shelley held his hand as they picked their way through the brush until, a short distance later, they stepped out from the woods.

Encircled by a wall of massive evergreens, he and Shelley stood on the edge of an isolated field of reeds, the withered stalks quivering and gleaming like crystal fila-ments bobbing on waves in the ocean. The wind swirled, the tree branches thrashed, and for a few glorious mo-ments, it seemed as if they were in the bottom of a stormy cauldron. The sky above had opened fully, and a pristine moon lay centered in a halo of light stretched from one horizon to the other.

Ivan lifted his head skyward. Already he had forgot-ten about the Hunterdon Central tournament and fight-ing with his father and McClellan and everything he was supposed to hate about this town.

"Oh, Ivan," Shelley said. She twirled, throwing back her head, raising her arms high. "I feel like I'm onstage. At Carnegie Hall, playing a concerto. And a packed house is all here for me. Clapping and cheering and waving." She ran back to hug him. "Thanks for bringing me here."

This was his special place. The only place in Lennings where he felt peaceful. All at once, emotions welled up in-side Ivan so that he could hardly contain himself.

"I want my name to live on forever," he said, hesi-tantly, reluctantly. "It's not possible, I know. No one lives forever."

Shelley lifted her head from his shoulder. "What do you mean?"

"Nothing."

"No, tell me," she said. "What're you worried about?"

For a while, Ivan didn't answer, his thoughts just out of reach to grasp fully.

"I don't know," Ivan said. "Of being forgotten, I guess."

"Forgotten? Why would you be forgotten?"

Ivan bent down and tugged at a reed. "I won the tournament today. Won it last year, too. And the year before that." He pulled the medal from his pocket and held it up. Suddenly, he reached back and threw the medal as far as he could. It flashed in the moonlight, then disappeared.

Shelley turned to him. "Ivan, why'd you do that?"

"They all look the same."

"So you just throw it away?"

"Throw one away, lose one, who cares? Does it erase what I did? Hundreds of years from now, the medals are gonna rust into nothing, but on March thirteenth, I'll be state champ. Forever. They won't be able to take that away."

Ivan walked toward the tallest trees that made up the far edge of the circle, where the reeds grew waist high. He pushed through, the ground stiff under his feet, leaving a path for Shelley to follow. Soon they came upon a wall of stones and crumbling mortar, stretching thirty or so feet before both ends sloped back into the earth. Ivan jumped on top.

"What's this?"

"Layaree's Wall," Ivan said. "It's old. Built before the Revolutionary War, I heard. Must've been important." On the other side, he jumped down. "I wanna show you something."

Shelley stepped over the wall, stood close, then leaned over Ivan's shoulder. Her warm breath tickled his ear.

Ivan's hand, hidden in the wall's moonlight shadow, felt for a flat oval stone just a few inches above the ground. "Every night this summer, I came here. I thought about her, all the time." He looked up at Shelley. "So I found a few sharp rocks and a piece of metal."

He was touching one stone in particular, so Shelley bent forward a little further. Just visible in the moon's illumination were the words ANNA KORSKE, carved deeply into the stone.

"I'm not gonna last forever," Ivan said. "Maybe this will." He sounded excited, like a son who had done a very good deed. "It'll be around after I'm gone. So she won't disappear. She'll be the only one here; no one else. Like she's special. Like she's immortal."

"It's beautiful," Shelley whispered.

Ivan looked at her. "Think so?"

Shelley nodded.

"Thanks."

Ivan sat back against the wall, pleased. Very pleased.

17

Light flickered from the muted television, while red and green bulbs on the Christmas tree blinked a kaleidoscope onto the wall. Carmelina lay nestled in Bobby's arms on the family-room sofa. She pulled a wool blanket up her legs. Bobby touched his hand to her stomach, then brushed the sheer material of her bra.

Carmelina whispered in Portuguese, and smiled. Bobby didn't understand what she said. But it was good, he was sure.

They hadn't left the sofa for a while, at times drifting asleep together, then awakening to catch glimpses of the approaching celebration. Bobby glanced at the television. Dick Clark flashed his world-famous smile and pointed toward the ball at Times Square. The thirty-minute countdown had begun.

Carmelina kissed Bobby's forehead, then dragged her lips along his eyebrows and down his temple, leaving a slick of saliva. "I love my present," she said, fingering a silver necklace around her neck. "I didn't thank you good enough." Her hand slipped down to his waist, untucked the bottom of his shirt, and tickled his stomach. "You're so thin . . . When're your parents coming home?"

"We have time."

"They don't know I'm here?"

"No."

Carmelina looked at him, seriously. "You didn't tell them I was coming over?"

He shook his head.

"Damn, Bobby, I'm supposed to be your *girl*."

"You are."

"Then why can't ya tell them we're together? It's like you gotta hide me. I wasn't invited for Christmas, and you didn't stop by, either. I had to make an excuse to my girl, Maria. She wants to meet ya. How you think that made me feel? I'll tell ya. Like garbage. Like there's something wrong with me."

"I'm sorry."

"Why doesn't she like me?"

Bobby shrugged. "I don't know."

Carmelina eyed him. "Know what I think it is? She don't think I'm good enough. Like I'm gonna trap her precious little boy. Damn, I got dreams. Did you tell her that? Did you tell her I got dreams for college, too?"

Bobby held her cheek in his hand. "Who cares what she thinks, Carmelina?"

"I do."

"Don't. Not tonight. We got the whole house to

ourselves. No parents, no curfew. You and me, all alone." He pulled down the edge of her bra. "Please?" he said. "Can we?"

She softened. "Can we *what*?"

"You know."

Carmelina pulled her blouse across her chest and folded her arms. "What would *she* think?" She smirked.

Bobby moved the blanket rolled between Carmelina's legs, then propped himself up on his hands. He inched forward so that his jeans pressed against her. He felt powerful, so much like a man. He closed his eyes, smelling the perfume of her skin. The image of Carmelina lying underneath him stayed vivid in his mind. They had made out all night. In the attic . . . on the stairs to the basement . . . in the living room . . . on his parents' bed . . . now his body wanted more.

"Bobby," Carmelina said, "you like to touch me?"

"Yeah."

"You like to kiss me?"

He nodded.

Bobby ground his hips into Carmelina, pressing her into the sofa cushions, then pushing still more, as if the clothing between them would give way. Carmelina arched, her hands slipping beneath his shirt, then down his body. She reached her mouth up, brushing her lips along the underside of his chin.

"Wanna take these off?" she said, tugging at his jeans.

Bobby stood up, watching Carmelina's eyes as he pulled off his pants. "What about yours?"

Carmelina didn't answer. A gentle twist of her body

made her blouse slip open again. She reached her arms above her head, squirming her hips, turning her head toward the inside of the sofa.

Bobby grabbed the cuffs of her jeans. The jeans crawled over her hips, then down her legs. He dropped them to the floor. Her white panties seemed to glow in the light of the television. They slipped off, as well. Bobby waited for a sign of hesitation from Carmelina, but he knew there wouldn't be any.

Carmelina pulled Bobby on top of her.

"This?" he asked.

She nodded.

"Now?"

"Right now."

Bobby pushed forward with his hips.

Carmelina bit her lip and held her breath. *"Oh Deus,"* she whispered.

"That hurt?"

She shook her head gently.

Bobby pulled back, then pushed forward again. Despite the chill in the living room, sweat quickly glazed his forehead and naked back.

"Bobby, you got—?"

"No, but you're okay, right?"

"Maybe we shouldn't . . ."

"A little more," he said, lowering his head. "Then I'll stop . . ."

Carmelina reached up and kissed his lips. "Okay . . ."

They moved together until their gasps for breath became one. Carmelina reached around his waist. Bobby was losing control. He opened his eyes. He tried to concentrate, but his thoughts were a wreck.

"Bobby . . ."

No, not yet! But it was too late. His mind let go. And his body, too. Odd grunts came out of his mouth.

Carmelina held on like she might never let go. Then Bobby was silent.

Bobby looked down at Carmelina. She breathed in, her chest rising, her mouth curling into a soft smile.

Bobby woke up. He strained his eyes toward the television. It was well past midnight. He looked at Carmelina. Her eyes were closed, her breathing shallow, her face serene. Her necklace glinted.

He sat up. There were parents to worry about. And a half-hour drive to Newark and back. His weight. The upcoming dual-meet season. Sleep. Christopher. College applications. Losing to Seitzer. His parents. And he was *sure* the room smelled of sex.

He nudged Carmelina. "We gotta get dressed." He reached for his jeans and found his underwear wedged between the sofa cushions.

For a few hours, Bobby had forgotten about the Hunterdon Central tournament, but now disgust over his loss in the semifinals returned with a vengeance. He had had the match won; he had been dominating. Then a split-second lapse in concentration and it was over. That he had come back to win third place meant little.

Bobby grabbed his shirt from the floor as Carmelina stepped into her jeans. Then she reached for her blouse and finished dressing.

Bobby stared at the television, idly pressing channels on the cable remote, one after the other. Finding nothing to distract him, he said, finally, "I better drive you home."

18

Ivan opened the locker-room door. He saw McClellan standing at the far wall, his arms folded. McClellan stopped mid-sentence and turned. "You're early, Ivan."

"Came to check my weight," he said.

"Mr. Holt and I were just—"

"Discussing the season," Holt said, stepping into Ivan's view. "We need a few more minutes."

Ivan studied McClellan, then Holt. Each was pathetic in his own way.

"We should move this to your office," McClellan said.

"That won't be necessary," said Holt. "Wait outside, Ivan."

Ivan stepped back and closed the door. He thought about going back to class, but the chance to hear Holt and McClellan going at it was too tempting to ignore. Ivan looked down the empty hallway, then inched the door open so that the muffled discussion was clear.

"Lewis," Holt said, "this year, Lennings High has a unique opportunity to shake its backwoods reputation."

"I know all about our reputation," McClellan said. "I've lived here twenty-five years of my life. You know what? Lennings *is* in the backwoods."

"That's what you think, Lewis. I don't. I see a school that's been overshadowed by the rival schools around us. We have no identity. No soul."

McClellan half laughed. "'Soul'?"

"Yes, soul. Some people see a school as walls and ceilings, the building and so on. Others believe a school is the administrators, faculty, students, and the learning that goes on. Still others point to the pomp and splendor, the music assemblies, the sports events, the people in a school, functioning like a living, breathing organism. I'm one of those people. I believe in the sophomore who plays magnificent piano recitals, the poet published in local magazines, the athlete who scores the touchdowns, makes the baskets, and, yes, pins every opponent. That builds self-esteem. That builds pride. That builds *soul*. I built it at my last school; I'll build it here."

"Lennings *has* that."

"Sometimes," Holt said. "Most of the time, not. I covet that soul. I want to nurture it. Bottle it and sell it, if I could. Lewis, I understand we've never had a state champ at Lennings. Nothing even close, for that matter. Until Ivan, of course."

Ivan smiled. He could almost hear McClellan's slow burn—the breaths rushing in and out his nostrils, the aborted first word of his response as he thought better of telling off Holt. It was pure delight for Ivan and would only have been better if he could have stepped inside to actually see McClellan's face, his anxious twitch. *Watch him like he watches me.*

"You're right, Garrison," McClellan said. "Guess I just never thought about it that way. After growing up in this town, wrestling here for seven years, coaching the last six, some things just elude me."

Gutless. The kind of sarcastic response Ivan expected from McClellan. *Don't go toe-to-toe with Holt; just lie down and let him slap you around.* Ivan shook his head. *No wonder we lose.*

"It's the big picture," Holt said. "Sometimes the staff members—bless their souls—lose sight of that. What happens in the classroom is only part of what makes up this school. That's why I can't emphasize enough how important Ivan is."

"He's just one athlete," McClellan said. "Just one of hundreds at Lennings. He's not bigger than the school. He's not bigger than our team."

Screw you, McClellan.

"No, no, he's more than that," Holt said. "I'm hoping we'll have a number of newspapers doing features on him. Very sad about his mother. It'll make a good human interest story. Get the Lennings name out there."

Screw you, Holt.

"And Lewis," Holt said, "I'll bet you'll get some good publicity yourself."

"Publicity?" McClellan laughed. "I don't need publicity."

"You do. Why deny it? We might go this entire season without a win. We're the laughingstock of the conference, the district, the county, maybe the whole state. But you do know the one glimmer of hope we have."

McClellan didn't answer.

"Ivan Korske," Holt said. "He keeps Lennings's wrestling from being an absolute, unmitigated disaster. And the irony of all this is that his success benefits you, Lewis, more than anyone else. You are redeemed. Exonerated. Pardoned."

There was silence. McClellan was beaten, Ivan knew; on his last legs; his mind scrambling for answers, surely, and, at the same time, begging for the battle to be over.

"I appreciate your interest, Garrison," McClellan said, finally. "But this is my wrestling program, and Ivan is one member of that program. Just one. No more, or less, important than anyone else."

"Don't be foolish," Holt said. "He's special. Damn special."

"No, absolutely *no* single wrestler is more important than the *team*," McClellan said, his voice on edge.

And again the locker room was silent.

It was the way McClellan had said it, desperate, as a humiliated opponent might wave a hand weakly in resignation. But Ivan knew, as much as he hated to admit it, that hadn't been the true intent of McClellan's words. McClellan had spoken with an unwavering dedication to the team and the program. His passion was undeniable.

But how could he? Ivan wondered. How could McClellan, in the face of five straight years of losing, still care?

Holt's shoes clicked on the tiled floor, then stopped. Ivan heard tapping on glass—the cracked window that looked out onto the school driveway, he figured.

"Too many cars at the front entrance," Holt said. "The damn buses won't be able to get out on time. I'm going to have to change the pickup system. That accident we had last month looks bad for the school. Maybe a few heads'll have to roll. People get complacent when they're in one position too long. It's good to muck up the water a bit. I think you understand."

"There's something to be said for continuity."

Holt chuckled. "Continuity means complacency. It means undeserved privilege. An organization needs its people to be hungry. When that desire wanes, the organization weakens . . ."

"And?" McClellan said.

"And it's time for practice," Holt said. "Mustn't sit on our laurels with an 0–4 season."

Ivan drew back from the door and kneeled down, pretending to rummage through his gym bag. The door opened and Holt stepped out. Then he stopped and turned back. "It's only mid-January, Lewis. Still early in the season. Enthusiasm abounds, right?"

"Sure," McClellan answered from inside the locker room.

Holt turned to Ivan. "Thanks for your patience. Good luck on Saturday. Maybe we'll get a win." He looked back inside the locker room.

Ivan watched as Holt strode down the hallway, head up, checking his lapels and the crease of his slacks as he continued away. So choreographed, so flamboyant. Ivan picked up his gym bag and was about to enter the locker room, when the door opened again.

McClellan didn't look at Ivan. He was clearly shamed. Ivan allowed a moment of pity, but that was all. McClellan's dress shirt stuck to his sweaty back and he shuffled down the corridor, head bowed slightly.

"I'll, uh, see you at practice in a few minutes," McClellan said.

19

It always started the same way.

Bobby sat on his bedroom floor, sports sections spread out around him. He had heard his parents like this before. Too many times before. Like a rumble of thunder, an ominous warning of a gathering storm. Bobby put down a pair of scissors and box-score clippings of his opponents and, for the moment, forgot about Millburn's undefeated record. He tried to close his mind to his parents' voices.

It didn't work. Never did.

There was a second rumble. Louder than the first. Then another. Gaining momentum within the walls of the house, rolling in with fury, like the storms at the family's summer house down at the Shore, filling the sky with black clouds, unleashing sheets of coarse rain. There, Bobby would lean against the bay window, feeling the thunder through the glass, the walls, his body. And wait for it to be over.

It was like that now.

Bobby stared around the room, not sure what he was looking for—something to throw, something to hit, something to shelter him from the fury. There was nothing. It'll be over, he told himself. Soon. Someday.

"Bobby?"

In the doorway, Christopher stood, head lowered, nervously rolling the bottom of his pajama top in his fingers.

"Can I come in?" He pointed at the notebooks and newspaper clippings. "I could help . . . maybe."

Bobby nodded. He was worried and scared, too. Christopher didn't say anything more, though Bobby knew questions would eventually make their way to his mouth. He wasn't sure how he'd answer. He couldn't explain the incessant arguments and vicious fighting, the detached coldness when it was over. His parents had been married twenty-three years—a goddamn lifetime—why now?

I can't make them stop, he wanted to say to his little brother. *I wish I could, but I can't.* But Christopher's eyes were welling and tears were not far off. His little brother needed comfort.

"Yeah, I can use some help," Bobby said, waving Christopher over. He pushed the newspapers aside so they could sit shoulder to shoulder. Christopher settled under his arm. Bobby held him tightly.

Downstairs, the storm quieted. Bobby opened a notebook in which he had marked the teams Millburn would face during the season. Under each, he had pasted relevant box scores and articles, and he had jotted notes in the margins.

"Why do ya do all this stuff?" Christopher asked.

"So I know about the guys I'm gonna wrestle," Bobby said. "I wanna know their records, how good they are." He ran his finger down the page to a box score. "Here are the weight classes. This says what happened in each match."

Christopher looked, but blankly. Bobby wasn't sure if it was because his little brother didn't understand or because the silence downstairs had gone on so long. Bobby thumbed through a few more pages, and for a time, it seemed the storm had come to an abrupt end. All was calm. Still, Bobby didn't relax. He waited. Always waited.

"What team's this?" Christopher pointed to a page.

Black marker outlined a half dozen box scores with "February 10" written in heavy black letters at the top. "Remember those mean guys from two years ago?" Bobby said. "That's Rampart. We're gonna—"

A crash of thunder. Punctuated with a crack of lightning.

"—beat them in a few weeks," Bobby finished.

The storm was back. And it was fierce. The faint enraged words Bobby could hardly make out before were now clear, snapping back and forth.

"Robert, goddamn you!"

"Shut up, Maggie!"

Then overlapping each other in one sustained shout.

Christopher's eyes were now wide with fear. Bobby thought of something else to say, but words were pointless.

"They fight too much," Christopher said in a hush, as if worried his mother or father might hear.

"Yeah," Bobby said, "they do."

Incessantly. His mother screaming; his father yelling. Doors slamming. Bobby wanted to blame someone, to know whose fault it was and be able some day, when he had the guts, to confront his mother, or his father. Then the rage, bottled up for so long, could spew out.

"Why're they so mad?" Christopher said.

"Don't know."

"Bobby?"

"Yeah."

"Do ya think Mom and Dad will have a divorce?"

Bobby looked oddly at his little brother. A precocious question, he thought. Then, so as not to give away his own fears, Bobby said, "Don't think about that."

"Stevie says it happens all the time. Then the dad moves away."

"Stevie's wrong. That's not gonna happen."

"Promise, Bobby?"

"Promise."

"Really promise?"

"Yes, *really* promise," Bobby said. "Why don't we watch TV?"

Christopher seemed happy with that. He jumped to his feet, walked over to the television on the dresser, reached up, and pressed the ON button.

"Loud," Bobby said to his little brother. "Put it up loud."

20

Ivan sat with Ellison behind the rest of the team. It was going to be a waste of a practice, he could tell right away, the kind that had to be endured, then forgotten immediately. Lennings was winless in eight matches, with the Hunterdon schools looming on the schedule. Guys were quitting, morale was out the window, and here was McClellan giving another one of his moronic speeches. Ivan thought about walking out the door.

"We've lost a number of matches, I can't sugarcoat that," McClellan said. "We should be in a better position at this point in the season. I expected a few victories. I know you guys did, too." McClellan fixed a hard stare at the team, but Ivan was sure no one gave a damn.

Except one wrestler.

As always, Phillip Hannen sat dead center in front of McClellan, following every word he said. During drills, Hannen often volunteered to practice with Ivan and

Ellison, getting thrown around the mat. Yet he never quit, no matter what drill, no matter how late in practice, no matter how much punishment he was taking. It was a quality Ivan usually admired. But to Ivan, Hannen was a kiss-ass, trying too hard, too often, to impress McClellan.

"Just three dual meets left," McClellan said. "We win a couple of these, and all of a sudden, the season is ours again. It's up to you. We have a clean slate. Our new season starts Thursday against North Hunterdon, then Saturday with Hunterdon Central. You guys are familiar with both teams. They're excellent, both ranked in the top twenty . . ."

His words were quickly drowned out by the churning of the boiler room machinery. But McClellan didn't fight it. He simply waved for the team to spread out on the mats. "Takedowns."

Ivan nodded to Ellison and said, "Let's get this going." They began alternating singles, doubles, hi-crotches. There was a familiar listless mood to the room. Ivan even felt sluggish himself.

And so, practice plodded along.

"Stand with the leg!" McClellan screamed. "Now run it!"

Ivan looked over. On the other side of the room, Jon Pico kept his head down on a single-leg, allowing his practice partner to sprawl back and counter with a quarter-nelson, driving his head to the mat.

"Damn it, Jon, you gave that position so easily," McClellan said. "At least make him work for it."

Pico sat up on his knees. "I thought I'd—"

"Don't tell me what you thought. You're not supposed to think; you're supposed to react. It's the end of January, for god's sake; we've been doing this for over two months. This stuff has to come to you without thinking. Like breathing." McClellan blew the whistle long and hard. "Take a water break."

A water break? Ivan thought, then said out loud, "Now?"

McClellan turned in Ivan's direction. "Did you say something?"

The team held still. Ivan stared at McClellan, knowing even a blink would be a concession. He wouldn't give McClellan that satisfaction. He stood tall. *Wanna start something?* The pounding furnace suddenly ceased. The room was quiet.

McClellan's nostrils flared, his jaw was rigid. "Don't want a break, Ivan?"

Ivan stood, fists at his waist. "Not sure we need it," he said, then, with more than a hint of disgust, "Coach."

"Why?" McClellan said. "Not sweating enough?"

"Not sweating at all."

Trickles of sweat inched down McClellan's forehead and disappeared into the ridge of his nose. "Maybe I need to make practice harder."

"Whatever," Ivan said.

"Maybe you need to work harder."

"Harder?" Ivan laughed. "I work my ass off every practice."

"Watch your language," McClellan said. "I don't tolerate that in this room, *my* practice room. You have a problem with the way practice is run?"

Ivan shook his head and smirked. He saw slack-jawed faces of the other wrestlers. He drew in a breath to say something snide but didn't. That was his concession.

"Does anyone have a problem with practice?" McClellan said. He waited. "I said, does anyone else have a problem with how practice is going?"

From the back of the room came a voice, "No, Coach."

Heads turned. Ivan recognized the voice without looking. *Hannen.*

"Good," McClellan said. "Okay, then. Get a drink of water and let's hustle up."

A few of the wrestlers hurried out of the practice room, but most of the team lingered to see what might happen next. Ivan continued staring down McClellan. He had hated him since freshman year. Always did; always would. Teacher-of-the-year awards meant nothing in this room. The wrestling room.

Soon, practice continued. Still, nothing changed. The Lennings team drilled moves as if going through the motions, waiting for practice to end, waiting for the week to end, waiting for the season to end. Once again, Ivan thought with great satisfaction: McClellan was the loser.

Then, something happened.

Ellison hit a hi-crotch, stood up with the leg, and ran the pike flawlessly. His execution impressed Ivan. Next to them, Lawrence Wright hit an arm drag to a double-leg that caught his practice partner by surprise. Behind them, Hannen gave his usual all-out effort. Grunts filled the room. The usual plodding from drill to drill evolved into a kind of dance, each pair of wrestlers hitting one move after another without hesitation.

Practice began to flow.

"One man on his back," McClellan barked. "The other man has a reverse half in." He strode around the room. "When you're on your back, it's survival—pure and simple—that keeps you from getting pinned. None of us should get pinned. At the same time, there's no excuse for the man on top to allow his opponent off his back. You have to have that killer instinct!"

There was *energy* to the room, a kind of palpable excitement that something good was happening, and for a moment, Ivan imagined that this was what it was like every day in the practice rooms of schools like Paulsboro, Hunterdon Central, Phillipsburg, and Highland Regional.

"Man on top, don't let him off his back," McClellan said. "Man on bottom, get off your back by bridging up, slipping an arm through—*anything* to keep from being pinned."

He blew the whistle. The fifteen-second shots continued.

"We're finally coming together," McClellan shouted. He was beaming, clapping his hands. "Let's keep this going. No letdowns. No relaxing."

Ivan looked around. The Lennings wrestling team was dancing, and McClellan was the choreographer. There wasn't a reason for what was happening. It had to be a mistake, a fluke. Nothing was "finally coming together." Blinded by five straight losing seasons, McClellan was confusing dumb luck for something greater than that.

But something *was* happening. Ivan couldn't deny that. Enthusiasm, tangible and sweet, filled the room.

"Damn good practice, Lennings!" McClellan shouted. "We'll finish up with a six-minute match. I want you to go hard, like this is the state finals. And we're going to practice the same way tomorrow and Wednesday, then wrestle this way against North Hunterdon on Thursday, and again in practice on Friday." He pumped his fist in the air. "And then you know what I'm gonna do? I'm gonna call the coach over at Hunterdon Central, and you know what I'll say? I'll say, Coach, I hope your boys have been practicing well, because Lennings is coming to town on Saturday."

When practice ended a half hour later, the team crowded McClellan, clapping wildly, hooting, hollering, drowning out the clanking pipes and banging boiler. Long faces were replaced with smiles.

Ivan stood to the side, neither clapping nor smiling. He grabbed his headgear and walked out of the room.

21

The top section of the Sunday *Daily Record* fluttered open and closed. Ivan stepped out onto the porch, then down the walkway. The cold did little to awaken him. With the newspaper under his arm, he scanned the horizon, disgusted by the thought that even the slightest hint of spring was buried well beneath the frozen ground and would be for some months.

Inside, warmth from the kitchen baseboard heater quelled the goose bumps that dotted his skin. Ivan handed the newspaper to his father after pulling out the sports section for himself.

"Will you eat today?" his father asked.

"Maybe tonight."

On the stove, a teakettle gurgled, then whistled. Ivan poured a cup of water over a tea bag, dropped in a sugar cube, and passed it to his father.

He wondered what McClellan was doing right now. He wondered if McClellan had hoped in some far-off corner of his most wishful thinking to open the sports section and see, in bold letters: LENNINGS SHOCKS POWERHOUSE HUNTERDON CENTRAL. The article would hail the match as one of the great upsets in New Jersey scholastic wrestling history. It would be the pinnacle of McClellan's coaching career. Of his entire wrestling career. Of his life.

Ivan turned to the High School wrestling results. He wondered if McClellan had yet done the same. He wondered how reality hit McClellan. In print, it had to be even more devastating: HUNTERDON CENTRAL ROLLS 47–4.

Great job, McClellan, you really got the team ready. Oh, yeah, were they ready.

Ivan pictured McClellan sitting, disgusted, shoving the newspaper off a table, rubbing his fingers into his forehead to smooth the frustration.

Monday's practice had surely given McClellan a glimmer of hope that he had made into a floodlight of improbabilities. He and the team had been blinded by a flash of unexpected excellence—a mistake, really—that could never have been maintained. *How stupid*, Ivan thought. Lennings on their touched-by-God best day couldn't beat Hunterdon Central, or North Hunterdon, on its absolute worst day.

"We have work to do," his father said. He tipped back the mug, then set it down.

Ivan stood up and moved to the kitchen window. *Why waste an ounce of energy thinking about McClellan, or the team, or the team's record? What's the point? Nothing changed last season, or this season. Or would next season. Not until McClellan is gone.*

Ivan looked up. His breath had fogged the glass. Beyond that, a ceiling of thunderclouds swept low over Lennings.

22

Bobby opened his crusted eyes and blinked. He took a moment to orient himself to the high school nurse's office. The air was stifling, his lips were cracked, his tongue as rough as sandpaper. He tried to swallow away the sour taste in his mouth, but his throat was too swollen. Pushing off a blanket, Bobby struggled to sit up.

He coughed, then coughed again—a throaty, hoarse cough that wouldn't stop, building to a crescendo that left him gasping for breath and his stomach muscles twisted in a wicked knot. A residue of sweat outlined an area on the green vinyl couch where he had lain down. He wiped it away with his hand.

Beyond the closed door, the hallway buzzed. He looked up at the wall clock. It was quarter after one—between periods. He had napped restlessly for two hours, perhaps a little more. A chill crawled over him. He bent forward, head in his hands, and flexed his muscles. Yet, in spite of the physical misery, only one thought filled his head. Rampart.

Yesterday's *Star-Ledger* headlined the upcoming match as A CLASH OF UNBEATENS, with an article highlighting "a key bout at 129 pounds between seniors Bobby Zane of Millburn, 8–1, and Rampart's Jim Caruso, 10–0." It went on to say, "The team emerging victorious on Saturday afternoon will undoubtedly earn the top spot in Essex County and a certain top-twenty state ranking."

Bobby had tossed the newspaper into the garbage. When it came to Rampart High, rankings and records meant nothing. Rampart and Caruso could have been undefeated or winless, it didn't matter. This was Rampart. Bobby could say, hear, and think about the name a thousand more times and it wouldn't change his feelings. His hatred was absolute.

The office door opened. Nurse Lowery, an elderly woman with a pinched face and wrinkled neck, walked in carrying a box of bandages. Wire-rimmed glasses dangled from her neck.

"Robert, I'm pleased to see you're awake," she said, setting the box down at her desk. "How are you feeling?"

"Much better," Bobby said in a rasp. He cleared his throat.

Nurse Lowery eyed him suspiciously. "Really?"

"Guess all I needed was a little sleep." Bobby clenched his stomach muscles, holding down another wave of nausea.

"You've missed a number of classes today."

"I'll catch up."

"Frankly," she said, nodding toward the office phone, "I think it's high time you call one of your parents and have them pick you up."

"No, thanks."

"I thought that would be your answer," Nurse Lowery said, "so I took the liberty of contacting your mother at work."

"Why?" Bobby said. "What'd she say?"

"Well, she certainly didn't seem surprised that you were sick. And she said she'd be down here immediately, if you needed her."

"I'm okay." Bobby smiled—a very weak smile, he knew, but it was the best he could muster. "I've got practice in an hour and a half."

"You, young man, should not even be thinking about exercising."

"Tomorrow is Rampart," Bobby said.

"Rampart?" Nurse Lowery sat down behind the office desk. "Ah, yes, I heard conversation in the teacher's lounge about this. Apparently this year is bigger than in years past." She shook her head. "Well, this is the second day in a row you've been in my office. Your temperature is sky-high, you're sweating profusely, and I'll bet you're doing your darnedest to hold down lunch."

"Didn't have lunch," Bobby said. Or breakfast. Or dinner last night.

"You're getting worse."

"I'm fine."

"Robert, you need to rest here on this couch, not on a wrestling mat."

Bobby muffled a string of coughs with his hand. "I'll be okay."

"If that's your choice," Nurse Lowery said. "But I'll tell you, you might not make tomorrow's match if you keep this up."

Like hell, Bobby thought.

Nurse Lowery held out two aspirin. "Your mother said it was okay."

Bobby popped the tablets to the back of his tongue and, with a mouthful of water, swallowed as best he could. He suddenly noticed how fierce his hunger was. He'd check his weight soon. Maybe he could have a couple of ounces of food. A slice or two of ham, maybe. Maybe not. He stretched out on the couch, propping his head on his varsity jacket.

The throbbing started again, and soon, so did the sweating.

23

Bobby held the phone away and muffled a cough, then turned back. "Can you make it?" he said. "I want you there."

He heard Carmelina sigh. "I wanna be there," she said. "You know that."

"Then, be there."

"I can't."

"Why not?"

"Bobby . . . ," she said. "I can't. My boss won't give me a day off."

"You sure?"

"I asked."

"It's Rampart," Bobby said, as if that was all he had to say.

"I know it's real important," Carmelina said.

"It's everything."

The phone was silent.

"I'm sorry," Carmelina said, finally.

"So am I."

It was well after midnight. Bobby stared at the ceiling. The mechanics for a single-leg played in his mind: driving through his opponent and stepping up with the leg, then running the pike and bringing him down to the mat. Heat rose from the neck of his T-shirt, and his hands clenched.

The desire to defeat Rampart went far beyond the wrestling mat. There was much more at stake. He hated Rampart for the people they were. Whenever he heard a snide remark about Italians being wise-guy Guineas or Nicky-Newarkers, he thought about Rampart. They were punks, and their arrogance was an affront to *good* Italians.

The aftermath of a match against Rampart two seasons ago still smoldered. Bobby remembered how Millburn's Stuart Brown sparked a 27–23 victory over Rampart in Rampart's gymnasium. Instead of giving up an expected pin—and six team points—against Rampart's captain, Brown held tough in an 8–1 loss, allowing Rampart only three points in the team score. It was the gutsiest wrestling Bobby had ever seen, something he would never forget.

When the match was over, chaos erupted. Three Rampart girls accosted a Millburn cheerleader in the school bathroom, while Rampart fans stood at the edge of the mat, taunting Millburn wrestlers. Afterward, a police escort did little to deter fans from hurling rocks at the Millburn team bus as it pulled out of the school parking lot.

The next day, officials from both schools agreed to suspend the rivalry for one year.

The whole scene had been a disgrace, Bobby thought. Disrespectful to sportsmanship. Humiliating, as an Italian. Rampart had to be punished. And so, tomorrow, he and his teammates would teach the whole goddamn town a lesson.

"Rampart," Bobby muttered, as if spitting out the sour, pasty taste in his mouth.

He ripped off his comforter, sat up, and opened a window. Cold gusts blew over his dehydrated skin. It was a wonderful relief, the best he had felt all week. Bobby closed his eyes, leaning on the windowsill.

It had been almost two days since he'd eaten. He was starving beyond hunger, and he couldn't remember the last time he'd gone to the bathroom. Maybe the night before yesterday.

Practice had been a nightmare. Between every shot, Bobby had taken a few extra seconds of rest and stalled to save energy whenever it wasn't too obvious. It wasn't the way he wanted to practice. He wanted to go hard every shot, every round-robin, every minute on the mat. But his body couldn't give that much. The aches, the chills, and the coughing had taken their toll.

Bobby switched on the closet light, squinting momentarily as his eyes adjusted, then set the scale at 129 pounds. He stepped on unsteadily. The balancing arm didn't move from the bottom. He tapped the counterbalance to 128 and ¾ pounds. Then an ounce or two under that. The scale arm finally balanced out.

One cup of water was all he could have.

His pewter baby cup in hand, Bobby looked toward the kitchen. The light was on.

He walked in, finding the kitchen empty. He opened the refrigerator, pulled out a bottle of seltzer and a lemon, and then reached for the cutting board. He sliced the lemon in half, then in quarters, and, for a time, was lost in thought about Rampart.

Then he heard something.

Bobby turned. He looked into the dining room. It was dark, and yet there was his father, sliding a half-empty glass back and forth.

"Dad?"

His father raised his head.

"Kinda late, isn't it?" Bobby said.

"It is for you."

"Can't fall asleep yet," Bobby said. He poured seltzer to the cup's brim.

"How're you feeling?"

"Fine."

"Mother is worried you've been sick."

"I'm fine."

"Why didn't you say anything?"

"It's nothing."

Bobby put the cup to his mouth and tilted it back. The lemon stung his chapped lips. Carbonated water ran over his tongue until the cup was empty. Not enough. It was never enough. But that was all the liquid Bobby would have until after weigh-ins. He set the cup down. He was still broiling inside and so hungry, he nearly heaved.

"I made it through practice," Bobby said. "Tough, though."

"Sure," his father said, his voice just a whisper. He rubbed his eyes. "Tough . . ."

"Dad?"

His father straightened up. "Had a tough break with one of my cases today. Sometimes things go your way. Sometimes they don't."

For as long as Bobby could remember, his father had never showed disappointment in a case, or conceded any loss. In fact, it had never occurred to him that his father *could* lose in a courtroom.

"Sometimes you have to be a little selfish," his father said. The glass slid back and forth. "Figure out what's most important to reach your goal and put what might block your path behind you. You're on the right track now, Bobby. You are. You need to keep everything together. Stay focused. Don't let anything, anyone, distract you. There'll be time to sort it all out later." He punctuated it with a nod.

"But even with all the preparation in the world, nothing is guaranteed," his father went on. "Never guaranteed." He wasn't talking to his son, Bobby was sure of that. "Understand?"

"Yeah, Dad."

"No, do you *understand*?"

"Yeah, sure."

"Beat this kid from Rampart tomorrow."

"I will," Bobby said.

His father took a final swallow from the glass, then smiled a melancholy smile. "You should get some sleep."

24

The sound of closing locker doors woke Bobby. The Millburn locker room was humid, a familiar stale smell filled the air. A catnap after weigh-ins usually made him alert before a match, but Bobby could tell right away he wasn't feeling better. Congestion blocked his ears, his head throbbed, and he couldn't cough up a wad of mucus caked at the back of his throat.

The locker-room door swung open. Coach Messina stepped in to say, "Millburn, get yourselves ready," then went out.

Fighting off shivers, Bobby dressed in his singlet and socks, his Yankees T-shirt, and, finally, his warm-up suit. Around him, in workmanlike fashion, teammates went through their pre-match rituals. In the corner, Big John mouthed the words to a song on his Walkman, while sophomore David Orenstein adjusted and readjusted his headgear. In the bathroom, Anthony rolled his shoulders;

Kenny bounced up and down on his toes. Most of the other wrestlers sat quietly, each in his own space in the locker room.

A few minutes later, Coach Messina returned. "Rampart's out on the mats," he said. "Listen up."

Everyone turned to the center of the locker room.

"We've waited all season for this match. And now we're on the edge of destiny. We can beat Rampart today, there's no doubt in my mind. And if we beat Rampart today, then we *will* be ranked number one in Essex County, and we *will* be one of the elite teams in the state. I can guarantee it."

Coach Messina stared around the locker room, hard.

"That is unless one thing stops you. A lack of absolute confidence. If confidence fails *you* today, then *you* will lose. If confidence fails *us*, then *we* will lose . . . The question you have to ask yourself is, after all the months of exhausting practice, after cutting weight and starving, after making every sacrifice and dedicating one hundred percent of your effort to put yourselves in this position, could your confidence be anything but absolute?"

He pointed in the direction of the gymnasium. "Those guys are not from Millburn. They don't have the pride, the training, the dedication. They don't have what it takes to beat you. If each one of you believes this *absolutely*, we will win as a team. Do you believe it?"

"Yes," a few of the wrestlers answered.

"Millburn, don't just say it," Coach Messina snapped. "*Feel* it! Are you going to beat Rampart today?"

"Yes!" the team shouted in unison.

"Good." Coach Messina leaned over and put out his arms. "Hands in!"

The wrestlers pressed against one another, their breathing halted, their hands clasped together.

Bobby *knew* no team was going beat Millburn.

Not today.

"Hoods up!" Bobby said.

In weight-class order, the Millburn team lined up behind Bobby and Kenny in the hall outside the gymnasium's side entrance. Bobby peered in through the door. Opposite sides of the mat were lined with folding chairs for the wrestlers and coaches. The Millburn cheerleaders were practicing their routines. Bleachers on both sides overflowed with spectators. The electronic scoreboard read: MILLBURN 0; VISITORS 0. The stage was set.

Bobby signaled.

The gymnasium ceiling lights dimmed, then shut down. The first . . . Then the second . . . Then the third . . . One by one until a single ceiling lamp illuminated the wrestling circle on the mat, leaving the rest of the gymnasium in darkness. A hushed silence came over the crowd.

Bobby looked into the eyes of his teammates, staring back from under their hoods. "Once around the mat, then start with takedowns," he barked. "Hoods up the *whole* time."

He signaled again.

Thundering from the PA speakers, the sullen voice and haunting cadence of the song "Renegade" began.

"*Oh, Mama, I'm in fear for my life, from the long arm of the law . . .*"

Bobby's heart jumped. This was it. Senior year. Captain of his undefeated Millburn team. In his home gym. Rampart on the other side. Everything on the line.

He whispered the next lines of the song to himself, as excitement shot up and down his spine. The chills he had endured the past two days were, at least momentarily, stifled by shudders of unbridled emotion.

Relax, Bobby thought. *Relax.*

But his breathing edged on hyperventilation. He had to force himself to suck air in as deeply as his lungs could handle.

"*Hangman is coming down from the gallows, and I don't have very long . . .*"

Bobby held up his hand. "One. Two. Three. Let's go!"

He led the team on a sprint through a narrow divide in the spectators, emerging from darkness onto the lighted mat, each wrestler whipping his headgear to the side and circling once. The music thundered. As Big John brought up the rear, Bobby and Kenny stood at the center circle. The team stopped, pairing off and alternating takedowns.

Watch me, Caruso! Bobby thrust his body into Kenny on a double-leg, lifting him high into the air, as if to say, "Look how goddamn strong I am." Kenny did the same, exploding into a hi-crotch, running the pike, and taking

Bobby down with such precision that everyone watching *had* to be impressed.

Bobby looked up from his hood, catching sight of his mother, father, and Christopher sitting with Mr. and Mrs. Jones. Bobby nodded to his father, who nodded back.

"Renegade" finished, and soon the national anthem, as well. The Rampart wrestlers lined the edge of the mat in weight-class order, their warm-up hoods hardly hiding the sneers on their gaunt faces. Bobby and his teammates stood on the opposite edge of the mat, sneering themselves.

The PA system boomed, "Welcome to Millburn for this afternoon's match with Rampart High School . . . Wrestling at 101, from Rampart, Ricky Imperiale." The Rampart wrestler sprinted across to the center of the mat.

"And from Millburn, David Orenstein." Orenstein marched, head down, body stiff. Halfway, the two wrestlers shook hands, then turned and went back to their teams.

"Wrestling at 108, from Rampart, Louie DiPaolo. And from Millburn, Steve Smith." Again, the two wrestlers met halfway across the mat, shook hands, and walked back to their places.

The announcer continued with the 115-pound and 122-pound matches.

Bobby stared at Caruso, noting the smirk on his face, the patch of whiskers on his chin, the slicked jet-black hair. Caruso snickered, then mouthed, "Poor little rich kid."

Bobby despised the Rampart team, the town, and everything it represented. He couldn't have held any more anger, and it all focused on the wrestler standing across from him. Underneath his warm-ups, Bobby's armpits were slick with sweat, his body quivered. He indulged in it.

"Wrestling at 129, from Rampart, Jim Caruso . . . And from Millburn, Bobby Zane . . ."

Bobby marched across the mat, buried under the roar of the crowd. He threw out his hand; Caruso threw out his. They slapped hands, then turned. As Bobby stormed back to his teammates, he said to Kenny, "Let's beat these assholes."

The introductions continued until the heavyweights were announced. Then it was time to start the match. The referee stood at the center circle, motioning for the two 101-pounders.

The Rampart fans rose as one, clapping and shouting, and stomping their feet, shaking the bleachers to their foundation. Rampart had won the first three matches, and now—ahead with seconds left in the 122-pound match—was about to hold a nearly insurmountable lead in the team score. The Millburn crowd, sensing the dual meet slipping away, belted out the school song while the cheerleaders shook their blue and white pom-poms, their cheers drowned out in the shrill that filled the gymnasium.

Bobby pulled off his T-shirt, tossed it to the floor, and strapped on his headgear. He coughed and shivered, then flexed his muscles to bring warmth to his body. The buzzer sounded.

Bobby stalked over to Coach Messina. They shook hands.

"Bobby, we're not wrestling well tonight. Someone's gotta step up and stop the bleeding. Are you gonna do it? Are you gonna be the one?"

Bobby nodded.

"Good," Coach Messina said. "Stay on your feet with him. Take him down, and let him up if you have to. Now go get him!"

Bobby marched through the gauntlet of shouting teammates, stepping onto the mat as his name was announced over the PA system. He met Caruso at the center circle. Caruso's eyes were cold, and his muscles rippled in waves along his shoulders, across his chest, down his arms. They shook hands. Months of preparation, years of hatred, came down to this.

The referee leaned in and blew the whistle.

They wouldn't know, Bobby thought.

He had a 2–0 lead—on a textbook double-leg in the first period—but they wouldn't know. His lungs were burning; his throat had nearly closed. It had caught up to him. The sleepless nights. The coughing. The chills. The aches. The shitty practices. But the Millburn fans wouldn't know. They wouldn't know that in a few seconds, when the second period ended, he'd want to throw up right there in the center circle. They'd see that their captain, Bobby Zane, was winning and think the match was turning in their favor. It looked good on the surface. But they wouldn't know.

"Time!" the referee shouted.

Bobby stood up, bent over, and hacked. And hacked again. He didn't bother looking toward Coach Messina, or his teammates, or his father, or anyone else. They couldn't help him.

"Rampart's choice," the referee said.

"Top," Caruso growled.

Bobby settled into referee's position, on his hands and knees; Caruso moved in on top. Off the whistle, Bobby exploded into a stand, looking to create space for an escape. He was giving it all he had, but his body was resisting. Before Bobby could get his balance, Caruso swept him easily back down to the mat.

On his hands and knees, Bobby braced. Caruso was well schooled, Bobby knew. All Rampart wrestlers were well schooled. And had there been a chance in hell that he, or his teammates, might have forgotten, Coach Messina had reminded the team all week in practice: "Stay off the mat with Rampart. Wrestle from your feet!"

So Bobby again stepped up. And just as quickly, Caruso tripped him down to the mat, then slipped in a half nelson. Instinctively, Bobby cranked down on the arm and rolled. Momentum carried their entangled bodies outside the circle.

"Out of bounds!" the referee shouted.

Bobby could only get to his knees. Fifty-eight seconds left on the clock. His chest was rising and falling with rapid, ragged breaths that wheezed in and out of his mouth. This time he did look toward Coach Messina.

"It's simple," Coach Messina said. "You escape, you win."

Again, Bobby and his opponent settled into referee's position. At the whistle, Bobby braced, holding off Caruso's attack. More time clicked off the clock. Then Caruso hesitated and Bobby stepped up.

It was a setup, a wily bit of deception. Caruso pulled Bobby's arm across his face, wedged his arm between Bobby's legs, and clamped his hands together. A cradle. And a damn good one.

Bobby kicked out his leg to break Caruso's grip, but strength his opponent didn't seem to have in the first period now appeared with a vengeance. Caruso squeezed the cradle tighter and rolled Bobby to his back. The ceiling lamps shined in his eyes.

"I got you, Zane," Caruso snarled in his ear.

Bobby strained to keep his shoulder blades off the mat. He twisted. And strained. And something inside him, borne from the hatred of Rampart, grew powerful. *You will* not *get pinned!* He arched his back, kicked his leg, and with an exhausting rush of strength, turned to his stomach.

"Back points, Rampart," the referee shouted. "Two points!"

Caruso covered Bobby on top. Bobby glanced at the scoreboard clock—nine seconds left. He could hear his teammates urging him to move. But he had nothing left, nothing at all.

Three seconds . . .

Two . . .

One . . .

As time ran out, Bobby was helpless. "Time!" the referee yelled. "Two-all tie, gentlemen."

The Rampart side of the gymnasium roared in delight, erupting even louder when Caruso threw his fist in the air. Bobby kneeled on the mat a moment, his head hanging. His worst nightmare had been realized.

"Let's go, Millburn," the referee said.

Bobby climbed to his feet, shaking his head. The referee raised both wrestlers' arms.

Bobby passed through his stunned teammates, past Coach Messina, past Kenny, who was preparing for his match. Behind the chairs, he slumped down. Sweat burned his eyes. Again, he looked toward the scoreboard. Both teams were awarded two points for the tie, and Rampart's margin remained. If Rampart did go on to win—which had become likely after his match—Bobby knew he had had an opportunity to stop the bleeding but didn't.

He gathered his warm-ups and slipped on his T-shirt. All the while, the sweat and frustration—and now tears—poured.

Jeers from the Rampart fans rang in Bobby's head as he sat among his teammates in the silent locker room, waiting. Eventually, Coach Messina entered. Bobby had never seen his coach look like this before. His tie was undone, strain showed on his face, and for a time, he stood silent and motionless before the team.

A minute or two passed.

Finally, Coach Messina spoke.

"Gentlemen, you will find that there are defining moments in your wrestling life, both good and bad, that come and go. You win today; you forget it tomorrow. You lose today; you forget it tomorrow." He stared at the ceiling. "There are also moments that have a way of staying with you forever. Moments that never go away. You can't soothe them. You might not think about them for a day, a week, a few months—if you're lucky, maybe years. Then they crawl back into your head. You try to forget it . . . Erase it . . . Bury it . . . But you can't."

He shook his head. "This loss, Millburn, will haunt you for the rest of your lives. We were undefeated, second in the county, on the verge of breaking into the top twenty of the state. Think about that—top twenty of the state. Maybe top ten by the end of the season. More importantly, this could've been one of the best teams Millburn's ever had."

Bobby hung his head.

"Instead, we were beaten by a bunch of guys that came into our building and spit in our faces. This was Rampart, for god's sake. If you can't get up for this match, you can't get up for any match. Adam," Coach Messina snapped, "were you even awake today? The kid you lost to was a freshman. And Big John, why in the world would you try to roll someone when you're up by two points with fifteen seconds left? Giving up three back points is inexcusable.

"And someone explain to me how one of our captains . . ."

Here it comes.

". . . ties a match when he is the better, stronger wrestler? Bobby," Coach Messina said.

Bobby raised his head.

"If you're going to be one of the top wrestlers in the state, you have to prove it every single time you step out on the mat. I don't care if you're sick, I don't care if you're hurt, I don't care what's happening outside of wrestling. Never any excuses, do you hear me?"

"Yes, Coach," Bobby said.

"No excuses," Coach Messina said, "ever again."

25

At the front of the classroom, Mr. Fitzsimmons slapped his hand on a stack of test papers.

"These were easy questions, people. Winter doldrums. Senioritis. I don't know what it is, but this class is—with a few exceptions—achieving mediocrity in a very grand fashion." He withdrew a piece of chalk from the desk drawer, rolling the thin white cylinder from one finger to the next. "Now, that's not what you or your well-heeled parents want, is it?"

The chalk squeaked with each slash against the blackboard. Bobby hardly noticed. Instead, his hand moved furiously, the ballpoint scratching words on the page of a spiral notebook.

Bobby Zane State Champ—129 lbs. Bobby Zane State Champ—129 lbs. Bobby Zane State Champ—129 lbs. Bobby Zane State Champ—129 lbs. Bobby—

Over and over, Bobby wrote. His hand didn't slow.

Zane State Champ—129 lbs. Bobby Zane State Champ—129 lbs. Bobby Zane State Champ—129 lbs. Bobby Zane State Champ—129 lbs. Bobby Zane—

Bobby glanced at the classroom clock. A half hour had passed, yet his textbook remained unopened. Still, he continued. Harder and harder, the pen digging into the paper, the muscles of his forearm burning, then knotting.

State Champ—129 lbs. Bobby Zane State Champ—129 lbs. Bobby Zane State Champ—129 lbs. Bobby Zane State Champ—129 lbs. Bobby Za—

"Mr. Zane!"

Bobby looked up, blinked a few times. His eyes focused. Mr. Fitzsimmons—ruddy skin, veined nose—glared at him.

"I can't help but notice all the writing you're doing today," Mr. Fitzsimmons said, the chalk again flitting back and forth between his fingers. "I'm intrigued."

"I'm, uh, taking notes," Bobby said.

"Oh, you are," Mr. Fitzsimmons said. "I'd really like to know on what, since all the answers are worked out in the textbook. Which, if you'd looked around, you'd have noticed all your classmates have been following."

Someone snickered. Bobby searched the room for the answer in a classmate's face, but all were blank. Then he squinted at the blackboard, a dizzying maze of symbols and numbers. It might as well have been blank, too.

Mr. Fitzsimmons smirked. "Mr. Zane, I'm waiting."

"Just, you know, being diligent," Bobby said, annoyed.

"'Diligent,'" Mr. Fitzsimmons said.

"Yeah."

"Really? Perhaps you should have been as diligent studying for this test."

"Perhaps," Bobby said.

And then Bobby simply didn't care. Irritated that he had to stop writing, Bobby didn't let the look on his face, or his voice, hide that fact. He spoke slowly and pointedly. "Mr. Fitzsimmons, I don't have a clue what's going on."

The teacher's smile turned sour. "Well, then," he said, "I would suggest that you check those extensive notes of yours."

"My notes?"

"Yes, your notes. Read those notes to the class. Or maybe you'd like me to," he said.

"No, that's okay," Bobby said, sliding his elbow over the notebook.

"You sure?"

"Yeah."

Mr. Fitzsimmons turned back toward the blackboard. "Do me a favor, Mr. Zane; stay with us in class. Calculus isn't a bunch of useless theories. It's life. It should be accorded the same respect as wrestling . . ."

Bobby shut out the rest of what Mr. Fitzsimmons was saying. He slid the notebook out from under his forearm and continued.

ne State Champ—129 lbs. Bobby Zane State Champ—129 lbs. Bobby Zane State Champ—129 lbs . . .

26

It was quiet, Saturday afternoon. Darkness crept into the bedroom. Ivan sat at his desk, staring at the Western Arizona application, some of the pages dog-eared but still unmarked. He listened for the Nova pulling into the driveway but heard nothing. So he opened the application, as he had done countless times before.

Ivan had memorized the questions by heart. *What has been your favorite class, and why? What has been your single most significant academic achievement? If you could have dinner with any person, living or dead, who would it be, and what would you discuss?*

Still, the pen in his hand wouldn't move. Frustration scrambled his thoughts. It was the middle of February, the season was coming to an end. It was time to make a move, time to be bold. *Finish the damn application*, he admonished himself. His fingers tightened, pressing the pen against the paper.

Nothing . . .

Ivan sat back. Earlier in the day, South Hunterdon had pounded Lennings, 45–6. For the third time this season, his victory kept the team from an embarrassing shutout.

From the start, Ivan had tied up with his South Hunterdon opponent, letting his opponent feel his strength, assuring him there wasn't a chance in hell of making it to the second period. Still, the South Hunterdon wrestler was game, sprawling hard at Ivan's every move, trying so desperately, and obviously, not to make a mistake.

Then it came: an awkward step, leaving Ivan an opening. Ivan shot in for a hi-crotch, pivoted, and lifted his opponent high off the mat. His speed was startling. Ivan held the position long enough to glare over at the South Hunterdon bench, before dropping his victim to the mat. The South Hunterdon wrestler tried to sit out, then hit a switch. Ivan countered both easily. There was an obligatory struggle, but once Ivan clamped in the half, turning his opponent to his back, it was only moments before the referee called the pin.

Ivan tried to focus on the application, remembering his last conversation with Coach Riker. "Y'all will get an answer from the admissions committee soon enough," Coach Riker had said. It was a done deal, Ivan figured. A third in the states guaranteed a spot in Riker's program, how could it not? "But nothin' happens until the committee gets that application," Riker said. "Send it in now, son."

That was two weeks ago. It was easy to put off the essays. Too easy, Ivan knew. There was always a good excuse. Go on a long run. Lift weights. Practice moves in the basement. Do push-ups and sit-ups. Think about Shelley. Something—anything else—could be done instead.

Ivan looked out the bedroom window. His father would be home soon. Maybe he'd have one more thing that needed to be fixed, or moved, or worked on. Maybe one more night would slip away.

No, Ivan thought, *time to get this done*. And so, he started at the top of the page.

Applicant's Name: Ivan Korske

Address: 1002 Farmingdale Road, Lennings, New Jersey 07002

Father's Name and Occupation: Josef Korske, Farm Maintenance

Living or Deceased: Living

Mother's Name and Occupation: Anna Korske

Living or Deceased:

Ivan stared at the last word for a long while. "Deceased," he said, as if saying the word for the first time. He said it again. "Deceased." *Dead. Expired. Departed. Passed. Gone.* His mother was now summed up neatly in one word.

Ivan threw down the pen and swept away the papers. They fluttered to the floor. He'd finish another time. When he could think more clearly. Later tonight. Maybe tomorrow. Or next week. Before the season ended. Sure, he'd do it then.

Ivan pushed his chair back—the legs scraping along the wood floor—and hunched over.

Why do they keep asking about her? What the hell do they really wanna know? Just rip open my guts and look in.

It wasn't just the college essays. It was the people in town. The kids at school. Teachers. They stared, sometimes briefly, but mostly with a lingering pity that made Ivan feel like a freak. So, he stared back. "She's dead, okay?" he wanted to yell. What was the point? They'd keep staring and whispering.

Ivan sat back, thinking, remembering, feeling memories of his mother fill his mind. . . .

● ● ●

Sunlight sliced through the canopy of trees to the ground where Ivan lay against a fallen tree trunk. The dirt was moist, almost cool, but otherwise, the August humidity was everywhere.

Search and destroy. The game that would bring Ivan neighborhood immortality. It was his turn to be prison escapee. To win he had to avoid being captured by Timmy and Josh before making it to his backyard where the golden sword of freedom, the crowned jewel of Farmingdale Road, stuck straight up in the grass. If he won, Ivan would keep the sword and the title of "Supreme Exalted Being" until the next game, whenever that might be.

The stakes were high, life-and-death, Ivan thought, since during all the times he and the Scotts had played, he had never won.

Not once.

His would-be captors were formidable. Timmy, though pudgy and not particularly coordinated, had straight-ahead speed, and Josh had a knack for knowing where Ivan was, without looking very hard. It was a weird psychic thing, Ivan figured.

But on this day, Ivan promised himself victory would be delivered. He held his breath, hearing Timmy's footsteps pass by . . . Then stop . . . Slowly, Ivan pushed up on his hands and peeked over the log. He watched Timmy, and the opening in the woods, measuring the distance in his head.

"See him?" Josh called out.

"Nah," Timmy yelled back, stripping bark off a fallen branch. "He's too chicken to show his ugly face."

Ivan inched up onto his knees, seeing Timmy take a step away from his direction. Then another. Ivan waited, setting his feet underneath his body, his hands holding on to the log for balance. His heartbeat throbbed in his throat. He might never get another chance like this. Ever. Timmy stepped again. Ivan's body recoiled.

Now!

Springing to his feet, Ivan broke toward the opening in the woods. He had a good jump—a great jump—and a clear path ahead. This time, he was sure, no one would catch him, and for a moment, he imagined himself pulling the sword from its resting place and hoisting it skyward.

But thoughts of neighborhood immortality vanished. On Ivan's left, Josh bolted from behind a thicket of trees. "There he is! There he is!"

Timmy was in pursuit, too. "You're dead meat, Korske."

Hurdling fallen branches and gangly roots, slaloming between trees and sidestepping rocks, Ivan ran as fast as he could. *You gotta get the sword! You gotta get it!*

The opening to the backyard grew larger, but Ivan could see Josh coming quickly from the left, while, behind him, he heard Timmy's sneakers hitting the ground step for step with his own. "I'm gonna win!"

The words had hardly left his throat when Josh's shoulder slammed into his rib cage, knocking him off balance. Timmy grabbed Ivan's T-shirt by the collar, trying to drag him to the ground. Still, Ivan kept moving forward, churning his legs, tearing from Timmy's grasp.

Yes, victory would finally be his.

Glancing over his shoulder, Ivan saw both boys fall but not the branch where he was stepping. His right foot caught first, and as he tried to step with his left, that one caught, as well. He hit the ground hard, his hands protecting his face. But nothing stopped his right knee from skidding against the jagged face of a large rock.

"Oowww!" he shouted, rolling to his side. He looked down at his red, scraped-up knee, then at the two brothers just a few yards behind him. "Look what ya did to me!"

Timmy and Josh got to their feet. "You're down, Korske," Timmy said.

"You cheated," Ivan said.

The two boys stood over him. "No way," Josh said. "We got ya fair and square."

"Lemme alone. Ya busted up my knee."

Timmy bent down to inspect the injury. "Aw, it's not that bad."

"Is too."

"Is not."

"You're not a doctor," Ivan said.

Timmy turned to Josh and made a face. "Look at the little *baby*. We weren't playin' rough or nothin'."

"That's not playin'," Ivan said. Blood rose from the gash in his skin. "You were tryin' to tackle me hard."

"Were not."

Josh rubbed the dirt off his elbow and pulled a leaf from his shorts' pocket. "We were playin' by the rules. And the rules don't change for little babies."

Ivan, his lean arms bracing against the ground, lifted himself to his feet. His knee had stiffened and with even a slight bend of his leg, the raw skin burned. A trickle of blood made the top of his sock red. Tears were coming, and coming fast.

Don't let 'em see you cry. Don't! They'll tell Shelley; they'll tell everyone in the whole entire neighborhood. And school, too!

"I'm goin' in," Ivan said, limping ahead of the two boys as they followed behind.

"Baby," Timmy said. "Ya can't cry every time ya lose."

"I'm not cryin'!" Ivan stared down the two boys as they crossed his backyard to the driveway. He heard their sharp laughter, each snicker needling him worse than the pain from his skinned knee. *They're laughin' at me; they're laughin' at me*. He wanted so badly to pick up a rock and nail them—Timmy, especially—right in their foul mouths, then punch them in the gut. He wanted to do anything to shut them up. And the snickers kept coming.

"See ya later, girlie," Timmy said.

"Jerk," Ivan yelled back.

"Crybaby," Josh said.

"Jerks," Ivan yelled louder.

The back door swung open, the thin wood frame slapping against the house. Ivan's mother, slender, in her blue shorts and white blouse, said, "Ivan, we do not use that language in this house."

"I'm not inside, Mama."

"That is enough. Boys," she said, looking toward Timmy and Josh, "your mothers would not like all this carrying on, now would they?"

"But Mrs. Korske—"

"No *buts*, Timmy. You are the oldest here; you should know better," she said. "Besides, it is too beautiful a day to be yelling at each other."

Timmy hung his head. "Sorry, Mrs. Korske," he said. Ivan loved that about his mother; *everyone* listened to her.

"Run along now, boys. Ivan will be out again after dinner." She looked down at Ivan, sitting on the back stoop. "And no more yelling for you, too, young man."

"My knee, Mama," Ivan pleaded. "It's smashed." He had held out as much as he could, but the tears now flowed like the blood from his wound. Ivan limped up the stairs. His mother knelt down, catching him in her arms. "It hurts," he managed between sobs. "It hurts a lot."

"There, there," she said. Her warm voice had returned. "I'll take care of you."

Ivan sat on the countertop, his spindly legs dangling off, checking himself for other scrapes. His mother went to the pantry, then returned with the medicine chest and a clean cloth. She ran warm water over the cloth, rubbed in some soap, and gently washed the exposed skin. Ivan flinched.

"That hurt?" his mother asked.

"No."

She smiled and applied a generous amount of iodine.

"Looks like paint," Ivan said. "Orange paint."

"It will go away," she said.

Ivan heard the sound of crunching pebbles coming from the driveway as his father drove up in the family's new Chevy Nova, the maroon hood gleaming in the sun. He worried what his father might say, thinking he was some kind of weakling.

Soon, the car door shut. His mother was coming back from the pantry when the screen door opened and his father stepped into the kitchen. Ivan was sure his father could whip any other father in Lennings.

"What is the problem?" his father said, wiping his brow with his forearm.

"Nothing," his mother said. "Our son is a brave young man, playing with those bigger boys."

His father said nothing, walking over to the refrigerator and pulling out a pitcher of iced tea. He filled a tall glass and drank it down in one long gulp. He filled the glass again. "You hurt your knee?"

Ivan wanted to look like a man in his father's eyes. He sat up tall. "Me and Timmy and Josh were playing out back."

His father turned on the kitchen faucet, putting his hands under the running water for a few moments. Ivan noticed dried blood of a half-dozen cuts and scratches on his thick fingers, and he saw the strain etched on his father's face when he made a fist. His father finished the second glass of iced tea, then looked at Ivan again. "And?"

"I was hidin' real good. And I had this chance to win. So I ran real hard." His voice cracked. "But they cheated, Papa, they cheated and tackled me."

His mother tore open a large Band-Aid, carefully touching one end of the adhesive tape just outside the scrape, covering the wound with the gauze, then fixing the other end. "There," she said, with a kiss on his cheek.

Ivan pulled back. "I'm okay, Mama."

"Did you win?" his father said, drying his hands on a dish towel. "Did you beat these boys?"

Ivan hesitated. His shoulders slumped. "Not exactly."

"Why not?"

"I tried, I really did. Both of them tackled me, or else I coulda made it."

His father walked over to the kitchen counter, kissing Ivan's mother on the top of her head. Ivan saw her smile, and he liked that. "Our son is strong," she said.

His father's hands were immense next to his knee. His father said nothing, turning Ivan's leg slightly one way, then the other, then looking straight at him. "Did you cry?"

Ivan prayed he wouldn't notice the tears on his cheeks.

His mother stepped in. "He did not cry," she said. "My son does not cry."

"It looks like he did."

"You are mistaken."

His father again stared at Ivan. "Did you cry?"

"No," Ivan said.

"See," his mother said, wiping Ivan's face with the other end of the moist cloth. "I made some sausage and peppers. Enough of all this talk. Let us eat."

Ivan jumped off the countertop and stepped to the kitchen table. His father put a hand on his shoulder . . .

Ivan gathered the pages from the floor, arranging them neatly. He looked down at the application. *Let's get this over with.* He read the essay question out loud, "'If you could have dinner with any person, living or dead, who would it be, and what would you discuss?'"

He had read the question silently a hundred times before, but hearing the words from his own mouth sparked something. *Living or dead.* He thought about it more. Did he dare write about his mother? Did he dare take the chance of spilling his emotions?

At the top of the first page, he wrote the date, then an inch below that his hand abruptly stopped. Sometimes he tried to shut out memories of his mother. He couldn't love her any more than he did right now, as he did yesterday, and the day before, and every other day of his life. And because he loved her so much, he couldn't keep the sadness at bay. Every day, every hour, every minute, held something that reminded him she was gone.

And what Ivan couldn't control confounded him. He could control any opponent. By ignoring them, he could control Holt and McClellan and the others on his team. But what Ivan couldn't control was the disease that had riddled his mother's body. And he couldn't control the relentless ache of having lost her.

"Who would you have dinner with?" he whispered.

Ivan again looked down at the pages before him. He remembered that day, long ago, when his mother bandaged the skinned knee he got playing out back with the Scott brothers, and he remembered a night, not long after, when he watched his parents kissing in the dark, their silhouetted bodies intertwined. The memories flowed easily, and suddenly he felt comforted. The pages would no longer stay blank.

Ivan picked up the pen, held it between his fingers, and let it move. Slowly, but with an unexpected confidence, he wrote: *I would have dinner with my mother, Anna Korske. . . .*

27

We gonna be together Saturday night?" Carmelina asked. "After I'm done with work?"

Bobby switched the telephone receiver from one ear to the other and propped another pillow under his head. It was dark outside, yet a tepid breeze blew through his bedroom window. Winter had given way to spring, if only for the day. Before practice, Bobby sat in the sun on the school patio, listening to the trickle of melting icicles. He was restless. Unsettled. All around him, it seemed, change was imminent.

"How 'bout we drive into the Village," he heard Carmelina say. "Ya know, walk around a bit, shop the stores, eat dinner. Well, I'll eat and you can watch, okay? Please, it's real important we talk . . . Bobby, are ya listening?"

"I'm tired, Carmelina," he said. "I gotta get to sleep."

"You'll come over, then?"

"Maybe."

"What's 'maybe'?"

"We got a match Saturday. It's the last match of the season. I'm sure Kenny and the guys'll wanna do something after."

"Maybe I wanna do something with you," Carmelina said. "Ever think about that? We should be together, Bobby; that's what boyfriends and girlfriends do."

He drew in a breath, loud enough for her to hear. "Look, Carmelina, the districts are in two weeks. I gotta focus. That guy I wrestled on Wednesday was a region champ last year, and I beat him badly. It would've been nice if you'd been there."

"Bobby, ya know—"

"Yeah, yeah," he interrupted, "you have to work."

"Ya know I do."

"Yeah, well, who knows how far I can go if I keep wrestling like this? Know how important that is to me?"

"Sure, I understand," Carmelina said, but it didn't sound like she did.

"Things'll change," Bobby said.

There was a hesitation. "When?"

"After the season."

There was a pause. "You're done with me," Carmelina said. "I can tell."

"That's not it."

"You're such a liar."

"I'm not lying," Bobby said. "I just feel like . . . like something really important is gonna happen soon. It's hard to explain. Carmelina, I don't know, maybe we should—" Something had caught his attention. Bobby covered the receiver.

He heard music. Bobby sat up and looked out the window at the back walkway. He could tell a light was on in the family room. He looked at the clock. It was quarter to eleven, yet his father wasn't home. He listened more closely. It was that *same* music.

"We'll talk tomorrow night," Bobby said into the receiver. "I gotta go."

"Why?"

"I just gotta," Bobby said.

"Now?"

"It's late and I'm thirsty and hungry and tired."

"You wanna break up," Carmelina said. "I can hear it in your voice."

"Carmelina—"

"Don't be an asshole, Bobby. Don't do this over the phone. Promise we'll talk in person. Saturday night. It's important. We'll figure everything out."

"Yeah, sure," Bobby said, before hanging up.

He walked down the stairs to the living room, where a bay window overlooked the front lawn. In the dark, he moved quietly along the silk sofa, then past two glass tables upon which sat some of his mother's treasured crystal figurines. The music started again.

Bobby crouched down, recognizing the voice of Dionne Warwick on the stereo. He had heard the music before but had never paid any attention, never listened to the words, never wondered why his mother played the same songs over and over, late at night, when his father wasn't home.

A car turned down Joanna Way, its headlights shining through the bay window. The crystal pieces sparkled and the light brushed his body, then disappeared. Bobby watched the car as it drove past their driveway, feeling relieved—and disappointed, too—that it wasn't his father. He crawled to the archway between the living room and the dining room. It felt wrong to *spy* on his mother. In her own house. Still, he sat back against the wall. The next song began.

"You see this girl," his mother sang. *"This girl's in love with you . . ."* Her voice was startling. Elegant. As elegant as she might look in her most beautiful evening dress. Bold. As bold as she had been some time ago, before this mess had started. *"Yes, I'm in love . . . Who looks at you the way I do . . ."*

Bobby peeked around the wall, through the dining room, into the family room. His mother, as if onstage, swayed to the music, eyes closed, smiling softly, the music climbing to a crescendo, piano keys pounding, Dionne Warwick's voice and his mother's overlapping into one, stretching the final note into one long wail.

The song ended, and another began. . . .

And then another . . .

Bobby's eyes welled up. Why was this the first time he had heard his mother sing? he wondered. Why had he never seen her dance before?

He thought for a while. Eventually, slowly, it was apparent that something about this made him feel older. He always wanted to act like a man, to be treated like a man, to live in a man's world. But this time, it was too much.

He wasn't ready to see his parents as people. They were his *parents*. But it was now so clear that he didn't know *anything* about his mother. What she thought about, or wanted, or dreamed of. And as he watched his mother in a way he had never done before, he wondered where she *really* wanted to be at that moment. It certainly wasn't in *this* house. On Joanna Way. In Short Hills, New Jersey.

Bobby's eyes clouded. Not much longer after that, he cried. He was confused and scared about his family. And especially his mother. And if it was true about his mother, he realized, it could be true about his father. It was obvious Bobby could only trust what he could control. And he could only control who and what he could trust. The *who* was himself. The *what* was wrestling.

Bobby stiffened. The music was still playing, his mother still singing. He wiped away the tears, stood up, and walked out of the living room—different from earlier. For the better? He wasn't sure. Did it matter? He was too tired for deeper consideration. His legs plodded up the stairs, heavy. The music faded when he turned the corner at the top of the stairs. He closed his bedroom door.

His world had changed.

28

The snowflakes pricked Ivan's cheeks, gusting winds rushing one way, then another. He leaned against the shovel handle and looked back. A fresh layer of white had already covered the walkway. His father would be home soon. He would not be pleased.

This'll never get done. It seemed like everything was that way. Like the application for Western Arizona. Whenever Ivan sat at his desk and tried to finish the dozens of intrusive essays and prying questions, he'd lose interest, thinking about wrestling, or Shelley, or stocking his hatred of McClellan. There wasn't much more he could write about his mother. Now, he had to pretend to care about school and classes and teachers. He'd write a paragraph, maybe two, then throw down his pen in frustration and mutter, "Screw it, another day won't make a damn bit of difference."

A trickle of sweat ran down his cheek. *At least I'll cut some weight today—*

Something hit Ivan. A snowball. His anger sparked. *What the hell?* And he spun around.

"Ha! Surprised you, didn't I?" Shelley shouted.

Ivan mustered a smile, but not much of one. Something was very wrong, he could feel it. Frustration had been building all season. Everyone was pissing him off; everything was pissing him off. Being on a lousy team. McClellan and his ridiculous pep talks. Now Ivan's anger had ignited. There was nothing he could do.

"Saw you from my window," Shelley said. "Thought you could use some company." She scooped snow into her mittens. "I'll get you again, Champ. I don't care how fast you are on a wrestling mat. You can't duck this." She raised her arm.

Ivan stood motionless.

"I will," Shelley said. "I swear I'll hit you with this." She pulled her arm back. "I got a pretty good arm."

"You'll miss."

"You sure?"

"Sure as McClellan's an asshole."

Shelley looked at him, oddly.

"Come on," Ivan said. "Take your best shot."

Shelley smiled, hesitantly. "Oh, you'll duck. Just when it's coming right at you."

Ivan shook his head. "I won't move."

Shelley packed the snowball, rounding it in her mittens. "Remember when we were little kids and I hit that huge pinecone at the top of the tree behind my house? That was on only my *second* try. Remember?"

Ivan unbuttoned his jacket and dropped it in the snow. He laced his fingers behind his back.

"Like I'm going to be distracted if you take your clothes off," Shelley said. "I've seen you in a singlet dozens of times, Ivan." She smirked. "It's no big deal."

"You *won't* hit me."

"How do you know?"

"I know."

The whipping wind blew beneath Ivan's sweatshirt. He shivered.

Shelley stood, arms at her side. A surge blew open the scarf from her neck. She quickly wrapped it around again. Her skin was red, her eyes slits, her mouth stiff when she spoke.

"Big deal, Champ, you took off your jacket. You still have on a sweatshirt, probably long underwear underneath. A stud would—"

Before she finished, Ivan pulled off his sweatshirt, his chest now bare. Shelley's smile withered as Ivan threw his gloves aside, too.

The frigid cold came at Ivan from every direction, feeling as if it scraped against his puckered skin. His first breath was halted by the spasm of his diaphragm. He fought it. And fought it. And fought it.

Until he simply refused to feel the cold.

Soon, he was breathing calmly, almost comfortably. Again, he clasped his hands behind his back, staring at Shelley. *What the hell am I doing?* He hadn't a clue.

"You're crazy," Shelley said; the lightness in her voice

was gone. "God, it's like twenty degrees out here. Colder with the windchill." She shielded her face from another swirl.

"Hit me," Ivan said.

Shelley turned away, then looked back at him, as if she couldn't believe what she was seeing. "Ivan," she said, almost pleading, "it's really very cold."

Ivan didn't flinch. Flakes bounced off his skin, and those that didn't melted in a moment or two. A thin cap of white had settled on his spiked hair. *What's happening to me?* He couldn't control himself. He was trapped in that muscles-flexed, heart-racing, supremely arrogant mode. As if he was about to step out on a mat for a match.

Shelley dropped the snowball. "You win. This is stupid—"

"Try to hit me." Ivan tried to hold back, but his voice was harsh. "You said you could. I'm giving you a chance."

"I don't want to."

"Why not?"

"I came out here to joke around, not watch you undress in a damn snowstorm." She shook her head. "Ivan, what's happened to you lately?"

"Nothing."

Ivan knew he was losing control. It wasn't just this moment. It was pushing Ellison in practice last week. Skipping home ec class the week before. Telling the reporter from the *Daily Record* to screw himself when he asked about last year's state semifinal match. But his mouth wouldn't stop.

"I'm standing here waiting for you to throw a snow-ball so we can see if you'll hit me in one throw like you said you would but I said you wouldn't."

"Put on your clothes."

"Throw it at me."

"No."

"Pick up the damn snowball!"

Shelley stopped and turned. "I'm going home."

As she plowed through the snowdrifts, Ivan thought—hoped—she might stop and turn around again. But she didn't. She crossed Farmingdale and continued up the driveway. *Please turn around. Please!* Ivan wanted to yell, but his mouth was silent.

The Petersons' front door opened, then closed.

Ivan was suddenly cold. *Friggin' cold.* His teeth chattered; his skin felt as if it were burning. He squinted into another wave of white, searching for his gloves, and his sweatshirt, and his jacket. His diaphragm jerked tight, and he could hardly draw in a breath.

Ivan ran up the front walkway, sliding on the ice-slick porch, his knee slamming into the front door. He fumbled for the doorknob, then stepped inside. The shivering was uncontrollable. He pulled off his shoes, stripped off his jeans, and raced up the staircase.

In his bedroom, Ivan tore through a dresser drawer, pulling out sweatshirts and sweatpants. His chest shook violently as he put on the clothes, then he ran to his closet, grabbed wool blankets, and draped them over his body. He sat against the heater. Utterly embarrassed. Utterly confused.

An hour had passed. Ivan heard the Nova pull up the driveway and, shortly after, his father walking around in the kitchen. He hadn't finished clearing the walkway of snow, and for that, he expected some kind of remark. Maybe something more.

Ivan dropped the blankets off his shoulders. He thought of Shelley. *Why'm I such an asshole?*

The telephone rang. Maybe it was her, Ivan thought. He got up and ran to the hallway, grabbing the receiver before his father did.

"Ivan?" said a raspy voice.

"Yeah."

"Coach Riker here. Got a few?" he said. "I'm sure y'all keep getting coaches 'round the country calling day and night. Pain in the rear end, I'll bet."

"No, Coach."

"How's the weather back East? Heard it's downright nasty."

"I'm used to it," Ivan said, watching down the staircase to see if his father was eavesdropping.

Coach Riker let out a hearty laugh. "Well, that dang cold can't last forever, right? We've talked a few times now, and I think it's at a point where we gotta get more serious about our university. Still liking Western Arizona, right?"

"Sure, Coach."

"How's it lookin' for the end of the season?"

"I'm fourteen and O," Ivan said.

"Good, good," Coach Riker said. "I've been talkin' to

the 158-pounder over there at Phillipsburg. Undefeated, too. Do some of my best recruiting in Jersey. Don't know if it's the corn y'all grow out there, but Jersey produces wrestling talent like a dang factory. And I know how good y'all are. Two-time region champ. Third in the state last year. Son, how'd ya'll do in the AAU freestyle championships last August?"

"Won the Eastern region qualifier," Ivan said. "Most valuable wrestler."

"And the nationals?"

"Took a second." *We went over this last time,* Ivan thought. *Why again?*

"Good, real good," Coach Riker said. "Well, let's talk a bit about our program. We gotta tough one here. Dang good wrestlers. Cream of the cream. We wrestle teams in the Pac-Ten and make trips back East against Lehigh and Penn State and so on . . ."

Ivan had heard this all before. Had read it in *Wrestling USA. Just tell me I'll be accepted.*

"We're all looking for only the best wrestlers to bring out here," Coach Riker said. "Now, son, I know athletically you can make it. I figure by your sophomore or junior year you'll be an all-American. But . . ."

But? Ivan's throat tightened. He held the receiver tighter.

". . . we ran into a kinda situation. A snafu, you might call it. Usually we gotta recruit our butts off to get the caliber of wrestler capable of competing with the teams I just mentioned, and do good enough in the classroom. Last year was different. This year, too. We got lots of quality wrestlers—too many—all with decent college boards and grade points. In fact, we got more wrestlers than our allotted scholarship number. Y'all with me?"

"Kind of."

"While it's great for our coaching staff, it's a bit of a problem for y'all. I looked at your transcript . . ." Papers shuffled in the background. "Son, your grade point just don't cut it. Can't get around it. Know what I mean?"

"I guess," Ivan answered. But that was the sort of candy-ass answer McClellan would give. "No, Coach, I don't know," Ivan said. "Didn't think grades were so important in wrestling."

Coach Riker didn't laugh this time. "Son, y'all aren't happy, I can hear it. There might be an answer. Y'all sent in your application, right?"

"I'm finishin' it."

"Get that in now. Deadline's coming up. I could pull some strings . . . Well, let's not get ahead of ourselves. I might be able to smooth talk the admissions committee. Maybe accept one of our recruits on an academic scholarship. That might open up a final athletic scholarship for y'all. I *might* be able to pull that off. From your end, since it's a bit late to fix your grade point, I figure there's only one thing y'all can do."

Ivan shut his eyes.

"I'm afraid it comes down to this, son. If y'all win the state championship, I'm sure I can convince the committee to accept you. Anything short of that, y'all be passed over. I know, I know, it's a dang slim margin of error—"

"That's crazy," Ivan said. "I'm better than the guys you're recruiting."

"Whoa, hold on now," Coach Riker said. "We got boys with better grades who are dang fine wrestlers."

"But not as good."

"I gotta consider the *entire* wrestler. Whether he can handle the social stuff, the academics, the travel schedule. I won't lie; it'll kick your butt. Does me no good to bring in someone who can't hack it, right?"

"But I shoulda won the states last year."

"Coaches here want you; make no mistake about that. Y'all are as good a recruit as we've seen in years. But our hands—my hands—are hog-tied. If you wanna come to Western Arizona, y'all gonna have to win the state championship."

"But—"

"Look, I gotta run. I'll be following the states closely. Good luck down there at Jadwin."

The phone clicked. Soon, a dial tone broke in. Up was down, down was up, and the world suddenly spun madly. Ivan stumbled into his bedroom. The room grew smaller, the walls closer, the ceiling lower. Arizona— bright afternoons running around the green campus, warmth, somewhere new and different—was now farther away than Ivan could possibly imagine.

"I shoulda been state champ," he whispered, hearing the scoreboard buzzer in his head.

On the shelves above his dresser, gold and silver trophies were lined up like plastic soldiers. Tournament medals dangled from each ledge. Thirty-three in all. Nearly all gold. Leaning against the back of the shelving were framed pictures of his two region championships. The trophies and medals should have remained buried in the bottom drawer, but Shelley had taken a Sunday afternoon to display them meticulously.

"Out in the open," she had said, "for everyone to see."

Ivan had appreciated her care. Now he despised the perfection.

He grabbed one of his wrestling shoes, wheeled around, and hurled it toward the dresser. The top shelf erupted in chaos, throwing the medals off their hooks and flipping them across the room, banging trophies against one another, falling to the dresser below, their plastic limbs and marble bases cutting into the wood.

The room was quiet.

Then suddenly, the top shelf came down on the shelf below, causing everything left standing to crash spectacularly to the floor. The last picture hit, shattering at his feet. The explosion of sound stopped. Ivan bent down and brushed off shards of glass. He picked up the silver frame, turned it over, and pulled out the photograph—the one of his mother. It was torn through the middle.

Ivan dropped to his knees. "Mama . . ." His stomach lurched, but nothing came up. He quivered and ached.

His father yelled, from the bottom of the stairs, "Ivan, did something fall?"

Ivan raised his head. "No."

"Come down now," his father said. "You must finish outside."

And if I don't? If I just walk down those stairs and say, "Papa, I'm goin' to Western Arizona, that's it, that's final, keep your mouth closed, and I don't wanna ever talk about this again"?

Ivan gnashed his teeth, knowing the truth was, the margin for error in getting into Western Arizona had suddenly become impossibly small. "I'll be there," he said.

"I did not hear you," his father said.

Ivan breathed in deeply, then shouted each word. "I'll . . . be . . . there!"

The walls pushed closer. The ceiling dropped lower. The room closed in.

29

Kenny pounded the mat. "How many more times are you gonna take me down?" He climbed to his feet and shook his head in disgust. "And why in the world are we over here? It stinks like rancid milk."

Bobby had picked this corner of the practice room on purpose, forcing himself to ignore the distraction, challenging the will of his practice partners. "Let's keep going," he said, flatly.

Kenny frowned, hands at his waist. "Yeah, sure."

They shook hands, and again, Bobby shot in deep on a single-leg, ran the pike, and covered on top. *Too easy*, he thought. Flat on his stomach, Kenny's defense waned. But Bobby wouldn't let up. He couldn't. It was too deep in the season and he was wrestling too well. Relentlessness had carried him to six straight victories—including four pins—since the tie at Rampart, raising his record to 14–1–1. Now, when Bobby was tired, he relived that

Saturday afternoon, the object of mockery for a delirious Rampart crowd, while the team he captained withered in defeat. The same putrid feeling of embarrassment filled his thoughts. It made him nasty, a pissed-off, arrogant machine set for one mission—to beat the hell out of anyone he wrestled. Every time.

So he jammed his left forearm against the back of Kenny's neck and serpentined his right arm underneath Kenny's right arm. Kenny's body twisted oddly as he let out a grunt. Bobby stepped to the side and began prying him with a deep half. This was his teammate, his co-captain, his best friend, but Bobby felt no remorse.

He settled his chest just under Kenny's shoulder, his right arm squeezed around Kenny's head. For a second, he noticed Coach Messina, arms folded, watching. Very satisfied, Bobby was sure. Chest to chest, up on his toes, Bobby first exposed Kenny's back, then held both shoulders to the mat. In a match, the referee would have signaled a pin.

"Time!" Coach Messina shouted. "Next pairs out on the mat."

But Bobby wanted to keep going. He *needed* to dominate Kenny, and Anthony, and everyone else in the practice room who stood before him.

Kenny sat up, his shoulders sagging and face etched in frustration. He ripped off his headgear and smacked it against the wall. "Damn," he muttered.

Bobby, too, unsnapped his chin strap. The eyes of his teammates were on him, and he relished it thoroughly.

Everything was coming together, there was no doubt about that. His quickness, endurance, strength, and every bit of wrestling talent had risen to the surface. Kenny had been the victim today, but next week it would be three opponents in the districts. And the week after, the regions. And the week after that, yes, the states.

In the locker-room showers, Bobby leaned his head forward, letting the stream of hot water flatten his hair and roll down his body. Steam rose to the ceiling. Most of the team had dressed and left long ago. Kenny stepped under a nearby shower, turned the handle, and waited for warm water.

"You've been whipping my ass," Kenny said.

Bobby pulled his head from the stream of water, snapped his hair back, and opened his eyes. "I had a good practice."

"Nah, it's more than just today. You've been whipping my ass for weeks."

"I've been lucky."

"Bull," Kenny said. "I know I've gotten better this season. I'm quicker and stronger, better on my feet. But you, you've changed over the past two months. You're at another level. I can't take you down; I can't ride you."

Bobby said nothing. He finished his shower and grabbed a towel. He sat half naked in front of his locker, not in any particular rush to leave. He weighed himself a few times, combed his hair, peed, then finally dressed.

Kenny dressed, too. He gathered his practice clothes

and stuffed them in a gym bag. "Wanna hang out?" he said to Bobby. "Maybe some of that friggin' talent of yours'll rub off."

"I gotta do something."

"Yeah?"

Bobby closed his locker. "I'm going down to Newark. To see Carmelina." He paused. "I think it's time."

"For what?"

"A change."

"Really?"

"Yeah."

"She got any idea?"

"I don't think so," Bobby said. "Maybe she does. Shouldn't be hard to figure out. We haven't gotten along. It's like eleven-thirty at night, I'm starving and so thirsty I can't even get saliva in my mouth, and we just sit there on the phone—silent. I'd rather be sleeping."

"This isn't the time to be screwing around," Kenny said.

They walked out of the locker room and down the hallway. They passed a display case dedicated to the history of Millburn's athletics. There were dozens of conference and county championship plaques, state title trophies, and team photos. Bobby stopped to look.

"Senior year, districts in a few days," Kenny said. "This is what it's all about. Bobby, you're looking real good on the mats. You'll win the districts hands down. I think you'll win the regions easily, too."

"Thanks," Bobby said.

"Then it's the states, Bobby. Crazy stuff happens at Jadwin. Always does. Guys come out of nowhere to win it all. But you can't let any distractions screw you up. Time to get mentally lean and cut away all that other garbage."

Bobby nodded.

"Anyway, I'm gonna go. I'll call you later." Kenny opened the school exit door, then stopped. "And Bobby?"

He turned.

"Let Carmelina down easy, okay?" Kenny said, with a slight grin.

Bobby buttoned his varsity jacket. Branch Brook Park was desolate. Clouds hung low, and the air was cold and wet. *An ugly afternoon*, he thought. He waited by the set of swings, where only a few months earlier, he and Carmelina had spent a Sunday flirting and kissing and touching. The rusted swings were still, the seats covered with remnants of the last snowfall.

"Eight days," Carmelina said. She was behind Bobby. He turned. "What?"

"You haven't called in eight days." Her eyes were red, her cheeks streaked from tears. "Forget that I waited around all night last Saturday."

"I couldn't get my dad's car," Bobby said.

"So you don't call?"

"It's been a tough week," Bobby said.

"Oh, I see," Carmelina said. "It's been a *tough* week."

"Coach's been practicing us hard. Really killer. I get home too tired to do anything."

"Too tired to dial a phone number?"

Bobby kicked at a patch of snow on the ground, spraying a mist of flakes into the wind.

"Well?" Carmelina said.

"Well what?"

"Stop actin' all innocent, Bobby, it's a simple question. Why don't ya call? I trusted you."

"I didn't do anything wrong," Bobby said.

"You're gonna."

"You don't know," he said. "You don't know what's going on inside me."

"I know you don't call." She wiped her eyes.

Bobby looked past the anger so clear on her face, seeing the beauty that made him first fall for her. "Let's sit, okay?" he said. He gestured to a picnic table not far from the swings. "Please."

After a hesitation, she followed. With the sleeve of his jacket, he brushed the snow from the table. Carmelina sat down. Bobby sat next to her.

"Sorry I didn't call," Bobby said.

"It hurts."

For a while they sat without speaking, shoulders touching. He smelled her perfume. It reminded him of stealing kisses in the mall fitting rooms and having sex Saturday nights at his house.

"You look thin," she said.

Bobby shrugged.

"Saw your name in the *Ledger*," she said. "They say you're real good."

"Always hoped one day I'd be really good," Bobby said. "And not just good; I'm talking about being one of the best in the state. All the days I've gone without eating. Filling cups with spit. Eating laxatives. Always feeling like throwing up. Always being thirsty. I figured one day it'd be worth it."

"Is it?"

"We'll see. I could be a state champ. Before, I dreamed it a million times." He drew in a deep breath. "Now I think about it for real. It's important to me."

"Is anything else?"

Bobby looked away. "I gotta be focused."

"You already are," she said.

"No one can keep up with me in practice," Bobby said. "Everyone on the team notices. Coach Messina, too. I can't let up. I gotta think about winning."

"Take this however ya want, Bobby," Carmelina said. "I don't give a damn about your wrestling. Win or lose, you get to drive home in a fancy car to a big house in a rich white town. You pick the college you want—your parents pay for it. You don't even gotta think about it. You wanna win, win, win, and all, but if you didn't, it wouldn't be the biggest tragedy in the world."

Bobby shook his head. Carmelina just didn't get it. That annoyed the hell out of him. They were talking about wrestling, for god's sake. It was nearly the only thing that kept living in his house tolerable.

"You wanna know what I worry about, Bobby?" Carmelina said. "I worry about us."

Us? There is no more us. "Carmelina, I got so many other things to worry about. Christopher. My parents. Everything's just—" Bobby stopped himself. "It all needs time."

"What about us?" she said. "When will you have time for us?"

"Soon."

"That's not good enough."

"Why?"

"We been goin' together four months."

"And?"

"Things happen."

Here it comes, Bobby thought. *She wants more time. She wants Fridays, and Saturday nights. She wants my mom to be nicer. She wants me to call more. More, more, more. Always more.*

Bobby stood up. There was only so much time in a day, in a week, in the rest of the season. He couldn't give Carmelina any more. Something needed to change. This was the moment. He'd let her down easy, just like Kenny said. Face-to-face. That was noble. Damn noble. She couldn't complain about that.

"I've been thinking," Bobby said. "Maybe we should—"

"Bobby . . . ," Carmelina said.

"No, no," he said. "Listen to me for a—"

"I'm pregnant."

Bobby wasn't sure he heard her correctly, but then knew he must've because he was suddenly very light-headed. "What?"

"I think I'm pregnant."

"You think you're—" He tried to spit the word out but couldn't. Everything he could see shimmered and his head spun madly. "How? We only did it a few times. Six times, right? Seven at the most. Damn, Carmelina, when you said you needed to talk about something, I just figured . . ." He looked up, feigned a smile. "Please say you're only joking."

"I'm late," Carmelina said.

"'Late'? Maybe it's a mistake. Girls miss their periods for all kinds of reasons. I'm right, aren't I right?"

Carmelina curled her knees tight to her body. "I'm over two weeks late."

Bobby bent over and dry heaved.

"What are we gonna do, Bobby?"

He dry heaved again. It took some time before he caught his breath. "I don't know." He covered his face with his hands, his fingers digging into his forehead. "I just don't know. I can't think, I can't fuckin' think at all . . ."

His body ached; his eyes welled up. He felt like crying, just sitting alone and letting the tears pour out of his body. He needed to be alone, away from everyone. Away from Carmelina. Away from his mother. Away from his father. Somewhere so he could forget his parents, and their fighting, and Christopher's cries, and now this.

"I gotta go and think," he said. "I gotta get outta here."

"Don't run away, Bobby. All you white boys come down to Newark and mess around. Have your little fun and leave. Run home like nothin' happened. Close your doors; don't answer phone calls. Don't be like them, Bobby."

"I'm sorry, Carmelina."

"Please don't."

"I gotta go."

"Go then," she said. "Leave me the hell alone."

Bobby took a few quick steps, then stopped. "It's not going away, Carmelina. It's not going away, is it?"

She didn't answer. She didn't have to.

Bobby remembered thinking a few weeks ago, something was going to change his life. He thought it would be wrestling. He thought it would be winning the districts, the regions, then the states. But none of those, it was painfully clear to him now, were going to be it.

30

Bobby stepped off the scale in his closet. Though he had weighed himself a half-dozen times over the past few hours, he felt compelled to step on again. He knew a quarter or half pound wasn't simply going to disappear, nor was weighing himself going to distract him from his new reality. Still, he set the counterweight. The scale arm balanced. One hundred thirty-one and a quarter pounds.

His weight hadn't changed.

Bobby walked into the bathroom and stood at the toilet, hoping for a trickle. Nothing. He swirled his tongue in his mouth, trying to gather spit. Nothing. His body was empty.

He looked in the mirror. A dehydrated, pale, remarkably thin person stared back through bloodshot eyes. He saw hopelessness in those eyes. He'd trade everything— even a state championship—to have that reflection be of someone else.

His eyes welled up with tears, and as hard as he tried to rub out the ache in his forehead, it remained. He leaned heavily on the sink. *I can't do this, I just can't. I'm not ready. Not for a baby . . . Carmelina, why were you so careless?*

He was pissed off at Carmelina, and in his anger, he entertained the idea that maybe she hadn't been careless. Maybe it was exactly what she had intended. Maybe she wanted to get pregnant by a white boy, a rich white boy from Short Hills. Maybe she wanted an easy way out of Newark. Maybe—

Bobby stopped himself. He hung his head, ashamed to look in the mirror again. Carmelina didn't deserve his accusations. She had plenty to lose, too. She had dreams. She wanted to graduate high school in June, just like he did. She wanted to attend college in the fall, just like he did.

He shook his head. How could he go to college now? Fathers don't go to college. And how could he possibly focus on the districts? Or the regions? Or the states? And how in the world was he going to tell his mother and father? This would only make his family's problems a million times worse.

His mother had been right all along. He hadn't understood her warnings. "Watch yourself with this girl, Bobby," she had said. "You're going to get yourself in trouble." And despite explaining every bit of what he felt in his heart, his mother told him otherwise. "You don't know yet what love is. But you have a lifetime to find out." And now he *was* in trouble. And he hated that his mother was so right.

It's all over. Everything is over.

Bobby thought he had plans set for the rest of the season, for the rest of his senior year. But his reality had changed. Carmelina wasn't suddenly going to disappear. Her being pregnant wasn't going away. And he had no plans for that.

31

W hat a waste," Ivan said.

Tacked to the locker-room chalkboard was a poster—CONGRATULATIONS LENNINGS! TIME TO CELE-BRATE!—stenciled in large maroon letters, with the names of the varsity and JV wrestlers written all around.

"Even the scrubs." Ivan snorted.

After twelve consecutive losses, Lennings tasted victory on the final match of the season. Ivan remembered the team erupting when the referee signaled a pin in the heavyweight match to seal the win, and afterward, Ellison's mouth in a howl of excitement, his arms thrown high in the air. And he remembered John Pico and Kerry Jackson whipping their headgear to the ceiling, while the wrestlers mobbed one another and fans spilled from the bleachers onto the mat. Families. Friends. Teachers. Classmates. It seemed everyone in town was there. Shelley was there, too, her face beaming. And still, Ivan had remained stone-faced. Jubilation surrounded him, smothered him. It disgusted him then, and now, four days later, even more.

One win, big deal. We only beat Liberty Hill. Did he have to remind them they were still the worst team in the county?

And, most of all, Ivan remembered McClellan shaking hands with each wrestler on the team, looking more relieved than satisfied. He shook Ivan's hand last, as if out of some stupid obligation, and said, "Great team effort today."

More of that rah-rah crap that got us so far this year.

Ivan hung his blue jeans and flannel shirt inside the locker and sat down. For the sixteenth time this season, he had pinned his opponent, breaking the record he had set the year before. But did anyone on the team say a thing to him? Not a damn word. They took what he did for granted, expecting him, without question, to pin every opponent.

Ivan looked at the poster again. He saw the names, printed in different colors and sizes, some in script, some in capitals. There was Pico's, Jackson's, and Ellison's. Ivan moved closer. He saw Walt Stone, Tim Kimble, Willie Franklin, Phil Hannen. Even McClellan's name was there. But not his own.

The locker-room door opened. Ivan didn't bother turning around.

"You're early," he heard McClellan say. "I've been going over the practice schedule up until the districts. Anything you think needs more work?"

"I'm ready."

"I'm sure you are," McClellan said. "What about the team?"

If they don't get it by now, Ivan thought, *they sure as hell won't get it by Friday night.* Stripped down to his underwear, he moved over to the scale. He felt McClellan's stare as he set the counterbalance to 132 pounds, then stepped on. The scale arm moved up.

"Friday night's going to be a real test," McClellan said. "Most of our guys haven't been to the districts before."

Ivan tapped the counterbalance to the right: 132¼ . . . 132½ . . . The scale arm balanced.

"You've been through this three times," McClellan said. "They'll be looking to you as their captain."

Ivan stepped off the scale. He pulled on his white T-shirt, the material rubbing against his dry, chafed skin, and stepped into his black shorts. The quicker he was dressed, the better.

McClellan gestured toward the poster. "A shame we couldn't put it all together a little earlier in the season. That might've turned things around. A case of too little too late, I suppose."

Ivan looked over his shoulder. McClellan seemed to be staring somewhere beyond the locker room.

"A victory is a victory," McClellan said. "At least we finally know what victory tastes like."

McClellan blew the whistle long and loud. The wrestling stopped. "Lennings, we're wrestling like garbage! Three months and you guys still aren't executing. Tim, how many times have we gone over the fireman's carry?"

Kimble shrugged. "Hundreds, I guess."

"And how many times have I said the arm goes up the crotch?"

"Hundreds."

"And how many times have I shown how to make it a throw, not a roll?"

"Hundreds."

"So why in the world did you *roll* with it?"

Kimble didn't answer. The other wrestlers stood around, while the furnace clanked, and pumped, and pounded.

"That's what I'm talking about," McClellan said. "You guys are thinking too much and reacting too little. This has to be instinct now. You can't think, *Do I throw a fireman's or do I roll with a fireman's?* Damn it, it just has to happen. Ivan," McClellan snapped.

Ivan shot a look at McClellan.

"What happens when you roll through on a fireman's?"

Ivan's eyes narrowed. *You tryin' to embarrass me?*

"I'll ask again," McClellan said. "What happens when you roll through on a fireman's?"

"Let's move on." Ivan didn't mutter or whisper the words. He spoke them loud enough that everyone in the room heard.

"Is that your answer?" McClellan said. "Come over here."

Ivan walked to the middle of the mat and stood defiantly in front of McClellan.

Before Ivan was set, McClellan drop-stepped hard into his midsection. McClellan held the position, clamped down on the overhook, and lifted his right arm between Ivan's legs.

"Here we lift," McClellan said. "Now the throw."

With one knee up and one touching the mat, he pulled down on Ivan's right arm while throwing his own right arm toward the ceiling. Ivan flew off his shoulders, landing hard on the mat.

"*Now*," McClellan said, "how do we do a fireman's?"

Ivan popped back up to his feet. Heat rose from inside his chest, his body suddenly wired to strike. He grinned, a tight, pissed-off grin. "Don't know."

"You don't know?"

"No."

"Three-time district champ, twice region champ, third in the state. I'll ask one last time: How do we do a fireman's carry the *right* way?"

Ivan said nothing. His thoughts were focused on ripping McClellan apart.

"Don't roll through," someone answered.

Ivan looked around. So did McClellan. The other wrestlers turned. Hannen stepped forward.

"Don't roll through," he repeated.

"Exactly," McClellan said. "Someone's been listening."

Ivan's smirk faded. He glared at Hannen. What gave

this freshman any reason to think he should even be in the same practice room as him? *Nice going*, Ivan thought, *I'm gonna whip your ass.*

But Hannen wasn't quite the pushover he had been at the beginning of the season, and he certainly wasn't just another sorry face in the practice room. In fact, Hannen had become a nuisance. Not that he was a threat to Ivan on the mat, not even close. But every practice, without fail, Hannen tried tirelessly to score a point on Ivan, as if one takedown or reversal would suddenly make him *somebody.*

"Split up into pairs!" McClellan said.

Ellison said to Ivan. "You and me?" But Ivan ignored him. Instead, Ivan pointed at Hannen. "You. Now!" Ivan cleared space on the mat, then stood in his stance. "You got all the answers, freshman."

Hannen crouched in his stance. "Only to Coach's question."

"Shoulda kept your mouth shut."

When everyone on the team was set, McClellan said, "Wrestle!"

Ivan stepped to his right, then pivoted to a duck-under to the left. Hannen tried to square off, but it was futile, Ivan was far too powerful. He lifted and tripped, driving the freshman down to the mat, digging his shoulder into Hannen's rib cage.

"Ahhh!" Hannen curled into a ball, gasping for breath. Wrestlers nearby stopped.

"You okay, Hannen?" Ellison said.

Hannen managed a nod.

Ellison said to Ivan, "Take it easy. We wanna leave some wrestlers for next year."

Ivan ignored him. "Done, freshman? I got the districts on Friday and no time to waste."

Hannen held a hand to his rib cage and grimaced when he stood. "Relax," he said, then added, with the smallest hint of mockery, "Champ."

Ivan quickly stood ready in his stance, waiting for Hannen to be set. Hannen adjusted his right knee pad and tucked his long-sleeved shirt inside the top of his shorts. He moved slowly, too slowly.

"You gonna wrestle, freshman?" Ivan said. "If not, then sit your ass down."

"Lay off me."

"What'd you say?" Ivan said, though he had heard him well enough.

Hannen suddenly smirked, as if he had had enough and was willing to live with the consequences. "I said, drop dead, prima donna."

The room fell silent, and for the briefest moment Ivan was startled. Never did anyone—not even opponents—show defiance toward him on the mat. Sometimes they did during weigh-ins, sometimes during introductions, but none *after* they had a taste of wrestling with him. Now, this freshman punk was trying to show him up.

"I'm sick of everyone thinking you're some kinda god," Hannen said. "I'm sick of hearing about you. And you know what? I'm sick of hearing about your goddamn family."

Rage exploded. "You're fuckin' dead," Ivan breathed. In that moment, Hannen was everyone and everything he hated. With startling quickness, Ivan bear-hugged Hannen and slammed him to the mat. The sound echoed in the practice room.

A knee pressed to his chest, Ivan reared back. His fist sliced through the air, striking Hannen above his ear, snapping his head back. He cocked his fist again and unleashed another punch, this time cutting a gash on Hannen's temple.

Chaos ensued.

Ellison tackled Ivan, allowing Hannen to scramble to his feet. Blood trickled into the corner of his eye. Hannen brushed it away with his hand. Seeing the crimson on his fingers, Hannen's eyes widened and he unleashed a fury of profanities at Ivan.

Ivan felt himself being grabbed from behind. He spun around. "Get your hands off me!" He was facing McClellan.

"We're not gonna have any more of this," McClellan said. "Out of my practice, Ivan! Right now!"

McClellan put his hands on Ivan's chest and shoved him away. Then a second time. Ivan stood his ground and raised his fists. An eerie silence cottoned the room as the team stood stunned from the chaos that had swept through the practice. No one moved; no one talked.

McClellan pointed to the door. "You're not bigger

than the team, Ivan. Don't even think about coming back. You're done!"

Ivan's eyes shrank into a tight squint. "Done? *I'm done?*" he said. "No, I'll tell ya what, you're the worst goddamn coach in the state." He scooped up his headgear and bolted out the door. In the hallway, his ears turned rigid, waiting for the slightest word, or sound, or muffled laugh.

Gimme a reason to go back in there. Gimme one good reason.

Ivan stalked the dimly lit hallway, his fist still cocked, his mind a hair trigger from going off again. All he wanted to do was hit something, anything.

Behind him, he heard McClellan say, "Lennings, we've got the districts this weekend. We're drilling takedowns now. You know the routine."

"Fuck you," Ivan yelled. "Fuck you all!"

His voice bounced from wall to wall, echoing. His teeth gnashed against one another. He sprinted two steps at a time to the top of the stairs, his feet pounding through the soles of his wrestling shoes. He wanted to turn around, tear back down the stairs, and face McClellan again. This time he'd hit him, and hit him hard.

Instead, Ivan charged past the empty classrooms, ripping off his T-shirt, reaching the locker-room door, and yanking it open. Only then did he look back down the hall. There weren't any footsteps, no one following him, cajoling him to come back.

Ivan stormed into the room and crashed both fists on top of the paper-towel dispenser. The metal caved in and the box shot to the floor, breaking apart, sending the roll bouncing under the chair and screws skittering under the heater. Before the box could come to a stop, Ivan stepped back and kicked through, lifting the box against the far wall, filling the room with a loud clatter.

Five minutes passed, maybe ten. Ivan couldn't remember his thoughts or whether he paced the room or slumped down on the floor. He looked around. The destruction surprised him. The paper towel dispenser couldn't be fixed, that was obvious. Ivan picked up the paper-towel roll and set it on the sink.

His legs shook. He slumped down on a locker-room bench, tired—suddenly very tired—confused and scared.

And again, he wanted to strike something. His fist curled. Anger flooded his mind as his eyes fixed on the poster. Every wrestler's name—but not his. Who the hell would embarrass him like that? He hated each one of them. He hated Hannen. He hated McClellan, most of all.

"Fuuuuck!" he screamed so loud, it hurt his ears, and for so long, his voice withered to a scratchy hiss. Ivan jumped at the chalkboard, ripping down the poster, tearing it in half. Then in half again. He stuffed what was left into the garbage can to lay among the used spit cups, bloodied cotton swabs, and wads of crumpled paper towels.

32

From her bedroom, Shelley pressed her face to the window, cupping her hands around her eyes. "Come down," Ivan said, in a forced hush. He gestured to the front door. Shelley moved away.

It was late. Ivan had waited at the end of the Petersons' driveway a long while for Shelley to walk in front of her window. His shoulders hurt and his legs ached. It was only hours since the blowup at practice, though it seemed like days ago. Ivan still hadn't gone home yet. He had spent most of those hours sitting in the cold on Layaree's Wall. He clenched and unclenched his stiffened hands.

Soon, Shelley appeared at the front door. "My parents are sleeping," she said. "What's up?"

"I need to talk to ya."

"Now?"

"Yeah."

"Let me grab my coat."

Maybe it was a mistake to drag Shelley into this mess, Ivan thought. Maybe he should tell her to forget it, that he would deal with it himself. Then he'd slip into his house without his father noticing. Hide in his bedroom. Spend some more time thinking. The answer would come to him then. *Something* would come to him then.

Shelley opened the front door again, buttoning her coat, swinging a scarf around her neck. "What's the matter?"

Ivan walked down the driveway, unsure where, or whether, to begin.

In quickened steps, she caught up with him. "Hey . . ."

"Today was bad," he said. "Real bad; probably the worst day of my—" He stopped himself. "Not the worst, but damn close."

Shelley followed him to the middle of the street. "What happened?"

"I'm off the team."

"Off the team? What are you talking about?"

"McClellan kicked me off the team."

"Off the *wrestling* team?"

"Yeah."

"Why? Why would he do that?"

"We're in practice, and I'm drilling with this freshman, a kid named Hannen. He's really doggin' it, trying to make me look bad. So I tell him. Then he starts in with me, saying crap." Ivan rubbed his knuckles.

"You didn't hit him, did you?"

211

"McClellan takes his side. What'd you expect? Bailed on me freshman year. Nothing new now. He's always been jealous—wishes he had half the talent I got. He was baiting me, pushing me. He knows I hate him, and he just kept pushing me . . ."

Ivan stopped, and for a while, neither said anything. Eventually, Shelley said, "Ivan, tell me honestly, whose fault was it?"

"They could care less about winning," Ivan said. "It's one loss after another. They all go home happy. No one does a damn thing about it."

"But you guys won on Saturday."

"Liberty Hill? You, me, Modine, and a few of the neighbors could beat that team."

"Oh, that's not fair, Ivan. Our guys were so excited, yelling, jumping around. The only one that didn't seem happy was you."

But Ivan was in his own world. "Don't even remember how I got to the locker room. I just went off. Smashed the paper-towel thing right off the wall. Cracked the mirror. I can't remember it all . . . It was like I was outta my body, watching me tear up the locker room. I was so mad—crazy mad—yet my brain was just kinda calm." He looked at Shelley.

"I'm tired, ya know," Ivan said. "Not sleepy-tired, but . . ." He tried to think of the right words. "Living-tired. Sometimes I wish I could just disappear for a long while."

Shelley moved close. "You can't."

"Maybe not." Then, without knowing really why, he said, "Ever think about dying?"

Shelley seemed startled. "No," she said. Then hesitantly, as if afraid to hear his answer, she asked "Do you?"

"I have these dreams sometimes—nightmares, really. Scare the hell outta me. I'm floating, arms crossed. The ground comes up underneath me—a casket surrounds me. Shovel after shovel of dirt covering my legs, my stomach, my chest, my mouth. And I'm gasping for air, but the dirt just pours down my throat. Choking me."

Shelley held his hand. "You've gone through so much."

"Wasn't my choice."

"But you survived better than anyone might've. God, you're so much stronger inside than I am. Than I'll probably ever be. And look what you've done with wrestling. You're the best in the whole state. Don't throw that away. Just apologize."

"To who?"

"Coach McClellan."

"No."

"Yes, Ivan," she said. "Tell him that freshman—what's his name?—was messing up in practice. It made you frustrated, so you threw a punch, but you didn't mean to."

"But I did," Ivan said. "I wanted to *kill* him."

"Ivan, your whole wrestling life is on the line. You can say what you want, but I know how important that is to you. You made a mistake, that's all. Tomorrow, I'm sure Coach McClellan will see things differently."

Shelley wouldn't let him off the hook, Ivan knew. But she had also helped ease what troubled him, if only for a while.

"Look, it's late," Shelley said. "I gotta get back. We'll talk tomorrow. In the morning, if you want—before you straighten this whole thing out."

They stopped at the end of the Petersons' driveway. Up one end of Farmingdale and down the other, all was quiet. The scarf slipped off Shelley's neck. She reached for it, but Ivan's hand was there first. He wrapped the scarf around her neck to the other side. He felt the warmth of her breath before it was lost in the cold. He thought to kiss her. In the middle of this mess, a kiss— a simple kiss—seemed okay. Maybe a little of Shelley would make up for a whole lot of wrestling. His lips moved toward hers. Slowly. He smiled, embarrassed, then glanced away but quickly looked back into her eyes, unsure what to do or say. But something inside was draw- ing him nearer.

"Yes?" she said.

"I, uh . . ." Ivan was distracted. Something else gnawed at him. He drew no closer, and for that moment, Shelley seemed disappointed. He could forget this after- noon, but not for long. He straightened up. "Ya know what? Ya know what pissed me off the most about this whole thing? I mean, this might be kinda dumb, but it pissed me off."

Shelley leaned into him, almost touching his lips with hers. "Tell me."

"That damn poster."

"What poster?"

"In our locker room. You shoulda seen it. Thing was stupid. Can you believe someone wasted time on it, all because we won one goddamn match? That's such crap. I just ripped the thing into shreds. Tossed it into the garbage, where it belonged."

Shelley turned away. She touched a finger to the corner of her eye. "I made it," she whispered.

Ivan wasn't sure he heard her right. "What?"

"The poster," she said. "I made it."

"No, no, I'm talking about this one in the locker room. It said 'Congratulations Lennings' in big letters. It had a—"

"Maroon and black border," she finished.

"You made—" Ivan stopped himself. *No . . .*

Shelley's voice was choked with hurt. "I spent so much time on it. Hours. I tried to make it look good because winning seemed so important to the team. Stenciling the letters, choosing the colors, filling in each one."

"*You* did it?" Ivan's voice was weak.

"Didn't you see my initials in the bottom corner? Next to your name." She wiped her eyes and sniffled. And sniffled again. "It's late."

A million thoughts came to mind, but no words came to Ivan's mouth. He watched Shelley run to the front porch and disappear behind the front door.

It was 1:32 A.M. Ivan leaned wearily against his bedroom window. He had managed to sneak inside the house and into his bedroom. Tomorrow morning, his father would probably hear from someone at work about him being kicked off the team. Bad news spread quickly in Lennings—any news spread quickly in Lennings. But Ivan would worry about that when it happened.

Across the street, Shelley's light was still on. "I should be really impressed with myself," Ivan whispered. "I screwed everything up . . . wrestling . . . Western Arizona . . . Shelley . . ."

He despised Hannen and McClellan with a fury he had never felt before. And now, Arizona might as well be a million miles away. But he worried mostly about Shelley. He wondered if she was crying. He wondered if she hated him. He worried that he had lost his best friend. For good.

33

In the hall closet near his bedroom, Bobby squeezed himself under the bottom shelf. He tried to sit but was only able to hunch sideways. He had on a rubber suit, sweatpants, and a sweatshirt, and had propped pillows along the walls and door as insulation, then covered himself with two wool blankets. It was pitch-dark, stiflingly hot, and so cramped, his neck ached.

He pulled slack on the telephone cord and put the receiver to his ear. "Yeah, I'm here."

It had been the same routine the past few weeks. He and Carmelina would sit on the phone and talk about nothing, break into an argument, then hang on in silence. Bobby was waiting for the fighting. It wouldn't be long now, he was sure.

"What are you *doing*?" Carmelina said.

"Sitting in the closet."

"Why?"

"To sweat."

"Don't ya sweat enough in practice?"

"You can never sweat enough," Bobby said. Each breath made the tight space hotter.

"So you sit in a closet?" she said. "Are you mental?"

"The districts are on Friday—"

"Yeah, yeah, I heard all about these districts."

"I gotta worry about my weight," Bobby said. A drop of sweat tickled his cheek, and dampness rose along the folds of his stomach muscles.

"You're lucky that's all ya gotta worry about."

Bobby said nothing.

"Don't wanna hear that, do ya?" Carmelina said. "Think I wanna have a baby? Think I wanna work in a damn department store, kissing rich white women's asses all my life?"

Bobby had expected this. "When are you going?" he asked.

"Oh, so now ya worry about the mess we're in," she said.

"Carmelina, just tell me when."

"Thursday."

"What time?"

"Four. Maria told me they make me pee in a cup. And take blood. Probably ask me a hundred questions."

"What kind of questions?"

"How the hell should I know?"

"Think they'll ask my name?"

"You wanna find out so badly, go with me."

"I can't go on Thursday, Carmelina. I got practice. It's the—"

"God-damn districts," she answered. "I'm not expectin' a thing from you, Bobby. I'll get a ride there and a ride back."

He paused. "I'm sorry."

"You're not sorry; why even say it?"

"I'd take you on Sunday, Carmelina, I swear I would," Bobby said. "I can't go on Thursday. I don't have a choice. I can't say, 'Coach, I gotta miss practice the day before the districts. Why? Well, my old girlfriend's pregnant.'"

"You're an asshole."

"Why?"

"It's just like Maria said . . ."

Bobby lifted off the wool blankets, letting the heat escape, allowing himself that small reprieve. Carmelina had him talking much longer than he wanted. Only ten minutes—fifteen, tops—he had told himself. Now it was almost an hour. He was hungry and dehydrated and so tired from all the fighting. He shifted his body, but there was no way to sit comfortably. He again covered himself with the blankets.

"Not listening, are ya?" Carmelina said.

"I'm here."

"I hope when you're sitting in your wrestling practice, you're thinking of what's in my belly."

Bobby made the sign of the cross and clasped his hands together. *Our Father, who art in Heaven . . . Hallowed be thy name . . . Thy kingdom come . . .* He finished one Our Father, then another. As he said the words to himself, the distraction gave him a hint of comfort. But the heat was too much, the blankets too heavy, the space too small. Though he was sweating a little, he was far too dehydrated to sweat enough.

"Say something," Carmelina said.

"Hold on," Bobby said, kicking the door open with his foot and knocking away the pillows and blankets. He sucked in the cool hallway air, then quickly stripped down, tossing the sweats and rubber suit to the tiled bathroom floor. The sweat on his naked body was slight. Much less than a quarter pound, he figured.

"Look, I gotta sleep," Bobby said. "I'll call you on Thursday. When you get home."

"Nah, ya mean after *your* practice."

Bobby shook his head. "Okay, whatever. When I'm done with practice."

"So you'll call me then?"

"Yeah."

"Okay, Bobby, you do that."

"I promise."

"Yeah, sure," she said. "I believe ya."

There was a click on the other end, then the dial tone cut in. Bobby hung up the receiver.

34

Ivan woke up exhausted and thirsty. It hurt his throat to swallow, and his head throbbed along his temples when he sat up. Still, it was better than he had expected. He looked at the torn photograph of his mother. He had made a promise to bury the state championship medal beside Layaree's Wall. He hadn't told anyone. Not even Shelley. But the chance to fulfill that promise vanished the instant his fist hit Hannen's jaw. Or maybe on the second punch. Or maybe, he thought, it was when he yelled, "You're the worst goddamn coach in the state."

That was it, Ivan knew. That was what he would hang for.

He had stayed up hours, trying to understand what had happened. He had considered everything, but in the end, it didn't make a bit of difference. He was no longer in control. As vile as it was, McClellan now held the key to whether he would ever be allowed to set foot on a Lennings wrestling mat again. Shelley was right. He would have to apologize, and apologize in a goddamn big way.

Ivan's jaw tightened. *I won't do it. A man gets on his knees for no one.*

There was a knock at the door. Ivan slid out from under the covers.

The door opened and his father walked in. "It is quiet up here." He eyed the room.

Ivan pulled the sheets to the head of the bed, then smoothed out the blankets. "I didn't wanna wake you."

"I am always awake before you."

Ivan grabbed shorts, socks, and a T-shirt from a drawer and stuffed them into his gym bag. He felt odd going through the motions. He glanced over his shoulder, but his father hadn't left the room. *Wondering where the Western Arizona application is? Not gonna tell ya, Papa. Look all you want. Take all morning. Doesn't make a difference anyway. Not now.*

"You came in late last night," his father said.

"I was at Shelley's," Ivan lied. It was easier than he thought. "Doing math homework. Got a quiz this week."

"You were very late."

"Does it matter?" Ivan said it stronger than he wanted. Already in deep enough trouble, a fight with his father wouldn't help matters. His tone eased. "Ya want me studying, right?"

His father nodded less than enthusiastically. Again, he

looked around the room. "You received a letter from Bloomsburg University. About your scholarship."

"Another time, Papa."

He could see his father stiffen. "Life does not always go the way you expect. I am pleased for your interest in studies. But these next weekends are too important. Do you understand?"

Ivan nodded.

"How is your weight?" his father said.

"Okay, Papa." Then, after it seemed there was nothing left to discuss, Ivan said, "I gotta get ready."

In the busy clatter of the school hallway, the slam of Ivan's locker went unnoticed. Past the water fountain, Shelley stood with some friends in front of her locker, setting down her books and hanging up her coat. She wouldn't look his way. Ivan waited a few minutes for the hallway to clear, but by then Shelley was gone.

Time to get this over with, Ivan thought. He muscled his way through the crowd, in full view of the furtive—and not so furtive—looks. They had heard. Ivan put on his best scowl. He walked past Holt's office, glaring at anyone who looked his way, and climbed the stairs to the second floor. At an office door marked HISTORY DEPART-MENT, Ivan raised his fist—noting the scrapes on his knuckles—and knocked.

When Ivan heard "Come in," from behind the door, he opened it and stepped inside the room. It occurred to him that he had never been in McClellan's office. The renovated janitor's closet was as cramped as he had heard. A bookshelf hardly hid a shadow of replastering where a sink had been, while cracks along the ceiling ran as extensively as a road map. A framed degree from Yale University and two mahogany plaques stood out. The engraving on each plaque read: PRESENTED TO LEWIS MCCLELLAN. VOTED TEACHER OF THE YEAR BY THE LENNINGS STUDENT BODY.

"Sit," McClellan said.

Ivan dropped his backpack to the floor and sat down. The room was hot, damn hot. *If it was any hotter,* he thought, *we could roll the damn mats out right here. At least I wouldn't have to drag my ass down to that dungeon.* Bones underneath his thinly padded buttocks cut through to the chair. He shifted to ease the discomfort.

McClellan took his time clearing his desk, stacking one pile of papers at the corner and placing another in a drawer. He had an air of smugness that Ivan had never seen before.

"That was a pretty disturbing scene yesterday," McClellan said.

"It was a misunderstanding."

"A 'misunderstanding'?"

"Hannen was jerkin' around."

"So you punched him?"

"He was doggin' it."

"So you punched him?"

"I let him off easy," Ivan said. "I bust my ass in practice every day. You know it; all of them know it. Maybe the others should bust their asses."

"What about self-control?"

Ivan felt himself getting angry, so damned pissed he was in this position. He was tempted to get up and leave. That would show McClellan, and everyone else at Lennings, that Ivan Korske doesn't kiss anyone's ass. "I thought winning was the point," he said.

McClellan shook his head. "You don't get it. Winning's never the sole reason for wrestling. You can lose and still have integrity and respect for others. But with you, it's always been about what's best for Ivan Korske."

"I win."

"What's that get you? A free pass to punch out a teammate?" McClellan said. "No, I have rules. I talk about them all the time so everyone is clear." He ticked off each with a finger. "One, the team comes first. Two, never use profanity. Three, no fighting. The rules couldn't be simpler. They help you as a person, and as a wrestler." Then McClellan smiled, a snide, fake smile. "But you don't like getting help, do you?"

Ivan's expression didn't change. *You want me to tell ya how much better ya made me? You wanna take credit? I won't let ya. I don't need your help. Never did. Never will. You know that and it kills ya.*

McClellan stepped out from behind the desk. "We're all influenced by one another. By teammates, teachers, parents, and coaches, sometimes—even people we don't like."

Ivan said nothing.

"You don't agree with me. I didn't expect you to. So let's cut to the chase." McClellan sat on the edge of the desk. "There has to be punishment. Principal Holt and the school officials want a suspension. They're a very straight-and-narrow group. You understand. Rules *were* broken."

McClellan was lying, Ivan thought. Holt would never suspend him, not with a chance for him to go to the states on the line.

"Maybe I should talk to him," Ivan said.

"To whom?"

"Holt."

McClellan smiled. "Oh, I see. You don't believe me. You can certainly take that chance. But let me tell you, Ivan, after Mrs. Hannen called the school this morning, all hell broke loose. School violence. You're lucky they let you in the building this morning. But I spoke to Principal Holt and he agreed to go by my recommendation. If I'm satisfied with the punishment, then he'll be satisfied with the punishment. Of course, if you don't believe me, you can walk out right now and take your chances."

Ivan rolled his eyes. "So I'll pay for the damage."

"Let other people worry about the bathroom," McClellan said with a sarcastic laugh. "I've given this some thought. Weighed all the factors. I'd like to see you wrestle through the end of the season. But I also want you to learn from your mistakes. I was thinking along the lines of an apology."

Ivan tensed but gave away nothing.

"You don't seem to want to."

"I'll apologize, if I gotta."

"To whom?"

"You tell me."

"I think you know."

Ivan shrugged. "Hannen."

McClellan shook his head.

Ivan sat back. "To who then?"

"Again, you tell me."

"The team."

McClellan walked to the office's back window. "It's a bit warm in here." He reached up and unlatched the lock, then pushed open the pane of glass. He rubbed his hands to wipe off any dirt. "Ivan, to *whom* do you need to apologize?"

It was then that Ivan fully understood the tone of McClellan's voice. Like a bully's. Like someone who had all the power and was ready to exploit it. This meeting was a joke.

McClellan smoothed his white dress shirt and straightened his tie. He came back to the desk and sat down again.

"You don't like me very much," he said, with a smile. "You don't think I'm a good coach. Probably think I don't know my elbow from my ass in the wrestling room. Maybe you even think I'm the worst goddamn coach in the county."

McClellan grinned wider. "I know you understand the situation here, but if you don't, I'll make it crystal clear. I want to coach a state champ—that's what I want. I'm that good of a coach, despite what you or anyone else thinks.

You and I also know I may grow to be an old man before I get that chance again at this school." McClellan's eyes never left Ivan's. "You hate this place. It disgusts you. You hate me, the team, the school, the whole damn town."

Bile bubbled up Ivan's throat. Only a hard swallow kept the bitterness down. He had underestimated McClellan, thinking he was a fool. Ivan stared at McClellan as fiercely as he would an opponent.

"What do you want me to say?"

"You know."

"Apologize?"

"Yes."

"To you."

McClellan grinned.

Drop dead. I'll never say I'm sorry—

Then Ivan cut off his rage. He was about winning, his life was about winning. He thought about his mother and father sitting in the Lennings bleachers; the roads he had run over and over, enough miles to make it all the way to Western Arizona; coming within a whisper of advancing to the state finals last year. Images of the past four years scrambled his thoughts; still, the answer *was* clear. The state championship was on the line, which meant more—just barely more—than winning this battle of egos with McClellan. There would be a time and place to tell him to screw himself. It would be soon enough.

Know what, McClellan? I'll apologize to ya. No sweat off my back. They're just words.

He took a deep breath. "I'm sorry Hannen and me got in a fight. I wanna come back to practice today."

McClellan said nothing.

Ivan straightened up. "I can win the states this year. You can't take that away. It's my only way outta here."

Still, McClellan said nothing.

Ivan leaned in. "Goddamn it," he said. "Okay, I'm sorry; I'm damn sorry yesterday ever happened and for what I said to you. I'm sorry, okay, are ya happy?"

A hint of a smile touched McClellan's lips. "Yes," he said. "That's what's best for everyone involved. And that's what's fair. Now write it down." He held out a pen and a piece of paper.

"Write it?"

"Yes, write it."

Ivan looked at McClellan's hands. He was exhausted and beaten, and it took all his strength not to vomit his disgust right there in the office. "If I write it, I'm back on the team?"

"Sure, sure," McClellan answered, pulling a stack of papers from the drawer and spreading it out on the desk with the other. "I'll tell Principal Holt what you and I decided here today. We'll get this whole episode behind us." McClellan's head was down, already marking the papers with a red pen. "Don't forget, get that to me by noon."

Ivan closed the door behind him. That was it. He stood in the hallway, leaning back against the wall, pen and paper in hand. He would write the apology, he would get it in by noon. It was over. He had sold his soul for the state championship.

35

Carmelina's sobs were clear through the phone. "Everyone was lookin' at me in school," she said, in halted breaths. "They knew, they knew. They knew where I was going. I'm telling ya, they knew . . . Their eyes, I could tell in their eyes."

"What happened with the test?" Bobby said.

"Nobody's ever looked at me like that," Carmelina said. "It was like they knew I was gonna do something really wrong. Was I gonna?"

Bobby covered the receiver and walked out of his bedroom to the top of the stairs. The light in his brother's room was off and everything was quiet downstairs.

"The test, Carmelina," he said. "What happened?"

"How could they know—"

"Carmelina, listen to me," he said, in a forced whisper. "What'd the test say?"

Carmelina didn't answer for a long time. Bobby thought she might have hung up. "Carmelina?" he said. "Carmelina? Are you there? What'd the test say?"

"I don't know," she said, finally.

"What do you mean, 'I don't know'?"

"I . . . don't . . . know. . . ."

"But you went to the clinic. Maria took you, right?"

"Yeah."

"So what'd they say?"

"This big black woman just kept smiling, telling me everything was gonna be all right. She just kept smiling . . . God, I don't know why. This wasn't a place for smiles. But she did. The kind of smile that was trying to hide somethin' real bad . . . I was so scared, Bobby, so scared."

"I know, I know," Bobby said. "I'm sorry you were scared—"

"Too scared."

"What do you mean?"

"I left."

"You left?"

"Maria took me home. I couldn't do it."

Bobby wanted to throw the phone through his bedroom window. "You gotta go back. This is serious, Carmelina. You can't just leave it alone. It won't go away. Tell Maria she's gotta bring you there again."

There was a long pause before Carmelina spoke again. "I'll go next week," she said, but the lie was clear in her voice.

"I don't believe you," he said. "Next time you'll just leave again. Maybe not even go."

"Then, you take me."

Bobby sat down on his bed.

"See?" Carmelina said. "You don't wanna bother. Just go on living your life, forget about me. And don't you worry, Bobby, I'll go next week to the clinic and I'll get the test done. And know what? *Maybe* I'll tell you whether you're gonna be a father or not. It's not your worry."

"Not my worry?"

"I'll deal with it."

"No, no forget it," Bobby said. "I'll take you next week. Tuesday night after practice. After you're done with work. I'll pick you up at the mall. I'll tell my parents I'm going to Kenny's, studying or lifting or something like that. They'll never know. Okay? Carmelina . . . Carmelina, are you there?"

"Yeah."

"I'll take you, understand? But you gotta promise me you'll go."

"Bobby, I'm scared."

He rubbed his eyes. "I'm scared, too." And he was— damn scared. "We'll go together."

36

I'm goin' running, Papa."

"Again tonight?" his father said, pleased. "That is two times."

"For the states, Papa," Ivan answered. "For the states."

Ivan closed the front door, ran down the porch stairs, and ducked into the shadows of the house. From inside his jacket, Ivan pulled out a large envelope. It was stamped and addressed to the admissions committee at Western Arizona. The application was ready to go. Or as much as it would ever be, Ivan knew.

Envelope in hand, Ivan sprinted down the driveway and onto Farmingdale. The application postmark deadline was tomorrow. He had cut it close and it had been a struggle, but Ivan had finally finished the essays and questions. Hastily, he knew. Sloppily, even. It all would have been much better if Shelley had helped. But he got what he deserved.

The fields of grass passed quickly and, soon, Sycamore Creek and Wellington Farms, too. Ivan neither noticed the cold nor the heat under the layers of clothing, nor any of the familiar surroundings. He ran fast, unusually fast. Despite practicing for two hours and having already run once tonight, his legs felt surprisingly light, his lungs large. Ivan didn't think about past matches, or future matches, for that matter. He just ran. Hard.

Streetlights illuminated the shop awnings on Main Street and the blue mailbox in front of Mr. Johnston's Florist Shop. Ivan came to a stop, stared at the envelope one last time, then pulled back the handle and dropped it in. The envelope was out of his hands; now everything was under his control.

Ivan looked around. Across the street, the Evergreen sign blinked. Trees rustled. The town's stoplight changed from red to green. He liked the solitude. Ivan crossed the intersection and jogged home.

37

Bobby sat hunched over on the locker-room bench—the hood of his warm-up suit draped over his head, his eyes closed—pushing aside worries about Carmelina and his parents and everything going on in his life outside wrestling.

"Be ready off the whistle . . . ," he whispered. "Be ready off the whistle . . ."

He looked up. Kenny also straddled the bench, deep in thought. Big John, a black T-shirt stretching across his broad frame, snapped and unsnapped the chin strap of his headgear. In the bathroom, Anthony splashed water on his face, then rolled his neck and shoulders. They were all nervous as hell, Bobby could tell.

Few doubts remained in his own mind. His record was 16–1–1 with twelve pins, numbers that hadn't gone unnoticed by the *Star-Ledger*. He was on an eight-match winning streak since the tie at Rampart—a match that seemed seasons ago. And much like that match, win-loss records meant nothing, from this point on, Bobby knew. All that mattered was who wanted to win more—him or his opponent.

Heat rose in his warm-up suit, collecting in the hood. *The hotter, the better,* he thought. Anything to make his muscles ready; anything to keep his heart racing. He stared down at the floor, feeling sweat accumulate on his forehead, then watched the droplets fall to the tiles. He swiped at the starburst shapes with the soles of his wrestling shoes.

The locker-room door opened. Kenny raised his head, and Big John sucked the last drops from a water bottle, then tossed it aside. Anthony came in from the bathroom.

Coach Messina's dress shoes clicked on the locker-room floor. "There's not much for me to say. The four of you are in here, the rest of the team is sitting in the stands. You made it to the district finals; they didn't. You qualified for the regions; their seasons are finished."

For some that might be enough, Bobby knew. They'd be satisfied as district runner-up. But not him. Not this year. Second place was *never* a victory, moral or otherwise. It meant he had lost, and *that* was unacceptable.

"For four months you've worked your asses off," Coach Messina said. "You've been the ones to come in early and leave late. You've run the miles after practice. You've done the push-ups and sit-ups perfectly. You've drilled twelve or thirteen single-legs when the others did ten.

"It's not magic, no sleight of hand. Winning means hard work. It always has; it always will. You guys have proved that. By the end of the day, across New Jersey, there will be thirty-two district champs in each weight class." His massive chest expanded with a deep breath. "Promise yourself you'll be one of those thirty-two . . . Hands in!"

Bobby squeezed between Big John and Anthony as the four wrestlers pressed against one another, sharing the same space; sharing the smell of sweat, anxiety, and Coach Messina's cologne; sharing the strength of his confidence.

"Let's have four district champs," Coach Messina said. He stared at Big John . . . Kenny . . . Anthony . . . and, finally, Bobby.

"There are *no* second places today."

The third period of the 122-pound championship match began, though Bobby paid little attention. He stood, jaw taut, eyes tight in a livid glare.

Kenny stepped beside him. "You ready?"

Bobby nodded. "If God came down to wrestle me today," he said, "I'd beat him."

The world could have been crumbling down around Bobby—and, he knew, in so many ways it was—but he refused to let it enter Millburn's gymnasium. Today, this was his temple, wrestling was his religion, winning the district title was his prophecy.

Across the gym, his opponent, Gerald Griffey, warmed up. His muscular black thighs and sculpted chest made his white and gold singlet seem two sizes too small. Teammates in street clothes stood by, patting Griffey on the back, gesturing in Bobby's direction.

Bobby shook his head, a smile stretching slowly on his lips. He pitied Griffey, a district runner-up at 122 pounds the year before. *In a few minutes,* Bobby thought, *he'll wish he'd stayed at that weight.*

A loud cheer swelled from the bleachers. Union High fans rose to their feet, stomping and whistling as time ran out and their wrestler celebrated an 8–4 victory, pumping his fist. Bobby's heartbeat jumped into high gear. He pulled off his Yankees T-shirt and tossed it to Christopher, then snapped the chin strap of his headgear.

The referee raised the Union wrestler's arm, then the two wrestlers cleared the mat. The PA system boomed, "Now wrestling in the 129-pound final . . . Bobby Zane, Millburn . . . Gerald Griffey, Elizabeth . . ."

Bobby shook hands with Coach Messina, then stalked onto the mat, stepping out onto a stage—his stage. Griffey met Bobby in the middle. Bobby put his left foot on his side of the center circle, adjusted his headgear, and set his stance. *Right off the whistle.*

The referee directed them to shake hands. "Let's have a good match, fellas. Don't stop wrestling until I say so." He checked with the timekeeper, then lifted the whistle to his lips. The whistle screamed.

Bobby shot out from his stance, catching Griffey flat-footed. Before Griffey could react, Bobby sucked his right leg in tight and stepped up to his feet, his head in Griffey's chest. He switched to a double-leg, lifted, and dropped Griffey to the mat. The match would be over shortly, Bobby knew, as he forced in the half.

Griffey knew it, too. He was a beaten wrestler. Done. Finished. And now, a half minute into the first period, a *two*-time district runner-up.

The gold medal sat in Bobby's open palm. He stared at the imprint on the front—two combative wrestlers encircled by the outline of New Jersey—then flipped it over. DISTRICT XI CHAMPIONSHIP 129-LBS FIRST PLACE was engraved on the back. Bobby closed his fist tightly.

He recalled last year, sitting in nearly the same position on his bed, while his mother and father prepared a celebration dinner in the dining room. That night, Bobby had glanced around his bedroom, jittery from winning the districts for the first time, not knowing what to do next, feeling like the world was his, like he could do *anything*. He had set the medal on his dresser, then stepped back to check that it could be seen equally well from his bed, closet, and door.

"I did it," he had whispered.

The district championship. He had reached his ultimate goal, a goal he had set at the beginning of the season. It felt a hundred times, maybe a thousand times, more glorious than he had ever dreamed. That he would lose in the semifinals of the regions one week later—and not advance to the states—was irrelevant. He had won the districts. Emotions overflowed, filling Bobby's eyes with tears. He had cried.

Last year's championship medal now had a companion. Same medals; different circumstances. While the first district championship, as an underdog third-seed with a 13–4 record, was unexpected, the second was a mere formality. Everyone—the crowd, Bobby's father, Coach Messina, the local papers, Griffey himself—understood Bobby would win the 129-pound finals this year. Those who didn't were fooling themselves. Perhaps the only raised eyebrows came from the devastating manner in which Bobby wrenched Griffey over and held his back flat to the mat for the pin. Thirty-two seconds into the first period. A television commercial's length of time.

Bobby heard his parents downstairs. Arguing, as always. He stripped naked, toweled dry his arms and back, and threw on a pair of sweats. He placed the medals side by side on the dresser. They glimmered in the vanishing afternoon light.

He wasn't satisfied. For four months he had cut weight, run hundreds of miles, done endless push-ups and sit-ups, battled his teammates day in and day out. The effort should add up to more. Instead, the medals reminded him of cheap trinkets he might've won at a Point Pleasant boardwalk arcade. But there was a reason the effort should add up to more, he knew. He hadn't reached the end. There was work yet to be done. It was all one long journey, at times glorious, like this afternoon, his hand raised high in victory, but mostly, as he expected tonight to be, utterly painful. In the end, he vowed, only one medal would hang from his neck: the New Jersey state championship medal.

The telephone rang. *Carmelina?* Bobby thought. He stepped to his nightstand. *Why would she call?* They had already agreed on when he would pick her up at the mall on Tuesday night. There was nothing else to discuss. He felt a nervous chill. *What if she's backing out?* He palmed the receiver but the second ring cut short.

Bobby expected his mother to call out with contempt, "Pick up the phone; it's her." But she didn't. Instead, he heard heavy footsteps move down the foyer.

"Are you coming down?" his father said.

"In a second," Bobby answered.

With a swipe, the two medals disappeared into his hand. The districts were over. Time to put them in the past. The state championship was the goal. He dropped the medals into a drawer with letters and cards from Carmelina, and photographs of the two of them together, then slammed it shut.

Last year's celebration had been spontaneous and genuine, a chance for him and his family to pull out their finest silverware and china, dress up, and enjoy dinner together. The day before, his mother had closed on a house in the Hartshorn section of town. Her smile that night matched the black slacks, white blouse, and Italian gold bracelets she wore. Bobby remembered—and always would—how wonderful dinner was, how proud his father was, how Christopher had said he wanted to be just like his older brother. It was his finest moment.

Stepping down the stairs, Bobby wished he could go

back in time, already sensing the anger between his parents carried over from an argument at the districts. *In the stands, no less. Why are we even doing this?* he wondered. *We could've had Chinese take-out. I would've been happy, Christopher would've been happy. At least two of us would've been.*

After his first district title, a warm hug and kiss from his father greeted Bobby when he had walked into the kitchen.

"Son, I'm so very proud of you," his father had said, wrapping his arms around him. All of the aches in Bobby's arms and shoulders had come to life, yet, he remembered, nothing felt better.

Christopher had jumped up from the kitchen table, hugged him around the waist, and said, "You're the best wrestler in the whole wide world."

His mother had followed with a kiss on his forehead. "Fix your collar." She'd stepped back and smiled. "My son, the district winner." She held out a wooden spoon with just a touch of tomato sauce on the end. "Try a taste." She tilted the spoon, letting him slurp a dribble of sauce into his mouth.

Now, at the bottom of the stairs, Bobby caught his reflection in the foyer mirror. A baggy sweatshirt draped off his shoulders, pants hung from his bony hips, his hair was a mess. The disheveled look went well with the scowl on his face. *It's permanent*, Bobby thought, *a Zane trademark nowadays.*

His socks squeaked on the tiled foyer floor. He held

a sliver of hope that his mother, father, and brother would immediately stop what they were doing to greet him, as they had last year. Part of him, though, didn't give a damn.

He stepped into the kitchen.

"Put these on the dining-room table," his mother said, handing him a stack of plates. Shaking her head, she slipped by him. "Damn it, I made a mess of this sleeve."

Bobby saw the splatter of sauce on her hand. "You okay?"

"I'm just fine," she answered, brushing off his concern as she rushed out of the kitchen. Her footsteps disappeared down the foyer.

At the kitchen table, Christopher had his arm deep into a box of crackers, intently watching the television, depositing one cracker after the other into his mouth like coins into a piggy bank. In the dining room, his father placed the utensils methodically, solemnly. Bobby figured that he, too, would have preferred to be somewhere else.

Clouds of steam rose from a pot of boiling water, while next to it, bubbles broke the surface of a pan of Alfredo sauce. Bobby put down the dishes and opened the refrigerator, wanting more than his usual ration of seltzer. As he reached for a can of Coke, he felt his father's firm hand on his shoulder.

"Solid win today. Should get you a good seed for the regions. Anything less than a second seed will be unacceptable."

His father had given this a lot of consideration. Too much. Bobby wanted to say, *How about a simple congratulations and leave it at that?*

"You've got that single-mindedness I've been telling you to have all season," his father went on. "It's all Bobby Zane. It's got to be that way."

Bobby answered with a halfhearted nod.

Soon, the dining-room table was set—utensils placed and china plates centered in front of each chair. Bobby's mother came back into the kitchen, wearing a long-sleeved shirt, the same one she wore when working in the flower garden during the summer. She had combed her hair, Bobby noticed, but it didn't change the harried look on her face.

She turned the stove off. "I'll strain the pasta."

While his father sat at the head of the table, Bobby took a seat to his left and Christopher to his right. His mother took the chair at the opposite end of the table. For much of dinner, utensils clinked against the dishes and glasses, but otherwise, an anxious silence filled the dining room. His mother and father said little to each other, passing dishes back and forth more often than words.

"This is good," his father said, swallowing a mouthful of pasta. His voice had little emotion. Bobby's mother acknowledged him with hardly a nod, crushing a red pepper between her fingers and sprinkling it on her food. *They might as well be a thousand miles apart,* Bobby thought. *Probably be better for all of us.*

"A shame Kenny lost," his father said, taking a sip of wine, then setting the glass down. "Anthony, too."

"They weren't ready," Bobby said. "I could tell."

After a half plate of fettuccine, Bobby set his fork down. His stomach had reached its limit. Though his hunger craved more, he couldn't force anything else down.

His mother gestured. "I hope you're finishing that."

"I'm done," Bobby said.

Her eyes narrowed. She, too, sat back. "Always starving yourself."

"No, I'm full."

"Well, there's a lot of food left," his mother said. "I worked too damn hard to let it all go to waste. Too hard."

Before Bobby could open his mouth, his father snapped, "We all did."

His mother looked up. "What's that mean?"

"You know what that means."

"No, tell me."

"It means we all helped out," his father said.

"Oh, *you* did?"

The dining room was instantly in a storm, and though these storms had become more regular, the speed at which this one hit was startling. Only a few hours earlier, Bobby had held his arms high, as Griffey lay flat on his back. An avalanche of cheers rushed over Bobby for those few fleeting moments, in front of his teammates, his hometown crowd, his family and friends, in his gymnasium. But it had been only a brief break from the winter-long foul weather.

The skies had closed again, reality rushing back. The black clouds of Carmelina's pregnancy from the east; his parents' rotted marriage, in a flash of wind and lightning, from the west. The two converging, raining down deception and bitter anger.

"Where'd you go last Thursday night, Robert?" his mother said, with a harsh laugh. "Come on, tell the boys."

His mother's challenge froze the table. His father held a tight smile. "I'm having dinner right now."

"I'm asking you."

"Let us eat, Maggie."

She slammed a plate down, shattering it into pieces. "I don't know where the hell you went!"

His father wiped his mouth with a napkin. "You're out of line with this one."

Through the shouting, Bobby heard the muffled cries of his little brother. He looked at Christopher, who sat in his chair, looking very scared.

Bobby put his hands up. "I'll eat, okay? I'll eat everything on the plate."

"No," his father said. "If you don't want to eat, don't eat."

Bobby jabbed his fork into the fettuccine, scooping the pasta sloppily into his mouth.

His mother smiled wickedly. "Where were you, Robert? Can't answer, can you?"

Christopher's head bobbed gently with each sob.

Bobby stared at his mother, his father. "Let's not go through this now," he said. "Not with Christopher—"

"No, Bobby, this is between your father and me."

"Drop it, Maggie," his father said. He sounded too even-keeled, oddly casual. He picked up his fork, lifted a few strands of fettuccine and twirled them, then guided the fork into his mouth.

"Who called before, Robert?"

His father didn't look up from his plate immediately.

"Who was on the phone?" she said louder. "I saw you pick up the phone. Tell me, who was on it?"

"No one. I told you the person hung up."

She shook her head. "I don't believe you for one god-damn minute. Who was it?"

"Someone hung up. That's the end of it."

"Maybe it was Carmelina," Bobby interrupted. "You know she hates calling here and having someone else answer. I bet it was her."

His mother smirked and shook her head. "Oh, no, it wasn't Carmelina. She called just when I got home. No, this was someone else. Robert, are you going to answer to our family?"

Bobby threw down his fork, the loud clank stopping both his parents from speaking another word. He hid his face in his hands. The muscles in his neck ached, and he was confused and too tired to face the fighting anymore. For a few moments, there was a tense quiet again.

Then Bobby raised his head. His tone was powerful. "Christopher and me are done with dinner. We're getting up from the table. Going upstairs. And getting away from this insanity."

With that, Bobby stood up from the table, tall and unflinching, not unlike his posture before the championship match that afternoon. Without looking at either of his parents, he held his hand out for his little brother. "Come on."

Christopher wiped away the tears and scooted off the chair. He held on to Bobby's hand tightly as they walked out of the dining room, through the kitchen and foyer, then up the stairs. In silence.

Bobby waited for his parents to say something, to yell at him for getting up from the table, or at each other for driving him from the table. But his mother and father said nothing, nor did Bobby hear plates being stacked, glasses being collected, or the faucet running. Maybe they just sat there, forced to face each other, no more games to play. Bobby chose to imagine them that way. That made for a better truth.

And while he held Christopher in his arms as they thumbed through comic books together in his bedroom, the silence remained.

38

Ivan stepped out of the Nova and watched his father walk to the mailbox at the end of the driveway. His father pulled out a handful of envelopes, most of which, Ivan knew, were letters from college coaches. We're this. We're that. We're the best. They all said the same things. *Have one coach write the letter,* Ivan thought, *and let the others sign their names at the bottom. It'd save a lot of time and paper.* For Ivan, the only envelope that meant anything would come with an Arizona postmark. And, as Coach Riker had told him, that wouldn't come until the end of April.

"We will go through these later," his father said. "For now, you will enjoy your victory. *We* will enjoy your victory."

Patches of soiled ice and snow dotted the front yard. Soon, these last signs of winter would disappear. Along the edging of the driveway, his father suddenly stopped and knelt down, dark blue work pants pulling taut over his thighs. "Too many stones."

His thick, scarred fingers picked at the pebbles that had spilled onto the lawn from the crush of the Nova's tires. Ivan wondered why his father would be concerned. If the two of them had worked for hours at removing the pebbles, they *might* have made a noticeable difference. Why now? Many questions about his father remained unanswered. For the time being, however, with the districts quietly behind him, Ivan didn't care about the answers.

"Papa, I'll rake later."

Perhaps what he said made sense. His father picked a few more pebbles, then slapped his hands free of dirt. Ivan reached out to help him stand.

"I am okay," his father said, a grimace on his weathered face. "I am not an athlete like you. Imagine if I had to do those moves you do."

"Bet you coulda when you were my age."

"No, you are special. You are a champion."

And he was. District champ for the fourth time, most-valuable wrestler for the second year in a row— both Lennings records. But neither meant much to Ivan. "I should've pinned that guy in the finals faster."

"He was a good wrestler," his father said. "Just because you pin a boy does not mean he is no good. You were not nervous, were you?"

"Nervous?" Ivan said. *"No."*

"It is good to be nervous. Nervous means you are alive. Nervous means something is important to you."

Ivan looked at him, oddly.

"You do not believe me. But you should. I know about nervous." He stopped at the walkway, letting Ivan settle under his arm. "How about sausage for dinner, with peppers that make you cry and onions as big as grapefruits? That is what men eat."

Ivan walked with his father up the front porch steps. The paint along the door frame was chipping. His father stopped to pick away a few curled flakes, dropping them to the porch floor. Always doing some kind of work on the house, but never catching up.

"When I was young, I thought I would run around this world, my own man. Alone. Like a conqueror." He paused and smiled. "Then I met your mama. She changed me. Made me a better man." The craggy features of his eyes and wrinkled cheeks smoothed.

"I was nervous when your mama and I married. And I was most nervous when you were born. You were so little in my arms. But I felt as alive as I would ever feel." He turned the key and pushed through the door. "And that is when the hard work began."

"When?"

"With you." He shrugged off his jacket.

"I wasn't hard work. Was I?"

"As you are now. Like this old house. Always a lot of work, never finished. Are you coming in?"

"Wait a second, Papa," Ivan said. "I'll be there."

Ivan, still standing on the front steps, pulled the front door closed and looked across Farmingdale at the Petersons' house. Their car sat in the same spot it had earlier this morning, but there was no sign of Shelley. They hadn't spoken in four days, longer than any time in their lives. Would she be mad forever? Would she continue to make him pay for that single mistake?

Behind Ivan, the front door opened and his father stepped out. "What are you doing?"

"Nothing."

"Come inside, then. We will eat."

Ivan took a last look at Shelley's window, wishing with all his heart that she saw him and felt his apology. He had searched for her after his finals match, but she had left the gym before he could find her. Wind blew across Ivan's face, drying his eyes. He blinked, but his eyes wouldn't stray from her window. Then, finally, he went inside.

39

His gym bag slung over his shoulder, Bobby pulled his jacket tight across his body and trudged up the walkway, toward the house. Lights were on, he noticed vaguely, consumed with thoughts about the weekend's region tournament and his top seeding. At the driveway, Bobby stopped. Oddly, his father's Jaguar was parked there, not in the garage. He started toward the back door of the house, when something in the car caught his eye. He looked closely. There was luggage—two pieces, maybe three—and overcoats were draped over the front seat. Boxes of law books were stacked in the back.

Bobby ran to the back door and bolted inside to the kitchen. "Hello?" he called out, sensing uneasiness in the house.

He listened; upstairs, his father was talking. To Christopher, he could tell. Bobby walked in farther and could see into the family room, where his mother was huddled on the couch, staring off somewhere faraway. A place Bobby could only guess.

"I'll be there Friday night." His father stood in front of Bobby in the kitchen. His eyes were bloodshot, his shoulders sloped. "And Saturday, too." He strained a smile, as if waiting for Bobby's response. "You know I'll be there to watch you win, right? You understand that. You understand that, right?"

"Sure, Dad," Bobby said, not really knowing what he was saying.

His father reached out to hug him. "You have to be strong, Bobby. This is your time. This weekend. And next."

His father's eyes were welling up. It was the first time Bobby had seen that. Their embrace released a pain that had overwhelmed Bobby. And he started to tear, thinking of one thing.

Betrayal.

An ugly word. And yet it was an intimate part of Bobby's world, explaining the mountain of anger he now had for his parents and what they had brought upon his family. All his life, they had taught "family this" and "family that." *What the hell's it all mean now?*

He had been duped. Tricked. Told the biggest lie in the world. What had once been pleasant memories, memories that defined his family, were no longer. Now they were painful. And if Bobby dwelled on them long enough, stomach wrenching. Worst of all, there was nothing he could do about any of it. He felt isolated, alone. *All you can control is yourself,* he had told himself. Now he even doubted that.

"Nothing changes, Bobby," his father said. "Call me at Grandma's. In the middle of the night if you have to. Call me at work anytime. I'll call home every day after practice to make sure you and Christopher are okay."

"But—" Bobby stopped himself. *But what?* What could he possibly ask? What could he possibly say that would make even the tiniest difference? Could any of this be undone? Was he losing his family at the same time his girlfriend was pregnant, while the region tournament awaited him in five days? Was he going crazy?

A kiss on his forehead lingered. So, too, did his father's voice saying, "Go comfort Christopher and your mother." Then he heard the click of the back door closing.

"Dad?"

Dazed, numb, his gut on the edge of nausea, Bobby stood in the middle of the kitchen, hearing the warm air whistle faintly through the heating shafts to each room as if the house were suddenly hollow, a shell of what it once was. The furnace in the basement pumped one more time, then shut off, and the final whoosh of heat breathed through the vents. And that was it.

Bobby walked into the family room.

40

A lightbulb illuminated the end of the corridor. Ivan passed the storage closet and turned toward the practice room. McClellan's footsteps echoed behind him. "We'll go an hour," McClellan said.

As Ivan drew closer to the pumping, whooshing boilers, he muttered, "You'll never make it."

For the third year in a row, Ivan was the lone Lennings wrestler to advance to the region tournament. Rumors were swirling around the team about a new coach—someone from a rival school—and the blowout Holt and McClellan had in the principal's office two days earlier. Everyone in school said McClellan's fate was now sealed. *The body's not cold*, Ivan thought, *and the vultures are circling*.

"I want you to be sharp today," McClellan said. "Singles, doubles—they all have to be crisp."

Ivan entered the practice room and switched on the ceiling lights, then dropped his headgear to the mat and sat down. He warmed up methodically, stretching his legs out front, slowly touching his forehead, then chest, to his left knee. Then his right knee. He didn't look up; he didn't say anything.

"The seeding meeting was last night. You're a first seed, which was obviously a given," McClellan said. "I have the brackets. You can look at them if you want."

Ivan didn't give a damn who was in his weight class—they were all competing for second place. The gap between him and the others was never more apparent. As was the tradition, wrestlers in the area preparing for the regions practiced at North Hunterdon High School on Monday and Tuesday. Hunterdon Central had eight wrestlers moving on; Delaware Valley, seven; Voorhees and North Hunterdon, six each; and Bridgewater West, five. Wrestlers from a few other schools were invited, as well.

The practices had the kind of competition that Ivan eagerly awaited, an opportunity to drill with the best talent in western New Jersey, something he never came close to experiencing in the Lennings wrestling room. As usual, he had been a closely watched participant, and as usual, he had dominated.

And now, McClellan was insisting on practicing an *hour* with him. *He's gotta be reminded he's thirty-three, not seventeen.* A weekend-warrior jog on Saturday or Sunday wasn't going to cut it against the state title favorite, 20–0 with sixteen pins, coming off a district tournament in which he dismantled his three opponents.

"You had good practices the past two days," McClellan said. "But I saw things we need to work on. Maybe you're tired, maybe a little distracted. Today should get you back on track."

Ivan's stoic demeanor gave way to an intimidating seriousness. His eyes narrowed. The muscles along his temples twitched. He watched McClellan on the other side of the room. It was one thing for McClellan to be a passive partner during drills; it was entirely something else to expect to go sixty minutes of live wrestling.

"Why we doing this?" Ivan felt like saying. There were other ways to hold practice. McClellan could have asked Ellison and some of the other Lennings wrestlers, whose seasons were already finished, to come in and train. Maybe a couple of juniors would've been interested in getting a few more practices before the spring track and baseball seasons began.

But Ivan knew the answer. McClellan wanted a piece of him. McClellan wanted to step back a decade and a half, when he was a Lennings team captain and one-time district champ, and prove that he had been good enough to wrestle with the best. Ivan laughed to himself. *I'm gonna wreck you, McClellan.*

"We goin' easy today?" Ivan said, with more than a hint of sarcasm. "I'm runnin' later, anyway."

McClellan looked at him. "You think this might be some kind of BS practice? Trust me, Ivan. It won't be."

Ivan bounced on his toes, his eyes alive, piercing—a glisten of sweat shone under the lights above. An intimidating sight. A singular focus. Thick veins ran on the undersides of his forearms, the paleness of his skin in stark contrast to his black shorts and black ASICS.

"Ready?" McClellan said.

Intensity ignited within Ivan, fueled by a chance to exact some revenge. McClellan had toyed with his wrestling destiny, holding it out like a precious gift to be given, or taken away. But no longer. They had come to an understanding, a truce, temporary at best, as if each held a knife at the other's neck until the season was finished. *You get outta my way,* Ivan thought, *and I'll make you coach of a state champ.*

"Takedowns," McClellan said.

Ivan adjusted his chin strap, then stood in his stance. They slapped hands.

Ivan stepped toward McClellan and struck. The execution of his drop step was precise, slipping underneath McClellan's arms, his shoulder slamming into his gut, stealing a breath from McClellan's throat, his arms instantly holding control of his legs. Ivan lifted, went head-side-around, and dumped McClellan to the mat.

That was the first takedown.

McClellan got to his feet, and again Ivan took him down with little effort, hitting a hi-crotch, then switching to a single and running the pike. A half-dozen more times, McClellan fell victim to Ivan's speed and strength.

Five minutes passed.

Then ten.

Then fifteen minutes of continuous wrestling.

Ivan's single-leg takedown shot out like a bayonet. His hip throws and leg sweeps were devastating. In the top position, he was smothering; on bottom, elusive. And when he was tired of wrestling with finesse, Ivan simply overpowered McClellan.

McClellan wheezed, and at every opportunity took an extra moment or two to catch his breath. Sweat washed down his pained, old face. Ivan shook his head. *Just give in and stop wasting my time.*

But McClellan wouldn't, so Ivan waited impatiently for him to be set. And then he dismantled him some more.

Then, as the room warmed and minutes passed, something unexpected happened, something Ivan couldn't have imagined in a hundred, maybe a thousand, years. McClellan held his own.

Soon, McClellan was pressing Ivan, countering moves ably, if just a half-step slow, and, at times, dictating the tempo. Perhaps it was years of wrestling coming back, the thousands of shots and drills over hundreds of practices and matches. Or perhaps McClellan was compelled by something deeper. A wrestler's disdain for being controlled, a wrestler's thirst for physical competition. After each shot, he picked himself up when it would have been so easy and reasonable to call it a day.

Forty-five minutes passed, drilling sit-outs, stand-ups, and pinning combinations; working takedowns. Ivan felt himself growing stronger. He'd tie up with McClellan, move him to one side or the other, then hit a hi-crotch to the opposite leg, switch to a double, lift, and drop him to the mat.

Again and again. Perfect technique, enviable execution.

McClellan climbed back to his feet, brushed the sweat from his eyes. Hunched over, he held on to the bottom of his shorts. His white shirt, now gray with sweat, was glued to his shoulders, chest, and back.

Ivan glanced at the clock, then at McClellan, a gesture that perhaps it was time for McClellan to quit.

Instead, McClellan snapped, "Let's keep going," taking in a deep breath before getting set in his stance.

Ivan reached out to tie up. But in a burst, McClellan faked an arm drag, dropped low, and dived in for Ivan's leg. He was in deep for a split second, holding the leg tight to his chest, head up, in a position that, years ago—when he was a high school senior wrestling a weaker opponent—would undoubtedly have resulted in a takedown.

But this was Ivan Korske. And this was fifteen years later.

Bearing all his weight down on McClellan, Ivan kicked his leg back, slipping from his loosened arms . . . then outstretched fingers . . . until McClellan was on his hands and knees, reaching helplessly. Ivan spun to McClellan's left, looking for the easy two points. But McClellan hit a duck-under and half sat to the right side, driving his shoulder into Ivan's hip and lifting up on his ankle. Still, Ivan was too quick. He kicked his leg through and squared off with McClellan.

Then Ivan set up a fireman's carry so beautifully, so

picture-perfect, faking an ankle pick to the right side and coming back with a drop step to the left. He had his arm up the crotch, deep, and McClellan draped over his shoulders.

"Step up and throw me!" McClellan said.

But Ivan didn't. Instead of lifting McClellan high for a throw, Ivan rolled through, tight on the arm and leg, as he did against his opponent in the first period of last year's state semifinals. The same move, the same position. And just like his opponent did, McClellan hooked Ivan's arms with his right arm and right leg, flattening himself to the mat, hoping to expose Ivan's back long enough for what would have been a takedown and two near-fall points.

McClellan was trying to hold him down, using all his weight, using every bit of his strength. And it occurred to Ivan that he was actually being *controlled* by McClellan. The idea of that made something in his mind go berserk. He arched mightily and turned. McClellan did his best to hold tight, but the battle was a short one. In the end, Ivan finished off the fireman's carry, covering on top for the takedown.

"Time," McClellan said, his face wrinkled with exhaustion. "You can't roll in that position," he said, between breaths. "You have to throw the man."

"It worked, didn't it?" Ivan snapped.

McClellan stood wearily against a wall, refusing to sit or to take a knee, or in any way show he was beaten physically. He had proved his point. He had wrestled with Ivan. He had shown he could do it.

That disgusted Ivan.

The short break ended, and soon the clock clicked to 4:15. They went another fifteen minutes, then called it quits.

Afterward, Ivan had time—plenty of time—to wonder, and worry, about how McClellan had nearly taken him to his back.

41

Bobby knocked on the bedroom door.

"Yes," his mother answered.

He turned the knob. His mother faced away from him, wiped her eyes, then looked over her shoulder. He hated when she cried; it always meant hard times had become impossible times. Only the worst could wear her down. Had this? Had she come to the end of what she could tolerate? He didn't cross the door's threshold.

"Ma?"

For a moment, she didn't answer. She dabbed her eyes again, then looked at him. "I'll . . ." A sob caught her breath. "I'll be fine."

"Need anything?"

She shook her head. "No."

"Can I borrow the car?" he asked. "I'll be back. Not too late."

His mother, seeming so frail, nodded slightly.

That was it. There was nothing else to say. So Bobby pulled the door shut, closing out his mother's hurt. Leaving her. He didn't mean to be uncaring. Or selfish. Just rational, his father might have said. What had happened to his parents, and as a consequence, his family, happened outside his control. And what couldn't be controlled, couldn't be worried about. At least not now.

It was almost seven o'clock. The escalator lifted Bobby to the second floor of the Livingston Mall. Carmelina would be finished with work, and together they would go to the clinic. *Then we'll know*, Bobby thought. *No more waiting. No more guessing.*

In the women's department, behind a mirrored pillar, he found a moment of privacy, where he made the sign of the cross, then continued toward the cosmetics counters.

Carmelina stood behind a glass display case, busily arranging perfume bottles in neat rows. A customer stepped away, and for a moment, the entire department seemed to open up for his entrance.

His eyes caught hers and Carmelina straightened up. *Let's get this over with*, he thought. He walked to the counter. "Ready?"

Carmelina pursed her lips. "Hello to you, too."

"You done?"

"Don't worry," she said.

Carmelina grabbed her purse and handed a register key to another saleswoman. She led Bobby through the department, back into the open atrium of the mall. She hinted at a smile—something Bobby hadn't seen from her in weeks.

"Thanks for showing up," she said.

"We gotta get going."

"Give me a minute."

Bobby sighed. "What do you wanna talk about now?"

"Just give me a minute . . . please."

Carmelina sat down on a bench outside Macy's. Bobby looked at his watch, then reluctantly sat down, too. She seemed too damn casual. He waited for her to say something.

"Bobby, we're not going."

He shot to his feet. "Carmelina, you can't do this. We gotta know. I can't keep worrying every moment of the day and night. It's driving me crazy!"

She patted the bench with her hand. "Bobby, sit."

He shook his head.

"Bobby—"

"No, listen to me for a second. I feel really awful, and I feel even worse for you. I know what's going on in there." He nodded toward her stomach. "And I know what's going on in your head, and I'm sorry that I'm part of what made this whole mess happen. But we can't wait. Not knowing is worse. At least if we know . . ."

Carmelina stood up and put her finger to his lips. "Bobby, I'm not."

He looked at her. "Not what?"

"Not pregnant."

"What?"

"I'm not pregnant. I got my period last night."

"You did?"

"Yeah."

"You sure?"

"Yeah, Bobby," she said. "I'm sure."

Bobby eyed her, warily. "You're not joking, are you? Tell me you're not."

Carmelina didn't say anything, and Bobby knew she was telling the truth. A stream of shoppers continued past them, though Bobby forgot for a moment where he was. He suddenly felt tremendously weak but tremendously light, and he thought that something wonderful had happened—or not happened—and it made him want to cry. He looked over at Carmelina again, catching the tears in her eyes, and suddenly there might as well have been a valley a mall wide between the two of them because he knew this would be the last he saw of her, and he believed she knew the same thing.

"God smiled on us, I guess," she said.

He nodded. What else was there to say?

42

Ivan pressed the doorbell and stepped back. He held the bouquet of flowers. He was thankful to be placing them in someone's hands, instead of at the base of a tombstone. If Shelley would take them.

He heard a voice and could see Shelley's figure approach, through the tiny door window. "Shelley," he said.

The door opened. Just a little. "Yes?" Shelley said.

"I'm sorry."

"Fine," Shelley said, then began to close the door.

"Other than my papa," Ivan said, "you're the most important person in my life."

Shelley hesitated.

"I'm not real good with words, you know that. I was an asshole, and I'll apologize for a week, or a month, or a year straight, if you'll forgive me."

Shelley then opened the door and stood, arms crossed. She shivered but said nothing. Ivan held out the flowers, which she took but did not embrace.

"I was outta my mind. McClellan, wrestling, Hannen—"

"It's cold out," Shelley interrupted.

"I'm trying to tell ya."

"No excuses, Ivan," she said.

"Everything coming at me—," he started, then stopped. "No . . . No more excuses."

"I probably shouldn't tell you this," Shelley said. Her eyes welled. "But I've been sick, really sick, the past few days, wondering how you could've done that to me. I wanted to do something nice for the team because you're part of that team and I'm proud of you. And you go and destroy it. Who are you to do something like that?" She shook her head. "No one's ever made me feel this horrible. Flowers aren't gonna make it better, Ivan." She handed him the bouquet.

Ivan gently nudged the flowers back. "Please . . ."

"I've always been there for you," she said.

"I know," Ivan said. "More than I have for you."

"This one hurt."

"In a million years, I never meant to hurt you. Especially you. You're family to me. Even more because you know me better than anyone in the world. You mean more than the state championship or Western Arizona or anything."

He let out a long breath, then said, with as much conviction as he had in his heart, "There's nothing else I can do but promise you that for as long as I live, it'll never happen again."

Then Ivan wished her good night and walked home.

43

Bobby's opponent was wiry and powerful and just a quick cut from escaping from his control when momentum carried both wrestlers outside the circle.

"Out of bounds!" the referee yelled. "Back in the center!"

Bobby ended up on his back. His chest rose and sank rapidly. He closed his eyes, feeling calm, given the circumstances—leading 7–1 in the third period of the Region 3 semifinals before nearly a thousand spectators in the Union High School gymnasium. He sat up, adjusted his headgear, climbed to his feet, and gave a nod to Coach Messina.

Coach Messina also stood, tugged at the pleats of his slacks, and said, as if it were just the two of them having a quiet conversation, "Fifty-one seconds and you're going to the states."

Going to the states . . . Bobby nearly smiled.

His opponent had proved to be formidable, and perhaps on a morning when Bobby had been wrestling less than his best, the match might have been a toss-up. But Bobby had taken him down easily with a leg sweep for an early 2–0 first-period lead. Then he'd let him up and taken him down again for a 4–1 margin at the end of two minutes. He followed that with an escape and takedown in the second period.

Bobby waited for his opponent to be set in the bottom position. It felt odd not being anxious that disaster might strike, that his opponent might find some way to reverse him to his back and capture the lead. But that simply wasn't a possibility, not with the way he had plowed through the districts, manhandled his teammates in practice all week, and scored a second-period pin in his region tournament first-round match.

His opponent was a beaten wrestler, frustrated that his attack from the top position hadn't materialized. Bobby smelled it, felt it, sensed it on a level beyond what fans could see. Wrestling was sometimes too subtle to be just visual, he knew.

So Bobby settled into the top position, knowing the most important fifty-one seconds of his life to date would pass quickly and uneventfully until the referee raised Bobby's hand in victory. And then he could look toward some other "most important" period or minutes or seconds of his life, and he would be a region finalist and he would be going to the states.

Going to Jadwin, Bobby thought, a moment before

the referee blew the whistle. He liked that. He liked that very much.

The gold medal, slightly larger than a half-dollar, sat in Bobby's hand. He stared at the front—two wrestlers encircled by the outline of New Jersey—then flipped it over: REGION III CHAMPION—129 LBS. Bobby closed his fist, then tossed the medal into a drawer, where it careened against the other medals, then fell silent.

44

Ivan flicked on the ceiling light. The basement was cold and drafty. He tied the laces of his wrestling shoes, swept dirt off the soles, stepped onto the mat, and began.

On his feet, he did singles and doubles, hi-crotches, ankle picks, duck-unders, and snap-downs. He used different setups: dropping his level, tap-and-go, moving side to side. Then combinations: arm drags and stepping in for the double, faking an ankle pick and coming with a hi-crotch to the opposite leg, shooting the single and switching to a double.

Despite the chill, despite the dehydration, Ivan was soon sweating.

The basement walls pushed outward and the ceiling rose toward the lights of Princeton's Jadwin Gymnasium. . . .

Ivan finished on his feet, with hip throws, headlock hip throws, pancakes, leg sweeps, duck-unders to a lift, singles to a lift, bear hugs, Japanese wizzers, and the fireman's carry.

The sound of hot water rushing through the house's piping grew louder, rising to a crescendo of screaming fans, the stands shaking under their weight. . . .

Down on the mat, Ivan sat out and turned in, sat out and turned out, sat out and did switches to both sides. He did wrist rolls, wing rolls, inside stands, outside stands, switches.

Under the gymnasium lights, Ivan stood on the center mat, waiting for the start of the 129-pound state finals. He paced back and forth like a caged animal, measuring his opponent. The instant their eyes met, he knew it was over; he smelled the fear.

They poised. The whistle blew. Ivan lunged forward and took his opponent down, threw in a half nelson, and squeezed. Closer . . . closer . . . closer . . . Until it was over.

His opponent lay motionless at his feet. The state championship was his. The roar of the Jadwin crowd was deafening. Looking out at screaming fans, Ivan lifted his arms. Behind eyes shut tightly, the image of victory remained etched in his mind.

"Ivan?" his father called from the top of the basement stairs. "Are you there?"

Ivan opened his eyes to silence. No crowd, no cheers, no state championship victory. He stood chained to an unfulfilled dream and haunted by the nightmare of last year's semifinal loss.

"Yes, Papa. I'll be up soon."

The door shut. Ivan walked across the floor and sat down on a wooden chair. It creaked under the weight of his body.

There wouldn't be anyone at the states more prepared than he was, he promised. And though Ivan figured, by the state finals, he might face someone equally tough—someone who might be Ivan Korske with another name, someone as starved to win as he was—he doubted it completely.

45

Coach Messina lay down a sheet of paper, the bracket for the 129-pound weight class. Sixteen wrestlers, the champions and runners-up from each of the eight region tournaments. "You got your wish," he said. "You're seeded third. You wrestle Schnell, from Paulsboro, in the first round on Wednesday night."

But Bobby was already looking ahead. "Korske's seeded first."

"You won't face him until the finals," Coach Messina said. "If he makes it that far."

Coach Messina was serious about that. Talent brought you to the states, he always said. But it was the wrestler who "caught fire" that made it through Wednesday's first round and Friday's quarterfinals to the semifinal and championship matches on Saturday afternoon.

Bobby looked at the bracket again, reading the names of the other 129-pounders, thinking how remarkable it was to see his own name alongside the talented wrestlers he had read about all season in the newspapers. And he must have looked, he hated to think, too respectful of the other wrestlers, because Coach Messina picked up the paper and tore it in half.

"Seeds mean nothing."

Then he ripped it in half again.

"The bracket means nothing. What matters is that you win four matches in a row. Four. That's all you need to think about."

46

The bedroom light remained on, while the clock on the dresser clicked past eleven . . . twelve . . . and one o'clock . . . Bobby stared at the ceiling, old matches rolling through his mind, thinking about how he would adjust for one opponent or another. He was dead tired. Still, Bobby wouldn't turn off the bedroom light because the moment after he fell asleep, it would be morning and the first round of the states would face him.

So Bobby stared into the darkness beyond the windows, and he studied the ceiling, and he looked toward Christopher's room. And he lay there, his mind racing. Very anxious. A little lonely. Thinking. No escape; no time out. The endgame approaching.

"What if I lose?" he said out loud.

It wasn't as if he hadn't ever tasted defeat. Once this season, five times last season. Before then, often enough. Bobby knew what it was like to have an opponent's arm raised by the referee, while he sulked at the side of the mat, wondering what went wrong in the match, what he could have done differently, more quickly, better.

Winning was different. He didn't think after he won; he just soaked it in. Like an August breeze down the Shore. Like a smoldering fire in the dead of winter. The feelings melted inside him.

"Losing isn't possible," Bobby told himself. Softly, at first. Then he said it again, more forcefully. And again. Until, finally, as if he were speaking to someone sitting at the edge of his bed.

Of course, losing *was* a possibility. It was real; it was life. Parents divorcing never seemed like a possibility, yet that had become reality. Life wasn't sugarcoated; there was no sound track to somehow soothe the pain. Bobby had learned that, had experienced it intimately.

For a moment, he entertained the thought of going downstairs, opening the refrigerator, and throwing down as much food as his stomach could hold. So what if he didn't make weight and forfeited away his chances? Shit happens sometimes. *Sure Coach Messina would be pissed as all hell, but he's not the one who has to deal with all this. It is my family that's a mess. It's my dad who doesn't live in the house anymore, my mother who's a crying wreck, my little brother who's crushed. A person can only take so much.*

Just go eat. The thought of eating was mesmerizing — the smell of food filling Bobby's nose, the taste washing over his tongue. His stomach quivered and he felt like throwing up.

But that passed.

Bobby managed a laugh. One minute, thinking about how much food he could shove down his throat and eat away his chances for the state championship; the next, so focused on a title he was sure he would win. *Insanity is what it is*, he thought. A roller coaster of utter confidence and deep panic, twisting and turning between giving in and stepping forward. *If people only knew*, he thought. *If they had any idea how screwed up I feel.*

So Bobby weighed himself a half-dozen times for no good reason except that he was comforted standing on the scale; knowing it was okay to remain motionless, holding his breath; it was okay to hear only the tap of his finger on the counterbalance until the scale arm floated and his weight was good.

Then he climbed back into bed. His stomach rocked, but he ignored it, concentrating on the beat of his heart moving through his thighs and shoulders, feet and hands, toes and fingers.

Then visualizing dozens of wrestling situations. On bottom, down by two with twenty seconds left. On top, behind by five, needing a pin in the last period. On his feet, score tied . . .

Eventually his eyes became heavy. His mind slowed. Bobby reached over and turned off the bedroom light. With the final whistle of the last match, he drifted asleep.

47

Shelley turned her head slightly, her eyes hiding in the moon's shadow. "Nice night . . . Too bad it's late," she said, her voice soft. "After everything's over tomorrow, maybe we can take a walk back to Layaree's Wall. Maybe get lost. Maybe the moon will be out again."

"Maybe," Ivan said.

"I'd say good luck, but I'm sure everyone's already told you that. I'd say, 'Hit that single-leg takedown well,' or, 'Don't forget to wizzer,' but I'm sure you have that covered, too."

Ivan smiled. He wondered if Shelley had any idea how he really felt about her. He had nearly thrown away their friendship. He would make it his life's promise that it never happened again.

On Wednesday, just before the lunch bell, she had walked up to him in the school hallway, sighed, then said breathlessly, "I can't fight with you anymore and I can't not be best friends with you. The past week has been horrible for me, just horrible; I accept your apology and I hope you accept mine for being so damn pigheaded."

And he did. Her timing was perfect. On the day of the first round of the states, it was exactly what he needed to hear. Later that night, Ivan put away his Fairlawn opponent, with a near side cradle, in the third period.

"And thank your papa for giving me a ride to Jadwin," Shelley said. "He was so proud of you today."

In the quarterfinals, just hours earlier, Ivan worked his Absegami opponent over for back points twice in the second period and followed that with an escape and takedown in the final two minutes, for a 9–0 win. Two matches down, two to go.

Shelley wanted to say something more, Ivan was sure. His stomach knotted, and it occurred to Ivan that he was only twelve hours or so from wrestling in the state semi-finals in Jadwin Gym in front of thousands of spectators, all eyes on him, with everything in life that he wanted in the balance, and yet here was this beautiful girl whom he had known for so long, stealing his thoughts, making him wish that he really did have all night to spend with her.

"You're a very important person to me, Ivan."

"You sound serious."

"It's been a serious night. Tomorrow will be even more serious. I just want you to know how I feel."

Ivan realized Shelley had closed the gap between the two of them and was coming closer. Right in front of him, hands touching his. Her eyes closed, her lips parted, her head tilted slightly. Shelley went up on the toes of her boots, her hands pulling him into her.

It was a moment that seemed to move slowly, allowing Ivan time to consider what was happening and remind him that *nothing* had ever happened between them. Ever. Though he had dreamed of her and fantasized about her and wished to *be* with her. And now that wall was about to crumble. Maybe. Maybe she'd kiss the corner of his mouth and it might be a kiss of good luck, or it might be the beginning of something more.

She was only a few inches from him, rising to his height. Then, just a breath away, about to kiss the corner of his mouth, delivering whatever message she might. Everything seemed right. So Ivan leaned toward her. His mouth parted, too, meeting her mouth full-on. Shelley relaxed against him, as he pulled her into his arms.

And they kissed.

"Sweet dreams," Shelley said, before leaving. "I'll be there tomorrow. To watch you win."

48

. . . and I knew you could do it," Bobby's father said. "People were yelling and screaming that there was only a few seconds left. And you scored that takedown. Beautiful, just beautiful. I knew you had him, just knew it."

Bobby sat halfway up the stairs to his bedroom, wondering if his father was talking just loud enough so that his mother, down in the foyer, might hear. And was she listening, wishing to push open the bedroom door, step into the foyer, and make amends? Or was she indifferently staring at the television, setting the volume loud enough to drown out voices in the hallway, while his father was posturing, his signal that this was still his house?

Bobby pushed those thoughts out of his head. His mother had spent too much of the past few days crying, and his father had done his best to set aside his own problems and spend time with his son who now was just a dozen or so hours from the semifinals of the states.

Bobby repeated that again—*semifinals of the states*. He

repeated it a third time just to make sure that his family's demise wasn't somehow distorting his wrestling reality.

His father suddenly stepped up and put his hand on Bobby's knee. "When you got that takedown, well I just . . ." He seemed at a loss for words, then shook his head. "Well, I yelled louder than I have in a long, long time."

And it had been a memorable match in the quarter-finals, with three lead changes and a last-second take-down to snatch the 7–6 come-from-behind victory over last year's state runner-up. Bobby jumped up to have his arm raised. He saw Coach Messina pumping his fist. Then he was mobbed by his teammates and classmates who had driven down to Princeton. Yet Bobby hardly re-membered, or felt, anything about the victory. He had been, and still was, numb. It was a wonderful feeling.

He looked up at his father, who was beaming, the hunch of his tired body straightened.

"You were really focused tonight," his father said. "There's been so much for you to worry about . . ." His voice faded. He looked embarrassed, even guilty. Then his voice raised. "But you overcame it all. I'm so proud of you."

And it occurred to Bobby as he sat there, partway to the comfort of his bedroom, partway down to the first floor—or what had been his *parents'* floor—that on the verge of the most important day of his life, he was not feeling particularly nervous. He was exhausted, to be sure, and maybe that was part of the reason, though Bobby didn't think so. It was more than that. Somehow, over the past half day, he had reached a narrow-mindedness that made little else matter. There was a semifinal match to be wrestled tomorrow against a wrestler from Pennsville. And when he won that, there'd be another match, the state championship, afterward. It was that clear-cut.

"This is no time to be nervous, or distracted," Bobby heard his father say. "If you've made it this far, damn it, you deserve to be there as much as Korske or anyone else."

Bobby yawned. He didn't mean to, but his attempt to muffle the yawn was slow, at best. His father stopped. "Tired?"

"Yeah, Dad, I am."

His father nodded. "I'll pick you up at quarter to eight."

"The semis start at ten. Coach wants me in the Jadwin locker room early."

His father grabbed the overcoat hanging over the banister, then glanced down the foyer at his bedroom. "Time for you to get some sleep." He started away.

"Dad?"

His father turned. Bobby lifted himself up and stepped down the stairs. He wanted to ask his father if he really had to leave. It just didn't make sense. This was his house. Just around the corner was his bedroom. He shouldn't have to go *anywhere*.

Bobby reached out and held his father. "I'm gonna win this for you."

His father squeezed, then let go. He walked into the

kitchen, then the lights went off and the back door slammed shut. Soon, the Jaguar's engine rumbled to life, fading as his father backed out of the driveway. Bobby moved to the living room, watching the car's headlights through the windows.

Then his father drove away.

Bobby opened his eyes, ending a restless sleep. He lifted the comforters and blankets off, the chilly air raising goose bumps. He looked at the clock: 6:54 A.M.

A day of reckoning. Only three months earlier, the dream of making it to the state semifinals hadn't even been in the realm of possibility. It would have been almost silly to even consider.

But he had made it.

Usually on a Saturday morning, he would hear Christopher in his bedroom, playing with his Matchbox cars. Instead, all Bobby could hear was the patter of drizzle on the bedroom window, faint yet comforting, and his own deep, rhythmic breathing.

Bobby rolled his neck slowly, feeling a twinge on the right side. He struggled to stand, then walked to the window. The dreary morning looked so damn appropriate.

In the silence of the house, Bobby shrugged off his clothes, peed a little, then stepped into the shower.

49

Clouds had rolled in overnight, carrying a thick mist that blanketed Lennings. Ivan stepped in on the passenger's side of the car and pulled the door. It creaked, then slammed shut. The Nova hadn't yet warmed up and wouldn't until they were well on their way to Princeton.

"Have everything?" his father asked, a wisp of breath curling from his mouth.

Ivan patted his equipment bag.

His father set the car in reverse and backed out of the driveway, then drove down Farmingdale, through the center of town, eventually turning south onto Route 31. Towns passed quickly. Destiny rushed forward.

For any New Jersey high school wrestler, advancing to the state semis would be a supreme accomplishment, undoubtedly the pinnacle of his life. To advance in consecutive seasons was a distinction worthy of the highest praise and a volume of pride. For Ivan there was little of either.

It was at this point last year when a chance at the state finals had been taken from him. This morning's match against his Boonton opponent wouldn't be close, he promised. He'd leave no chance for some timekeeper's screwup.

"Did you sleep?" his father said.

"Long enough."

Soon, mist became rain. His father turned on the wipers. Warm air was finally blowing from the heater vents. Ivan closed his eyes and settled back.

"You had a call yesterday," his father said. "From this Coach Riker."

Ivan opened his eyes. *We gonna fight now, Papa?*

But his father was calm. "He explained the problem with their scholarships. You have been very anxious for the past weeks. You are not like that. I always expect you to have much confidence. Now, you are angry, like the world is against you."

"It feels that way."

"It should not," his father said. "It should not at all."

Ivan stared out the windows, watching the splash of rain from the passing cars and the clouds that seemed to hang just above the roadway. "I gotta win today, both matches. Then everything will be okay."

"Losing is not the end of the world," his father said. "I do not want you to lose. But someday you will, and when that day comes, it will not be the end." He shook his head. "Losing is not death."

I know what death is, Papa. I lived in the same house with death, fightin' it, fightin' it with my mama. It beat me; it took her away. Don't worry; I know death.

"I know what you are thinking," his father said. "It is sad she is not here today. It is painful. I think of her always."

Ivan nodded. Yes, he understood pain, too.

"Days pass, but it does not get any better, I know," his father said. "Every day is one more that she has missed. I wish I could tell her about you. She would be very proud. Not only for your wrestling, but for the man you have become. You understand that, yes?"

"I guess."

Minutes passed in silence. Princeton drew closer. The rain lightened, then eased, then stopped.

Ivan thought about what his father had said. At once it seemed like the oddest and most right time to bring up his mother's death. On their way to Jadwin Gym. They hadn't said much, but it was everything that needed to be said. And Ivan felt healed, if only a little.

So he again sank back into the cushions of the seat, thinking of only one thing. Stepping up on the championship podium. Holding the gold medal. Absorbing the cheers. Raising his arms above the world.

50

Bobby looked up at the top of the building facade: JADWIN GYMNASIUM. The mecca of New Jersey high school wrestling. In the morning light, it was majestic. With his father and mother behind him, and Christopher trying to keep up step for step, Bobby walked to the front entrance. A line of spectators was already formed.

"I'm gonna hold your water bottle, right?" Christopher said.

"Of course," Bobby said.

"And your warm-ups?"

"Sure." Bobby put a hand on Christopher's head and tousled his hair. "You're my good-luck corner man." Then he gestured to his father. "I gotta go in." His father nodded.

Bobby entered through the competitors' door and crossed the lobby. Inside, the cavernous arena opened up. At the center of the floor were two mats, side by side. At ten o'clock, the semifinals would begin with the two 101-pound matches competing simultaneously, then the 108-pound matches, and so on until the heavyweights concluded.

Bobby noticed the glances from spectators and wrestlers who were milling about. He wondered if they knew his name. Did they think he might not belong here? That he was a fluke? Bobby shrugged his varsity jacket higher on his shoulders and straightened up.

A hand fell on his back. "How're you feeling?" Coach Messina said.

Bobby turned and nodded. "Fine."

"Before you get ready to weigh in, let me talk to you a second."

Coach Messina led Bobby to a corner of the gymnasium. His eyes were more intense than Bobby had ever seen them. Different from when the team wrestled Rampart. Different from when Bobby won the districts. Different from a week ago at the regions.

"For four years you've been wrestling under me, Bobby. I've seen you develop from a young kid wanting to get some exercise during the winter into a damn fine wrestler. I've watched you become a great captain, perhaps one of the best we've ever had at Millburn. And in the past month, I've seen you raise your talent to a level deserving of the state title. Take a look around." He gestured toward the stands, the mats, the building itself. "There is only *one* Jadwin.

"Remember the first time you wrestled in a Millburn

singlet? Remember what it was like each time you stepped out in front of your family and friends? They're nice memories, even special. But in all my life, the greatest moments I ever had were the two times I stood on the center mat of Jadwin with my hand raised as a New Jersey state champ. Nothing else comes close. Nothing. And, I'm sure, nothing ever will."

For two seasons, many years ago, the legend of Dean Messina began in the districts, grew during the regions, and reigned supreme at the states. Bobby knew every bit of that legend and wanted every bit to reach as high as his coach had.

"I'm proud of what you've accomplished this season," Coach Messina said. "And now what you've done here in Princeton. You're the wrestler that I imagined you'd become. But don't let it end in the semifinals. You've come too far. You can win this morning, and you can win this afternoon, too. Be ready right from the whistle. This is a big day for Millburn. A big day for the team. A big day for me. But most of all, a big day for you."

Coach Messina held his shoulders. "Are you ready for the state championship?"

"Yes."

"Are you sure?"

"It's mine," Bobby said.

51

Ivan did indeed lift his arms high. He pumped his fist and let out a sharp, "Hell yeah!" There would be no timekeeper's mistake, no early whistle, no semifinal loss this time. Ivan stood at the center of the mat—his Boonton opponent hunched in disappointment—waiting for the referee to raise his arm in victory. Then Ivan stalked off the mat, nodding approval for another devastating win.

"Good job, Ivan, good job," McClellan said. "The monkey's off your back."

"Goddamn right," Ivan said, surprised he even answered McClellan.

He scooped up his warm-ups, gave Holt an obligatory nod, high-fived Ellison, and found a spot where everyone in Jadwin could see him. He hugged his father, then Shelley. His record now stood at 23–0. Twenty-three wins, no losses, one match away. He pulled down the straps of his singlet, his bare chest heaving, his muscles swelled with blood. He gulped down some water. Ellison stood next to him.

"Who won the other semifinal?" Ivan said.

"The guy from Millburn. He looked tough. He's got a good single."

Ivan looked over at Zane and the crowd of people around him. "Someone's gotta tell Cinderella it's midnight."

Ellison smiled. "That's your job."

52

All that was left was time.

The season would end, win or lose, after the next match—the state finals. Bobby looked over at Christopher, curled up, head resting against his father's knee. His mother had gone out into the lobby to buy a hot chocolate. Big John and Kenny sat a few rows behind Bobby. He heard them laughing and joking with Anthony and the others.

Some of the senior girls had driven down to Princeton. A few teachers and coaches, as well. When they caught his eye, they waved, or smiled, or nodded. None dared say anything.

A few minutes earlier, Bobby had looked at the 129-pound bracket. A tournament official had filled in: *Zane, Millburn, decisioned Brandel, Pennsville, 6–5.* A simple notation. He saw the other semifinal. *Korske, Lennings, decisioned Marshall, Boonton, 10–3.*

Space for the finals result was blank.

So Bobby sat back, allowing himself a few moments to remember his semifinal match, which finished only an hour ago, but which seemed like days or weeks ago. And he remembered looking up at the scoreboard, seeing forty-nine seconds left in the third period. He had been wrestling well, perhaps the best of his life, yet was losing 5–2.

"Keep wrestling," the referee instructed both wrestlers.

Even holding the lead, Bobby knew his Pennsville opponent wouldn't stall. There was no honor in that. On their feet, they circled each other. Brandel looked ragged; Bobby felt worse. At the edge of the mat, Bobby stepped in to tie up. Instantly, he lifted Brandel's elbow, slipping his head under and past his opponent's armpit, then arched. But Brandel turned sharply and squared off, and again the two wrestlers faced each other.

"Twenty seconds left," Bobby vaguely heard Coach Messina yell.

Time was running out. And somehow Bobby sensed that even in fifty years, even if he managed to be someone significant and do something important with his life, he had had one chance for wrestling immortality—and it was slipping away. He was sure a loss right then would haunt him for as long as he lived. He would never get his chance for a state title.

Brandel reached his arms out, and Bobby saw an opening. He stepped left, then shot to the right side, posting Brandel's elbows and drop-stepping under. Before the

Pennsville wrestler could react, Bobby was in low on the knee, quickly gaining control.

"Takedown!" the referee yelled. "Two points, Millburn!"

Fueled by the desperation of each passing second, Bobby bulled forward, breaking Brandel down to the mat, working his hand under his opponent's arm and onto his head.

The Jadwin stands shook, and Coach Messina was shouting, "Half, half, half!"

Bobby came out to the side, driving with his legs, his wrestling shoes digging into the mat. He heard Brandel's grunts as Bobby inched his back closer to perpendicular. The referee poised to count back points. Bobby's arm and wrist were aching, his thighs were burning, but Brandel was going over.

Closer . . .

And closer . . .

Brandel bridged frantically, lifting his shoulders off the mat. Turning . . . Still, the referee hadn't called back points. Bobby knew the buzzer would sound any second. The crowd roared. The stands rocked. Coach Messina was shouting, his father howling, Christopher screaming.

In a single moment, Bobby summoned every bit of strength he had in himself from the years of drilling and practicing and weight lifting and running, and he remembered in a flash the anger he had for his parents and the pain he felt for his little brother and all the storms they had both endured and the utter mess with

Carmelina, and he knew that another moment like this would never pass his way again. So he funneled all the energy and emotion and passion, and he squeezed Brandel's shoulders close to the mat.

"Back points!" the referee shouted, as the buzzer went off. He gestured with his fingers. "Two points, Millburn!"

They were the most beautiful words Bobby had ever heard. In an instant, everything he could see, hear, and feel floated and bobbed like ripples on a pond. Imperfect, distorted, colorful. Seeing what was happening through his own eyes, yet seeing it all from somewhere way above.

Bobby was on his feet, raising his arms—but not fully—waiting for confirmation. Sweat stinging his eyes, he looked over at the referee.

"Did I do it?"

And the referee nodded. Bobby's arms shot skyward, head back, body arched. His mind swirled as he succumbed to the flood of victory, not thinking any thoughts, not hearing, not seeing. Pleasure and relief washed over him, and he was suddenly exhausted but somehow stayed upright because his body was floating, rising, and the championship medal, he knew, would later sit in his hand, lifted skyward, glinting in the Jadwin ceiling lights, then draped around his neck for the world to see.

Through tight eyes, he saw Brandel at his feet, the referee nodding, Coach Messina clapping, his teammates jumping up and down, adding to the thunderous applause from the thousands in attendance, stomping their feet, cheering at the tops of their lungs. Jadwin Gym seemed tiny. And through it all, Bobby heard one voice force its way through the rest.

"That's my son, that's my son! That's him! He's going to the finals!"

Bobby saw his father at the corner of the mat, a smile as wide as the gymnasium, a smile Bobby hadn't seen for many months. Beside him, Christopher jumped around, arms swinging, Bobby's warm-up suit whipping around. Bobby's eyes caught his—excited, bulged—and he could read Christopher's lips. "My big brother won! My big brother won!" He also saw his mother. She was crying. . . .

Amid the madness, Bobby looked over. Brandel still hadn't moved, his eyes shut tight. He remained on his hands and knees, head on the mat.

The referee tapped Brandel on the shoulder.

Brandel struggled to his feet. He hadn't looked up yet, and still didn't when the referee raised Bobby's arm in victory and the crowd roared again when Bobby leaped into Coach Messina's arms.

Bobby had reached the end—the state finals—and he felt alone. Alone among people. In the crowded hallway of Millburn High. In the standing-room-only gymnasiums of the past three weekends. On the phone with Carmelina. At the kitchen table. Sitting in Jadwin Gym next to his father, mother, Christopher, and teammates.

No matter how hard anyone tried, no matter what

they said, the feeling of solitude didn't change. None of them could step into his shoes. None of them could pass the burden on to themselves. None of them could step onto the mat with Korske for the state finals. He had to.

Bobby was alone. And all that was left was time.

53

Ivan glanced up. In bright red lights, the scoreboard clock counted down the time left in the 122-pound championship match.

41 . . . 40 . . . 39 . . .

He paced and stretched and bounced on his toes, but as much as he tried he couldn't control the anxiety that roiled his gut. In thirty or so seconds, he would reach the edge of that destiny to which his entire being had been dedicated.

His stomach tightened. His muscles jerked tight. *Hold it together,* Ivan told himself, knowing shortly he would be exposed for all the gymnasium to see, and that might as well be the whole world because nothing of any relevance existed outside Jadwin Gymnasium.

There were perhaps twenty seconds left in the match, but Ivan would not glance at the clock anymore. To do so would make him a slave to the clock, and Ivan would not be a slave to that, or anything else. Or anyone else.

McClellan moved beside him. "Ready?"

"Yeah."

"Just in case," McClellan said, "when you're in deep on the fireman's carry, remember to make it a throw."

"I know."

"If you roll, he'll hook your arms and legs."

"I got it," Ivan snapped.

"Good."

As the clock ticked toward zero, fans for the soon-to-be 122-pound champion stirred, then rose.

Ivan watched, while at the other side of the gymnasium Zane knelt down in prayer. *Pray all you want; it's not gonna help.* Then Zane adjusted the chin strap of his headgear, slipped it over his hair, brushing aside a lock before snapping the halo secure. Ivan continued to stare, waiting to see if Zane looked at him.

He did. And it angered Ivan. But he relished that anger, knowing it would push away any fatigue or hunger or thirst that might derail his quest. So he fixed his eyes on Zane until his vision narrowed and there was no gymnasium, no teammates, no coaches, no family. Just Zane and him. Two warriors. Two enemies.

And Zane still stared, pulling off his T-shirt, slipping the singlet straps over his shoulders. On another day, at another time, Ivan might have acknowledged Zane's impressive run to the finals, but now he hated Zane. He wanted to hurt him, to deliver him pain, to make him regret the moment he stepped on a wrestling mat with him.

"Three . . . two . . . one . . ." the crowd chanted, then

exploded as the buzzer sounded, ending the 122-pound state championship match.

Bobby's heart beat so powerfully, so rapidly that he could hardly sense when one beat ended and the next began. His body churned, muscle against bone, muscle against muscle, skin seemingly ready to tear at the seams.

Bobby watched Korske rolling his neck and ankles, whipping his arms behind his back, then rotating them in circles, and all the while his muscles quivered under his skin. Korske looked like a menace, like a pissed-off bully. Not any different than what Bobby had seen at the Hunterdon Central tournament in December. Bobby pulled off his warm-up pants and tossed them to Christopher.

"Win, Bobby!" Christopher yelled, fumbling with the water bottle, Bobby's clothing draped over his shoulders.

Bobby slapped hands with Kenny, Big John, Anthony, then nodded to his father. He faced Coach Messina for their last prematch handshake. The man who had taught Bobby how to wrestle, who had taught him how to be a great captain, and who then helped merge the two together.

Coach Messina's massive hands held Bobby's shoulders. He nodded with confidence as he spoke, as if intending to chase away any lingering doubts in Bobby's mind. "Time to win the states," he said, simply, then released Bobby.

Bobby walked to the center of the mat, where the referee stood waiting.

"Stay focused," McClellan snapped.

Ivan looked at him, really looked at him, not with hatred in his heart, not with the usual disdain he felt, not with the pity he always had for McClellan. Everything in his life was riding on this match, there was no time to waste on McClellan. And, Ivan figured, if McClellan gained something because he won the state championship, so be it.

"I know how painful your mother's death was, but you're not doing this for her, Ivan. You're not doing this for your father, or the school, or the town. You're doing this for one person: Ivan Korske."

McClellan pressed a finger to his chest. "You deserve this more than anyone. You've worked harder than anyone here. You've sacrificed too much, pained too much, given of your soul too much to lose. No one's going to beat you on that mat. Not today."

Ivan snapped his chin strap. He had lived these six minutes in his mind a thousand times, now it was time to live them in real life.

A voice came over the arena PA system. "Now wrestling for the state championship in the one hundred and twenty-nine pound weight class . . . Ivan Korske of Lennings Township and Bobby Zane of Millburn Township . . ."

———

A roar filled the gymnasium. Bobby looked at Coach Messina, barely able to make out his words. "It's your time!" Coach Messina was shouting.

Under the cascade of ceiling lights, Bobby nodded, then he stepped onto the mat. At the center circle, the referee shook Bobby's hand, then his opponent's.

"Gentlemen, follow my instructions and keep wrestling until the final whistle," the referee said. He motioned for Bobby and Korske to place a foot on the center circle. "Ready," he said, raising the whistle to his lips.

Only an arm's length separated them. Bobby stood in his stance, left foot forward, knees flexed, hands forward, elbows tight against his body; Korske did the same.

The waiting—months, weeks, days, hours, minutes—had passed. The state championship, all that they each had hoped and dreamed for, would await the winner at the end of the next six minutes. Six impossibly long minutes. Then absolute bliss. Or complete devastation. The dream was before them. Immediate. Inescapable.

"Wrestle!" the referee barked, punctuating it with the whistle's shrill.

And the state championship match at 129 pounds began. . . .